THE BILLIONAIRE'S GIFT

A HOLIDAY ROMANCE

LAURA LANIER

CONTENTS

BLURB

Loss. Love. Realizations

Blaine Vanderbilt may only be thirty-years-old, but he' managed to make a fortune in the retail market as the founder of a chain of discount stores he named Bargain Bin.

The tall man with smoldering good looks has a hard heart. He's led his life thinking there is no harm in running a business that puts others out of theirs.

Until his elderly father passes away and leaves him with the question— should he make some changes to how he's been living?

It has Blaine wondering about all he's done, not only in his business life, but in his love life as well, as he's been as cold with women as he's been with other business owners.

He decides the time has come for the tides to turn and he makes a plan to change his ways completely. Step one is making sure the children who are stuck in the Children's Hospital in his hometown of Houston have a great holiday. That's where he meets the woman who may be his saving grace or his worst enemy.

Can Delaney Richards accept Blaine for the man he is becoming, or will his past bad deeds be a thing she can't forgive him for?

A TIME FOR THANKSGIVING BOOK ONE

A Holiday Romance

By Michelle Love

1

BLAINE

November 5th:

The sound of light drops hitting the canvas rooftop of the black canopy fill my ears along with my heart. It feels as if it's raining inside of me too. Today we are laying my father to rest in the grave next to my mother's. She died when my youngest brother, Kent, was born—a rare thing nowadays. That happened twenty-five years ago. It doesn't hurt nearly as badly as it used to.

But with pops' death, the pain is coming back, biting at me with a vengeance. It's been a long time since anything has hurt me. It took me years to harden myself to the point that I was unbreakable. And in one day, pops managed to break down that whole steel structure that had surrounded my heart.

Like a grizzly bear with a huge fist, pops slammed into the protective barrier that shielded me and my feelings from any pain. He was taken away from us so suddenly. His fatal heart attack at fifty-seven has left me, my younger sister, Kate, and the youngest of us, Kent, alone in this world.

I'm the oldest, and I assume the others are going to be looking to me for the first time in their lives as a role model. I have never been what pops would call a good role model to them. As a matter of fact, he would use me as an example of how not to be.

I'm a billionaire at the tender age of thirty. I've worked on my little empire since I started college. I mastered in business and managed to hedge in a group of like-minded investors to help me with my endeavor.

With the initial investment of money, I managed to build a great business. My first store, Bargain Bin, in downtown Houston, my hometown, it was a complete success. Only a year and a half later, I had the money to open another store in Dallas.

At that time, I wondered, if the stores I was opening in the big cities were working so well, why didn't I try opening one in a smaller town? Not a tiny town—a midsized town.

So I opened the next Bargain Bin, number three, in Lockhart, Texas, population 13,232. Just the right size to find out if my idea would work.

One by one, my stores took over the market in that town, just the way I thought they would. There was some controversy about my store coming in and ruining business for the locally owned, small-town stores that were already established there, but I didn't care. Business is business. No reason to take anything personal.

The thing about Bargain Bin is that I will beat any price on anything. Sure, I have to really search around the world for the cheapest products, but it's working for me. I have stores all over the United States now—quite a feat for a man my age.

Pops wasn't in love with my way of doing business or with how I treated women either. He told me on more than one occasion that my heart was cold. He was right. I had to agree with him on that.

Just like anything that you want to keep for a long time, freezing is the best way to accomplish that.

A squeaking sound brings my mind back to what it should've always been focused on instead of roaming away from the sadness in front of me. My sister leans into my side and runs her arm around me as she sniffles. "I'm going to miss him, Blaine." We watch as my father's gleaming, titanium casket is lowered into the dark ground.

Not exactly sure what to do, I look to my brother, who is on the other side of her, for the appropriate response to such a thing. As always, he helps me out as he gestures for me to put my arm around her and pat her on the head.

I mimic his movements and say, "There, there, Kate. Things will be all right. You have me." And just like that, Kent has me taking the place of Pops, as he was mouthing the words for me to say to her and I was doing it, trusting him without thinking.

"I do?" she asks. "Do you promise, Blaine?"

Narrowing my eyes at Kent, I tell my little sister, "I promise. Whatever you need, you come to me. I'll be here for you."

Kent gives me a smile and a thumb up, and I give him the bird. He's always been that thorn in my side as the baby of the family and the guy who tries like hell to make me see my evil ways, as he calls them.

My stores mostly employ people with disabilities. As those people are all on some type of disability government assistance, they can't make too much money. So, I make sure to pay them only what their particular amount can be. I don't want to mess up their assistance, after all.

Kent thinks I'm a terrible person for doing such a thing. He calls it exploitation. I call it doing smart business. He can call it what he wants—he isn't in charge of how I make my money.

Which brings me to the fact he and my sister make very little of the green stuff that makes the world go around. Kent is currently a truck driver. He hauls oil from Point A to Point B. Over and over, he does the same damn thing, day in and day out. It is a nightmarish way to make a living, if you ask me.

Kate works at a daycare, taking care of snot-nosed brats every day. That, too, sounds like something out of a nightmare to me. Pops used to help them out with their bills when they came up short, which I told him wasn't really helping them at all.

But now I guess it's up to me to step into pops' shoes and the role of the head of the family. It was a role I've never wanted, but he's left it wide open and empty. With the way my little sister is holding onto me, I can see I'm needed.

2

BLAINE

Walking into our father's home without him greeting us at the door like he'd always done is more than odd. The home that was once small and cozy feels empty. Even though there are the same things in it there have always been, it feels empty without pops.

"I hate this," Kate whines as she flops onto his old, threadbare couch.

I asked my father on several occasions to let me buy him a house, but he was full of stubborn pride and would never let me. I gave him a Cadillac last year. It was the first thing he ever accepted from me. He had always wanted one, and I suppose, when I gave it to him for Christmas, he let a bit of that foolish pride slip away so he could drive the car he'd always dreamed of owning.

I recall feeling a spark in my heart that Christmas day when he finally accepted something from me. It felt good. Most of the time I feel a whole lot of nothing. It's better that way.

"So now what do we do, Blaine?" Kent asks as he opens pops' little fridge next to his easy chair. "Beer?"

I nod and he tosses me a cold Natural Light beer, then Kate holds up her hand for one, too. The three of us sit and all of us pop the beers open and take long drinks. The resounding, *ahh*, fills the room, making us all smile as we had all decided to make the sound our father would make after his first drink of beer after a long day at work.

"I wonder what in the world the Bar-B-Que Shack will do without pops to cook all of their meat for them. He was the absolute best at it," Kate says.

"I wonder if there're any leftovers in the kitchen icebox," Kent says and gets up to go and see.

I'm anything but hungry. But I can see my younger siblings need the normalcy to help them get through this. "If there's not any, I can call in an order and have it delivered."

Kent calls out from the kitchen, "No, I want pops'." The sound of bottles being moved and things being shuffled around as he digs through the refrigerator tells me he's digging deep to find any leftovers. "Ha! Yes, I found some."

"You have no idea how old that is, Kent. Don't eat any of that," Kate shouts at him, then gets up to go inspect the food our little brother is about to put into his mouth, no doubt.

I get up and follow her to make sure the idiot doesn't eat something that might kill him. We've had enough tragedy already.

Kent is smiling as he holds up the box with a date from three days ago written in black Sharpie across the top of the white Styrofoam lid. "Today is the last day to eat it. Come on—it's brisket, pops' specialty."

"Are there any beans in there?" Kate asks as she takes over the search in pops' fridge for things that will remind us of him.

I give in and say, "If there's potato salad in there, pull it out too. I like the way the old man made that too."

While Kent puts the meat on a plate and pops it into the microwave, Kate finds beans and potato salad, then pours the beans into a bowl and places it on the counter. "Zap these next, would you, baby bro?"

"Sure, I can handle something this easy," he says, then takes another drink of his beer. "Do you guys remember the first time we got into pops' beer fridge?"

"My ass still hurts," I say with a laugh.

Kate laughs as she puts the potato salad in a bowl and places it on the table. Since everyone else is doing something, I decide I need to help, too, and get up to get us some plates, silverware, and napkins.

"He did get you two boys the worst. I was crying before he ever spanked me. When the actual spanking came, I hardly felt it, but it didn't stop me from wailing like a banshee," Kate says as she takes a chair. I place a plate in front of her and put a spoon in the potato salad.

"We never did that again, though. One spanking was enough," Kent says as he puts the steaming plate full of brisket on the table, then goes back for the beans as the microwave beeps.

"It wasn't the spanking of myself that stopped me. It was hearing you two cry like you were being beaten to death that stopped me. That was the last time any of us were spanked, I do believe," I say, then place the last two plates on the table and take my chair.

"I never got another one," Kate says as she starts making her plate.

"Hey, wait!" Kent shouts at her. "We have to say grace, Kate."

She puts the spoonful of potato salad back in the bowl and nods. "You're right. Especially today. Man, I can't believe he's gone. I just can't believe it," she says and picks up the napkin I gave her to wipe her eyes, which are springing leaks.

"Hey, no crying at the table, sis," I tease her. "You know the rules in pops' house. Only good words are spoken at the table. Now tell me your best time with pops."

She nods, then takes a drink of her beer. "My best time with pops, huh? There are so many of them, I don't know if I can pick a best one. But I think one of the top best times I had with pops was when he took us fishing."

Kent puts the beans on the table and sits down. "Yeah, fishing rocked with him." He reaches out for our hands, and we each take one, then he looks at me. "You get to do this now that he's gone, Blaine."

"Say grace?" I ask as I shake my head. "I don't know what the hell to say."

Kate makes a snorting sound I assume is some kind of a laugh. "Just say what pops used to say. Wing it, Damien. I don't think the meal will burst into flames, having one of Satan's disciples praying over it."

I hate when she calls me that name, and she knows it. It's no secret that all of my family thinks I'm heartless and must be demonic to do the things I do in business and in my personal life too. The name calling is something I usually don't put up with, though.

The occasion calls for me to laugh her off, so I do just that. "Okay, Kate. Let's see what I can come up with. Bow your heads and close your eyes," I tell them and watch to make sure they do. Then I bow too. "Lord, you've gained an angel in our father today. We know he's safe and happy in your hands now. We've found this food he prepared before he left us. Now, we know it's three days old, so if you could bless it to be sure it doesn't make us sick, we'd all really appreciate that."

"Say something about us being thankful, Blaine," Kent whispers.

"And we are thankful, Lord. Not only for this food, but also for having our father for the amount of time you let us have him. He will be missed. He was a great man, a kind man, and a wise man." A knot forms in my throat and I have to stop and clear it. "Amen."

This not crying at the table is a lot harder than I thought it'd be!

3

BLAINE

November 10th:

Hurrying to turn the lamp on beside my bed, I sit up, trying to catch my breath. As the light comes on, illuminating my bedroom, I look around to be sure I'm really in my home on my estate rather than in my childhood bedroom with my father sitting on the edge of my twin bed, talking to me.

Every damn night since we buried our father, I've had the same dream. Pops comes into my bedroom, the one I had as a kid, and sits down and starts talking to me about right and wrong.

My head is aching with how much has been put into it, even though it's not real at all. My heart is aching as well. I don't recall ever feeling as much as I have in the last five days.

It's hard to believe my father is more with me now than when he was alive, but that's how I feel. Yesterday I went to the corporate office, and when I found one of the employees from the Houston store in the reception area, I stopped to talk to him—an unusual thing for me.

He told me he'd asked his manager for some time off with pay so he could go see his younger brother in the hospital. The manager had told him it was against our policy to give employees leave with pay for anything.

I had to take him into my office because he started crying, and I found myself feeling terribly for him. He told me his ten-year-old brother had been diagnosed with the same disease that hit him at that exact age. He explained how the disease changed him, taking away his ability to walk and leaving him paralyzed from the waist down because it attacked his brain. It also took away some of his mental capabilities, and he wanted to be with his brother to help him understand things.

The young man told me things that made me see life in a new way. He told me he wanted to tell his little brother how he was still a viable human being and that he would be one too. Walking and being able to use your brain as well as you used to isn't as hard as it seems to be. At least he gets to keep on living.

I sat there and listened to him tell me things I'd never taken the time to listen to from any employee before. And I found myself writing out a policy to allow leave with pay for certain things—family = members facing challenges with their health being one of them.

And before he left my office, I had him give me his parents' phone number so I could call them. Without even thinking, I told them I'd be paying for their son's hospital bills and anything he needed to help him deal with this terrible thing he'd been afflicted with.

Danny Peterson gave me something that day—he gave me an insight into what kinds of things he and others like him face. I felt as if I'd been given a gift—the gift to understand others and have empathy—I've lacked my whole life.

With pops coming to me in my dreams every night, I'm feeling like I need to make a lot of changes. It's as if I'm being given the opportunity to start on a new path—one I didn't realize existed before.

Looking at the clock on my nightstand, I see it's six in the morning and make a snap decision to call my brother and sister to see if they'd like to come with me to breakfast. It's early enough to catch them before their workdays begin.

Kate answers on the third ring, "What's up, Blaine?"

"Me," I say. "I want to take you and Kent out for breakfast. I'll have my driver take us and afterward he can drop you both off at your jobs, or you two can come with me to visit this kid in the hospital if you want to take the day off. I'd like to hang out with you both."

"I can't afford to take the day off. But breakfast sounds nice. I'll get up and get ready."

"I'll pay you for the day you'll be missing. Come on, go with me to the hospital. I don't want to go alone," I cajole her.

"I'll call and see if that'll be okay, then. See you soon."

Next, I call Kent.

"Hey, what are you doing calling me this early?" he answers his phone.

"I'm up and want to take you and Kate out for breakfast. You think you can take the day off? I'm paying your missed wages if you'll take it off and come with me to visit this sick kid in the hospital."

"I'm in," he says without hesitation. "Where do you want me to meet you?"

"I'm getting my driver to take us, so just get ready and make yourself look decent too. I want us to look respectable when we go to the hospital," I tell him, then end the call.

With a pretty great day ahead, I get out of bed and feel kind of lighthearted. I usually don't feel a thing like this when I start my days. My plans usually consist of getting online and making sure I'm getting the cheapest products possible.

It's nice to have such a gratuitous plan for my day, and as I go to the bathroom, I think of another thing I should do—take Danny's little brother some kind of toy or something to make his hospital stay a little more pleasant.

I don't have a clue what a ten-year-old would like, though. Maybe Kate will know since she works with kids. All I know is, I have a pep in my step that I don't usually have. It's oddly amazing and I think I like this feeling.

Stepping into a warm shower, I have to fight to settle my brain down. So many thoughts are moving around inside my head—

thoughts I've never had before. I suppose it's my father's death that has me thinking about making changes in my life. A pressure is on me to get things moving in a new direction. A good direction.

As I wash my hair, I think about how my brother and sister are living. They're making a living doing honest work, and I should be prouder of them for how well they've turned out. I never tell them anything like that. I actually say opposite things to them about working so hard to earn a buck.

I need to let them know that not only am I proud of them, but I'm here to help them do anything they want to do with their lives. Anything at all. I wonder how they'll react to that.

My money has often been called the devil dollars by them. They may not want that money helping them to get where they want to be.

But then again, with my changing attitude, they might start thinking of that money differently. All I know for sure is that I need their help to figure out how to make things right again—how to keep making money, but stop hurting others while I do that.

I hope they can figure out how to help me.

4

DELANEY

"I need you to have that PICC line in before I get there, Nurse Richards," the doctor in charge of the neonatal unit for the day orders me.

"I'll have it done. Don't worry. I'm about to start a double shift, going to the opposite side of the hospital for the next eight hours to help out over there with the older children. If you need me for anything, then just call me and I'll come back over here."

"Okay, thanks. I appreciate it," he says, then ends the call.

I head to the small room where a tiny newborn is having a difficult time staying with us. The poor baby was born with a hole in her heart that's going to have to be repaired if she's going to have a chance at surviving.

To add to her problems, she's developed an infection and antibiotics will have to be pumped straight into her tiny heart. Her mother and father are with her in the little, dark room, and I find them holding each other as I come inside. "Good morning."

They let each other go and turn away from the little incubator that holds their daughter. "Good morning," her mother says. "What's the plan? Do you know yet?"

"I'm going to be putting in a PICC line. It's not going to be easy to watch. If you two would like to go down and get some breakfast from the cafeteria, now would be a good time. I promise to have her calmed back down as soon as possible," I tell them as I move about the room, getting together the things I will need.

"I'm staying," the young mother says. "If my baby's in pain, then I need to be too."

Her husband wraps one arm around her and stays silent. I look over my shoulder and offer the same words I offer all the parents of the sick children I take care of. "There's no reason to look at things in that way. Staying strong for her is much better than suffering along with her. That way you can come back in here and let her feel your calmness rather than you being upset after hearing her cries."

"She's right, honey," her husband says, then takes her out of the room.

As I look down at the sleeping baby, I feel terribly about her condition. I don't understand why these things happen to anyone, much less children. I do know this medicine will help her and that gives me the strength to do the hard part—make her cry.

In the beginning, five years ago, when I become a pediatric nurse, things were so hard for me. Even giving children shots that prevented them from getting horrible diseases was hard for me to do. Day by day, little by little, I came to terms with what I was doing for them.

A bit of pain one day, opposed to a terrible illness, is worth it. And I have exceptional abilities to calm them back down. The baby moves a little in agitation as I move her around to position her.

The door opens and in comes the other nurse to hold her still for me. "Hi, Betty. You ready?" I ask as she washes her hands, then comes to us.

"I suppose so. Let's get this over with. I totally hate this part of our jobs," she says.

I nod in agreement, take in a breath, and hold it as I push the needle into the baby's chest. Her scream comes out as I do. Then my mind shuts off so I can help her without feeling terribly about it.

.   .   .

THREE HOURS LATER, and a couple of coffees, too, I'm on the other side of the hospital, checking on the third-floor patients. With a quick knock on the door, I grab Samuel Peterson's file hanging next to it, then go inside as I look it over. "Good morning," I say as I come into the room where a ten-year-old little boy is fighting pneumococcal meningitis.

A very tired father sits at one side of the child's bed and another young man sits in a wheelchair on the other side. "Good morning," he says to me. "I'm Danny. Sammy's brother. How is he?"

"His numbers are going down, which is a good thing," I tell him as I look at his chart. "I'm here to get his vitals, so we can see if he's still improving. If you don't mind my asking, Danny, what happened to have you in that chair?"

"The same thing," he says, then blows a chunk of blonde hair out of his eyes. "Only thing different is my parents got him to the hospital three days earlier than they realized they needed to take me. We're all hoping he doesn't end up like me."

With a nod, I start taking Samuel's temperature and hear the sound of someone clearing their throat. It's a deep sound with a smooth edge to it. "Can we come in?"

"Sure," Danny tells the man. "Hello, Mr. Vanderbilt. It's a pleasure to see you here today."

"I wish things were better," the man says.

I turn around to grab the blood pressure cuff and stop as I see one of the most handsome men I believe I have ever seen before. His light-brown eyes land on mine without any words coming out of his mouth.

There's a nice-looking younger man behind him and a woman too. I quickly get back to my task at hand and try to stop envisioning the built man without any clothes on. *Shame on me!*

"Dad, this is the man who owns the whole company of Bargain Bins, my big boss," Danny says.

Oh no! Not that asshole!

He's my family's mortal enemy. I never realized he was so attractive. I've only seen a few pictures of him in the paper. But I hate this man. He's the reason my parents live in public housing and I have to help them just to make ends meet.

When he opened a Bargain Bin in my hometown of Lockhart, Texas, he drove my parents, who owned a small tire shop, completely out of business. They lost their home, and in just a matter of three years, were on welfare.

That man is as close to the devil as they come!

"I brought your brother a video game. I had no idea he would be sleeping," the devil man says.

"Yes, he's sick with meningitis. I do hope you've been vaccinated," I say as I busy myself with taking care of the poor, sick boy.

"All of our vaccinations are up to date," the young woman says. "Our father made sure of that. Even after we all grew up, he still kept records and called us after he'd scheduled our appointments to get them done. He died last week."

My ire is quickly smashed by her news. I turn back to look at the three of them and notice they all have a resemblance to each other. "I'm sorry to hear that. Your father, you said? All three of yours?" I ask.

The great-looking man who ruined my family nods, making his dark-blonde hair move around his chiseled face in such a way that it makes my knees weak as he says, "Yes, we're siblings. I'm Blaine, this is my sister, Kate, and that is our brother, Kent. I know how deep that bond goes. When Danny came into my office yesterday, he made me realize how important it is to have them around when things get tough."

"Yeah," Danny says. "Mr. Vanderbilt gave me time off with pay to come and be with Sammy. He's not a bad man like everyone says he is."

I stifle a laugh as the evil man's perfect eyebrows arch. "I have a lot of changes to make. I think I have been kind of a bad man. But thanks to my father passing and you, Danny, I think I've seen a light."

I doubt that, or perhaps it's the light from the fires of hell, where the man is sure to go, he's seeing!

5

BLAINE

I can't stop looking at those green eyes. They're so dark, it brings to mind emeralds. Her fiery-red hair is pulled back into a sensible ponytail and her deep-green scrubs actually make her look even prettier.

Moving further into the hospital room, I lean against the counter I'm sure she's going to have to come to in order to get something for the poor, sick boy sleeping in the bed.

She's so beautiful. She has to be married, so I search her quick-moving hands for a wedding ring and find her fingers without a single ring on any of them. *Good!*

"So, how long have you been a nurse?" I ask her.

She looks over her shoulder, but not directly at me. "Five years." Her words are short and I have the distinct sense she's judging me.

The sound of a voice comes over the hospital's PA system, "Nurse Richards, you're needed in the neonatal unit."

The gorgeous nurse looks up and sighs, parting her naturally ruby red lips as she does. "Okay. Either I'll be back to finish him up or another nurse will come in to do it." As she turns away from the kid in the bed, she looks at me for a second, then hurries out of the room.

I find myself watching her as she goes and wishing she didn't have to leave so damn fast. Then Kent takes my attention as he snaps his fingers in front of my face. "Earth to Blaine."

"Huh?" I ask, then blink and shake my head, then look at Danny and his father. "You two fellas want to come with me to the cafeteria to grab something to eat? My treat."

Danny nods and his father shakes his head. "I'll stay with Sammy. I don't like to leave him alone."

Kate steps up to the plate. "Mr. Peterson, I'd be more than happy to sit with him while you go get something to eat. I work at a daycare. I'm really good with kids. And I don't think he's about to wake up, but if he does for some reason, I'll call my brother, and he can let you know, okay?"

"Come on, Dad. You haven't left this room since you brought him here," Danny tells his father.

"Come on, Mr. Peterson," Kent tells him. "I saw peach cobbler when we walked past there on our way up. It looked good. And I saw one of those ice cream machines there too. I bet some of that cobbler with some ice cream would really hit the spot."

The man nods and gets up. "It does sound good." He looks at Kate, who goes to take his place. "You will call if anything happens?"

"I promise," she says as she pats him on his shoulder. "Now, go eat something, Mr. Peterson. It's important to keep your strength up."

As we leave the room, I see the pretty nurse talking to a doctor. Her hands are on her hips and she seems to be irritated at the man. I eavesdrop as we pass them and hear her say, "Look, that's not cool. I was with a patient. You can't have me paged just to talk to me. It's over and done with, Paul. I'm not playing your head games. I'm a grown woman with a good head on my shoulders. You still want to see other women, and that's cool. Only thing is, I don't want to be one of many —I want to be the one."

Purposely, I hang back behind the others so I can listen to what they're talking about. The doctor says, "And you might be. I have to have something to compare you to in order to make that decision."

"And there you go," she says. "We just aren't meant to be, Paul. So,

I'm going to get back to work after I grab a much-needed fourth cup of coffee, and you are going to stop your shenanigans."

"Fine, Delaney. But you're going to be the one who regrets ending what we have. You'll see," he tells her.

I hang back even more, in hopes of letting her catch up to me, since she said she was going to get coffee. And now I have an in with her, as I have something to offer her.

Her footsteps are soft but fast-paced as she walks up behind me. I hear her stepping off to one side and take a step that way too. A huffing sound comes from behind me and I stop. Turning around, I act surprised. "Oh, sorry. I thought I was getting out of the way for the person coming up behind me so fast. Seems I managed to get right in your way. Where are you off to in such a hurry, Nurse Richards?"

She narrows her beautiful eyes at me, the long, dark lashes nearly touching her high cheek bones as she does. "How do you know my name?"

"They called you over the speakers only moments ago," I say and place my hand on her elbow to steer her forward as I start walking again. "So, where is it you were headed?"

"The cafeteria," she says, then looks at my hand on her arm. "And you?"

"Same place," I say with a smile. "Allow me to get you something. Name your poison."

Her tone is sharp as she snaps, "Coffee, and no, thank you. I can get my own coffee. I don't need your charity, Mr. Vanderbilt."

"Call me Blaine," I say and move my hand from her elbow to the small of her back as we turn into the doorway of the cafeteria. "And may I call you by your first name, Delaney?"

She stops and glares at me as if I've called her a bitch or something other than her name. "How the hell do you know my name? That didn't come over the PA system!"

"As I passed you talking to that doctor in the hallway. I heard him call you that. It's such a pretty name," I say as I escort her to the coffee machine and see the case of pastries beside it. "Donut?"

"No, just the coffee, and like I said, I'll get it myself." We both reach out to pick up a large cup and our hands touch. She jerks hers back as if she was shocked or something. "I said, I'll get it!"

"Sorry," I say with a grin. "I want one too."

"Oh, well, I didn't realize that," she says with the tiniest look of embarrassment on her sweet face. "You go ahead."

"Ladies first," I say as I wait for her to get the cup.

She takes one and fills it up, then I do the same. We both reach for the sugar at the same time, bumping hands again. I laugh and she growls. "We seem to keep getting into each other's way."

"I'd like to think we think alike, not get into each other's way." I reach for the pumpkin-spice creamer and offer it to her first. "I'm putting this into my coffee. Would you like some?"

She nods, but frowns. "I was about to use that one too." She holds her cup of steaming coffee out, and I pour it in, stopping at the same time she says, "That's enough. Oh, you stopped. Okay."

"We do think alike," I say as I drop a stir stick into her cup.

"Hardly," she says. then walks away from me.

I grab a donut from the case and follow her. I saw her eyeing them and know she wants one. Just as she gets to the counter, I slap a twenty on it. "I got this."

She huffs, "Fine!"

The older woman who is behind the cash register gives her a shake of the head. "Not a very nice way to thank someone for a kind gesture, Nurse Richards."

"If you knew who this man was, you'd understand," she says, then spins away from me.

Why does she act like she hates me?

6

DELANEY

His hand on my arm doesn't slow me down one bit. "I'm busy."

"I know that," his silky, smooth, deep voice says from beside me. Then he's steering me to a booth and sliding me into it without me understanding how he's doing it. When he slides in next to me, I find I'm trapped between his huge frame and the wall. *Damn it!*

"Look, Mister."

His finger touches my lips, and I fight the urge to bite it. "Blaine. And you have something you want to say to me so badly that it's making you act a little crazy. So, what is it? What have I ever done to you to make you form an instant opinion of me?"

I drum my fingers on the table in an attempt to control my anger at the man who really does seem clueless to his evil ways. "Look, Blaine, your ways of doing business have left a trail of bankrupt people behind you on your road to success. You have climbed on top of their nearly-dead bodies to rise to the top of the business world. I, for one, do not care to hob-knob with a person such as yourself. Call me judgmental if you want to."

"Okay, I will," he has the audacity to say to me.

"You ass! You ruined my parents' tire business in Lockhart. Do you recall that at all? I bet you don't. I bet you gave less than a flying fuck who you ran out of business when you opened that damn store there." I sip my coffee to try to calm down. Something about this man has all my red flags waving at once.

"I see now. So you are validated in your opinion of me. I can understand you a lot better now. You see, communication is the key to any happy relationship," he says with a smile—a very nice smile that's hovering on the edge of the best smile I've ever seen on a man in my life. Only, that smile is on the face of the most horrible man I've ever encountered.

"Great. So let me out so I can go on about my life." I pause and think about what he just said. "And the word 'relationship' has no place in this conversation."

"Oh, but I think it does. How about you let me take you out tonight? It could help make up for what my business has cost your family. And I don't know if your parents ever told you everything about my business, but I always offer to buy out the inventory of the businesses I happen to tread on with my discount stores."

"Yes, they did tell me. You offered them fifty thousand dollars for their inventory that was worth twice that amount. So kind of you, Damien," I say with a smirk on my lips.

"Damien?" he asks, and his frown tells me he's been called that before. "I am not the Anti-Christ. I have done some business dealings that I'm thinking more about now. I am a man who is in the beginning stages of changing my ways. Since my business has directly affected your life, I'd like very much if you would go out with me so we can talk and I can come to a better understanding of what I need to change."

"Change?" I ask with a huff. "You need to change everything. Close the damn stores down. That's what you need to do."

"That's a bit drastic, and frankly, it would be very mean of me to suddenly end the employment of thousands of people. So some other suggestions would be appreciated, Delaney," he says, then his damn hand is moving across my shoulders as he lays his arm on the back of the seat.

Even the way he smells is expensive and it really pisses me off. "It's not my job to educate you on business ethics. With your obvious education in business, didn't you even have one business ethics class?"

"I've had several," he says with a smile. I can't believe he can sit there and smile at me. *It's pretty damn obvious what I think of him!*

"Well, you learned nothing from them. When you opened your first two stores, you did so in huge cities that could handle that kind of competition. Then you decided to go for the jugular of our country, the mid-sized towns, and that's where you went wrong," I let him know, since he seems so damned oblivious to the fact.

"But those places are where my company makes the most money. It's just good business sense, that's all. Surely you can understand that, if your parents were business people, themselves," he says, then picks up the donut he bought, pulls a chunk of it off, and holds it near my mouth. "Would you care for a bite?"

"What?" I ask, and he pops the piece into my mouth. I have to chew the delicious thing up and swallow it, and I'm so damn mad at him for invading my mouth, it's not even funny. "Don't you ever do that again."

"What, share my food with you?" he asks, then pulls a piece off for himself and eats it as I glare at him, secretly hoping he'll choke on it.

"No, shove food into my mouth without my permission," I correct him and wiggle to try to let him know I want him to let me out of the damn booth. "I need to get back to work. You are more than aware that I need to go finish checking out Samuel Peterson."

"Oh, yeah, that." He gets up and holds his hand out for me, but I ignore him and get out on my own, turning to grab my coffee. As I walk out, I find him right next to me. "I'll walk you back."

I huff, as I have no idea how I'm going to shake this man. "Do whatever you want. You always do, anyway."

"You don't know me at all—don't really know me. The man

behind the business. I'm telling you, I'm changing things. I really am. I'd love to get to meet your parents and get some insight into how I can make things better."

I stop and look at him with amazement. "Oh, you would, huh? Would you like to go to the nice, three-bedroom home they had before you ran them out of business? Because that's gone. The mortgage company took it when they couldn't pay anymore. Now they live in a one-bedroom, tiny home in government housing. I'm sure they'd love it if you stopped by. My mother could make you a government cheese sandwich and give you a jelly jar with tap water in it. Want to know why?"

He shrugs and kind of looks like he doesn't. "Why would that be?"

"Because they are dirt poor now, thanks to you!"

I storm away as he stands perfectly still. I leave him with the sight of my extended middle finger and hope he finally gets how I feel about him.

7

BLAINE

"And she shot the finger at me and left," I tell Kent as I pay for the Petersons' food.

The cashier looks at me and says, "She's usually a very nice woman. I can't understand what's gotten into Nurse Richards. Maybe it's because she's pulling a double shift and hasn't slept in quite some time. She still has three more hours until her shift is over and she can finally get some rest."

"I'm sure my brother just rubs her the wrong way," Kent offers. "He's not exactly the nicest guy all the time."

"You should show her how nice you can be," the cashier says, then points at a flyer tacked on the wall behind her with a picture of Santa on it. "It's the holidays and the hospital always welcomes people who want to do nice things for the children here at The Children's Hospital. Maybe that would show her the man you're trying to let her see."

"You are a genius," I say as I look at her nametag. "Mildred."

She looks at her nametag and laughs. "I borrowed this one. My name's Shirley. And thanks, Mr. ...?"

"You can call me Blaine. Blaine Vanderbilt," I tell her, then her smile fades pretty damn rapidly.

"The owner of Bargain Bin, right?" she asks.

I nod and find I'm not feeling so proud as I've always felt about owning that company. "Yes. Have you had a bad past with any of my stores?"

"Only that every damn thing I've bought from there is the cheapest shit ever made and breaks almost right away," she says. "The latest thing I bought was a television stand that broke as soon as I placed my brand-new television on it, sending it to the floor and breaking it too," she tells me.

I reach into my pocket, pull out a thousand dollars, and place it on the counter. "Sorry about that."

She looks at the money as she shakes her head. "Keep it. If you really want to make me happy, change the return policy your stores have. It's the strictest policy I've ever seen with the shortest amount of time to return the few things it allows."

Feeling a bit shell-shocked with so much hate thrown right into my face, I nod and turn to leave. "I really am sorry."

Kent puts his hand on my shoulder and walks with me as we leave the cafeteria. "Man, I'm sorry. You're here to try to do a good thing and a lot of flak is being tossed at you."

"I hate to admit it, but I kind of deserve it. I have a ton of changes to make, Kent. And I need your help, as well as Kate's, to make things right again. What do you say to working for me, instead of driving a truck? It would mean a nice office at the corporate headquarters and a boatload more money than you make now."

"Boatload?" he asks as he seems to be contemplating my offer. "How many figures are we talking?"

"Six or seven, at least. Bonuses when sales increase—the normal things consultants get in the retail business. So, you kind of sound like you'll consider it," I say as we turn the corner to walk down another hallway.

"If you really mean it about making changes, then yes. I will consider it. It's time you made some changes, Blaine. You've been going down a bad path for too long now. Many people have been hurt. It's time to fix things. That's what pops always wanted. He wanted you to do things the right way."

"I know. When I would stick around long enough to let him give me an earful, he'd get on the soapbox every damn time. It annoyed me, to be honest. But what I wouldn't give to have that man back and listen to him even one more time."

As we turn to go into Sammy's room, I notice Delaney's head turn our way, then snap back to look at her patient. "Visiting hours are over," she snaps.

Kate hurries across the room to us. "Time to go."

"I'll be back tomorrow," I tell Danny, then walk over and put a hundred-dollar bill into his hand. "Take care of them, son. Your little brother needs you right now." I look at his father and nod. "And so do your parents. I'll see you tomorrow. I hope to meet your mother. I'll bring her some flowers."

"Thanks, Mr. Vanderbilt," he says as he beams a happy smile. "I sure will do my best. And there better not be anyone who ever says a bad thing about you when I'm around or I'll give them a reason for!"

Delaney makes a huffing sound, and I laugh as I run my hand over Danny's head, messing up his blonde, shaggy hair. "Thanks, buddy. You're the best." Turning around, I find the lovely nurse has turned too, and we're facing each other, quite by accident. "And it was lovely meeting you, Nurse Richards. I'll be seeing you around. I plan on helping this family out a lot."

Sarcasm is dripping off every single word as she says, "Isn't that just the nicest thing I've ever heard."

Her gaze is a little on the sinister side. *And they call me evil!*

Stepping around her, I follow my brother and sister out of the room and hear the soft sounds of her feet behind me. A hand on my arm stops me, and I turn back to look at her with a smile. "Yes, Nurse Richards?"

She makes sure to close the door behind her, then her finger starts shaking in my face. "You listen to me, Blaine Vanderbilt. If you think coming to see this kid will get you a date with me, you had better think again. I will not be swayed by your act of kindness. I know all too well who and what you really are. Coming here and plying this family with gifts will not get you what you want."

My sister and brother look on with surprised faces as she reads me her riot act. I take her wagging finger and hold it. "I'm not doing this to impress you, Delaney. But how cute that you think I would spend my precious time doing that just to get to you. It makes me think you might have a little internal battle with what you want to do. Perhaps my being around so much might have you seeing the real man I am becoming, and that might just scare you a little."

"The only thing that scares me is the fact that you would stoop to making people think you care about them to get a piece of ass!" she snaps.

"Oh, baby, I'm not after a piece of ass. If I was, I wouldn't even bother talking to you. You'd be in one of these empty hospital rooms, in the bed, with your feet over your head, screaming my name, if that's what I wanted. Believe me, I know." I let her finger go, and she lets it fall to her side as she stares at me. "Now, I will see you tomorrow. I hope you come to work with a better attitude. I overheard some of your co-workers saying you had to work a double shift and you've been up all night and won't get to sleep for another three hours, so I'm cutting you some slack. Now, if you'll tell me your address, I'll have your dinner delivered to you so you don't have to worry about that either."

"I don't want a thing from you, Vanderbilt," she says but her words have lost their hard edge.

"Suit yourself. I'll bring you something for breakfast in the morning, then," I say, then turn to leave.

"Don't bother," she calls out after me.

"It's not a bother at all, Nurse Richards. Not one bit."

I like her spunk. *I think it might be just what I need in my life!*

8

DELANEY

The egotistical maniac is walking away from me with his broad shoulders swinging casually as he goes. For some reason, my eyes won't stop looking at him as he walks away. His blue jeans fit him way too well and show off his muscle-bound legs that are thick as tree trunks.

When he told me if he wanted a piece of ass he would've had it, I kind of believed him. A glimmer went through his light-brown eyes that told me as much. His body hardened just slightly, and I could almost smell the testosterone coming off him in waves of undulating pulses that I'm sure have drowned many women.

He's never had a serious girlfriend, based on anything I've ever seen in the media. I've seen him in pictures when he was dressed to the hilt, looking nothing like he did today, at a few events with gorgeous creatures on his arm. Never was one mentioned as anything except his escort for the evening.

I must admit, he is something to look at. I find myself straining to catch the last glimpse of him before he turns the corner. Then he's looking at me, and I hurry to look away. *Shit!*

"See you tomorrow," I hear him call out, then, when I look up, he's gone.

"Thank God! Now I´ll go find someone to take my shift tomorrow. It'll mean I'll have to work double the next day, but I'll get switched to another department and not have to meet up with him anymore." I walk over to the nurses' station and check the schedule.

Beth comes up behind me and asks, "What do you need, Delaney?"

"I need to get the hell out of this wing for the next week. What can you do to help me?" I ask the nurse who makes our schedules.

"Out of this wing? Why?" she asks as she looks over the schedule.

"A man has a hard dick for me. He's going to be here most likely every day to see a patient in this wing. I know it's just to get to me, so I want away from here." I look over her shoulder and see that Rhonda is working the cancer ward. "See if she'll switch with me, please. I have to get away from the man."

"You sound worried," she says as she looks at me with concern. "Is he a threat?"

"Not in the way that's illegal, no." I look away and wonder what my problem really is, then find the words coming out of my mouth. "He's sexy as hell, the most handsome man I've ever met, and he's rich. I'm afraid my good sense will go out the window if I'm around him too much. When you throw in the fact that he's been pretty damn nice to me, it's apparent I can't trust myself."

"That sounds amazing," she says as she looks at me like I'm insane. "That does not sound like a man you should be hiding from in this vast hospital."

"He's the owner of Bargain Bin, the chain that ruined my family's business. He's the enemy. Get it now?" I ask as I tap the computer screen to show her Rhonda is on call and in the sleeping quarters. "I'll go see her, to ask her in person, if you're cool with the change."

"Your enemy, huh? Not a lot of people have enemies, Delaney."

"So is that a yes?" I ask as I walk away from her.

"I guess so. But you should really reconsider this and get to know the rich, handsome man, even if he is your family's enemy," she calls out after me.

I shake my head and wag my finger behind me as I head out to find Rhonda and divert myself from this path Blaine Vanderbilt is right in the damn middle of.

The break room is full as I turn to go inside to get to the sleeping quarters that are behind it. There's food set out on the long side table we use when it's someone's birthday or when it's some other special occasion when we all bring in food for a celebration.

"Wow, who's birthday?" I ask. "And where's the cake?"

"Look, Delaney, lobster bisque," the janitor, Billy, shows me as he pulls up a spoonful of thick, creamy goodness. There's a large chunk of lobster right in the middle of it. "And you are the reason for this feast."

An intern comes up to me with a card. When I open it, I see the food is a gift from Blaine Vanderbilt for all of our hard work here at the hospital. My name is the only one on the card, as he wrote that I was a special nurse who was aiding his friend's family in their terrible time of need.

"What a crock of shit!" I say, making everyone look at me with slack jaws.

Paul comes up behind me and looks at the card over my shoulder. "Uh, oh. Seems someone is smitten with you, Delaney. Now how did that happen so fast?" I turn to find his hands on his hips as his eyes dance.

"I'm not sure. I suppose it's because I hate the man. You all enjoy. I won't take a bite of the food the evil man who owns Bargain Bin sent. But if you guys want to eat the food from the devil, go right ahead. Much like Eve when she ate the apple in the Garden of Eden and it became her downfall."

"Halloween was last month, Delaney," another one of the nurses I work with calls out to me, then shows me a pretty delicious-looking, tiny cake. "Evil, devil, and words like that have no place in November. It's a time for thanksgiving. Come on, try some of the food. It's all fantastic."

I make my way through the people and find the woman I'm looking for at the back of the room eating a large plate of food. "Hey,

Rhonda, I'd like to talk to you about switching schedules for the next few days or so."

"And why is that?" she asks, then places a huge bite of some type of sandwich—it looks like roast beef—into her mouth.

"I need out of this wing until the Peterson kid is released. So can you help me out?" I ask as I watch her eat.

She nods, then swallows before she says, "Just one thing, though. I want out of that ward until after the first of January. I hate all the hoops we have to jump through when the hospital lets people come up to visit the cancer patients during the holidays. It just poops me out and the charge nurse over there can randomly stick you as the aid to any one of the crazy celebrities who come in to visit the kids. I hate it."

"Deal," I say without hesitation. "I'll take that over trying to fend Vanderbilt off any day."

"I have to tell you that you are a crazy woman, Delaney. If that hot piece of man-meat was after me, I'd roll over quick and in a hurry for him."

The smell of roasted chicken wafts past my nose as Paul comes up beside me, a chicken leg roasted to perfection waving in the air as he says, "Unless a man is willing to drop down on one knee and pledge his undying and committed to love to Delaney Richards, he doesn't stand a chance. Vanderbilt went wrong when he simply asked her out on a date. Yes, Delaney, I heard about that."

Fantastic. I'll be the laughing stock of the entire hospital now!

A CHILLY FALL BOOK TWO

A Holiday Romance

By Michelle Love

Intrigue. Lust. Passion

All of the charm in the world doesn't seem to be helping Blaine win the good favor of the feisty red-head, Delany Richards, who he finds so intriguing that she's consuming his thoughts.

Delaney is fighting an attraction to the gorgeous man, but her family's loss overpowers her desire for the man who ruined the family's small tire shop in her hometown.

When Delaney's boss lets her know she is the one who will be at Blaine's side as he makes visits to the children in the hospital, she's forced to hang out with the man all day as he visits the sick children.

Their mutual attraction is hard to deny, but her will is strong. Can Blaine prove he's a changed man and win her over?

9

BLAINE

November 15th:

"The background check has cleared, Blaine. You can start your charity work at The Children's Hospital today," my secretary, Blanch, lets me know.

"Great," I answer her over the intercom in my office. "Can you call Kate and Kent in their offices and send them in here, please?"

"Will do, Mr. Vanderbilt. And would you like me to bring in the coffee service for your meeting with them?"

"That would be very nice of you. Please do that."

I've been practicing my please and thank you's as often as I can. Turning over a new leaf means changing the usual way I talk to people too. I used to think there was no reason to use gratuitous remarks when you are dealing with people in business.

Kate is the one who is in charge of helping me with my hard edges. Kent is in charge of helping me figure out what I can do to make my business fairer to the local economies. So far, we've yet to come up with much.

The door to my office opens up and my brother and sister come inside, followed by the coffee cart, complete with pastries for our morning meeting. "Good morning," I say as I sit at my desk.

"It's nice if you get up and greet the people who come into your office, Blaine," Kate tells me.

I nod. "I'll try to remember that."

She shakes her head and grabs Kent by the arm before he can make himself a cup of coffee. "Wait! Blaine, you need to practice doing that. Then it will become a habit and you'll do it automatically. Get up, come shake our hands, greet us with a smile, and say some nice words."

With a sigh, I get up and go with my hand extended to do her little exercise. I take her hand first. "Good morning. My, don't you look pretty today? Tell me, how did you sleep last night?"

I earn another shake of her head, sending her blonde curls bobbing away. "Blaine, that's too personal. And the pretty remark might be considered flirty or sexist. Stick with the normal, 'good morning, lovely to see you' thing. Okay. Now, try to do better with Kent."

I turn to find Kent waiting with a tight-lipped expression. "How do you do, sir?" I ask as I shake his hand.

"Not very well, Mr. Vanderbilt," he says as Kate and I both look at him with confused expressions. "I'm trying to give you the chance to interact with someone who's not having a great day, Blaine."

"Oh, I see now. Okay," I say, then take a step back. "What seems to be the trouble, old man?"

"Not 'old man,'" Kate corrects me.

"Fine. What seems to be your malfunction, jackass?" I laugh, but it's only me who's laughing.

"Come on," Kate whines. "Be serious. Watch me." She reaches out to shake Kent's hand. "Good morning, Mr. Vanderbilt. How is your day going?"

"Terribly," he says with a fake frown. "I bought a bag of tools at your store today, and when I opened it, I found it was missing three of the tools the label said it had in it. When I went to the customer service counter to return it and get a refund, I was told they don't issue refunds on electronics. I told them they were tools, not electronics. The lady pointed to the one electric thing in the picture of the tools inside of the bag—an electric screwdriver—and gave me a smile."

I start laughing, and then Kent really frowns at me. "That's crazy," I say as I pour myself some coffee.

"And that really happened to me yesterday, Blaine. At the store right here in town, that happened to me. We have real trouble here," he says, then makes himself a coffee.

"You should leave the cart, Blanch," I tell her. "It looks like this is going to be a lengthy meeting."

With a nod, she leaves us, closing the door behind her. Kate picks up a cinnamon roll and an apple juice, then takes a seat. "My advice is to make up a new refund policy comparable to any of the other large chain stores. After we get that done, then I will implement a training program for the customer service employees."

"That sounds like progress," I agree as I take my seat again. "And I've been cleared by the hospital to do some charity work there for the holidays. Today I will begin. So can I count on you two to work on the refund policy?"

Kent leans forward and says, "I think we need to stop buying everything so damn cheap, Blaine."

"Whoa, that's my main thing. I buy things cheap so I can sell them cheaper than anyone else does." I shake my head as I lean back in my chair.

"Well, the cheap crap shows up in the stores either broken, nearly broken, or missing parts. I know you're making it all work and the customers keep coming back, but it's not fair to keep taking people's hard-earned money for the same crap over and over again," he says and gives me a little smile at the end. "What if that was you?"

"Me?" I ask, then lace my fingers behind my head and lay my head on them as I look up. Pops invasion into my dreams hasn't slowed down one bit. His words are getting easier to recall when I wake up. Some of them are making an appearance in my memory with Kent's suggestion. *What if that was you?*

"You don't even use the things you place on your stores' shelves, Blaine," Kate tells me, then takes a bite.

"I can afford better," I say as I look at her. "I work hard to get what I have."

"So does everyone else, Blaine," Kent says, and his words hit home.

"You know, I need to say something to you both. I don't think I've ever told you before. I am proud of you two. I know you both work really hard. Maybe even harder now that you've taken consultant positions with my company. I just wanted you to know that."

The looks they give me make my heart pump a little faster. *This being nice thing really is great!*

10

DELANEY

"Do you like the green jello better than the red?" I ask a very tired and terrible-feeling thirteen-year-old girl who's just come back from her daily chemo treatment.

The dark shadows beneath her pale-blue eyes show me just how tired she really is, and it breaks my heart. I'm trying my best to get her interested in anything. When people space out the way she has been doing for the last week, it means they're thinking about giving up the fight.

"I don't care," she mumbles as I tuck the blanket in around her.

"I'll bring you some of each. I made them into jiggly Thanksgiving figures—turkeys, pumpkins, and cornucopias. I'll bring you one of each," I say as I plump her pillow, then lay her back down. "What do you think about that, Tammy?"

"I think I'd like to be left alone."

The poor girl only has her mother for support, and I'm afraid that's just not cutting it. She is the first person on my list if a good-looking celebrity decides to come in and visit.

Since the last of her hair fell out, she's been a shell of her former self. So I decide I'm going to go find her a wig that looks like the hair she used to have and bring it to her this afternoon. Maybe that will perk her up.

"I'll let you take a nap, then I'll be back at lunch time with a surprise for you, Tammy."

"Why?" she asks with a bland tone.

"Because I love you. You're my most favorite patient. You're nice and quiet. I really think you just need something to look forward to. So I'm going to surprise you every day."

Just as I turn off the overhead light so she can sleep, I hear her whisper, "I just want my mom."

Her mother has been so busy working—trying hard to make enough money to pay her ever-growing hospital bills—that she's had very little time to spend with Tammy.

"I know, baby," I whisper, then leave with a heavy heart. I wish like hell there was something I could do to help her.

I have to wipe a tear that's managed to escape me as I walk down the hall toward the nurses' station to see who's next on the list for me. "Use me where you need me the most." I hear a familiar man's voice.

When I go around the corner, I see him. "You!"

"Hey, you!" Blaine Vanderbilt greets me with a huge smile. He has on dark-brown scrubs, like he's a nurse or doctor or some shit, and a pilgrim hat. I don't know how he's managing to still look so damn handsome in that stupid hat, but he's pulling it off.

His hand moves with ease to the small of my back as he moves us away from the nurses' desk. "What are you doing?"

He looks at the charge nurse over his broad shoulder. "I'll follow her around today."

"No, he won't!" I say and try to stop, but his hand moves around to hold my elbow, and somehow, he manages to keep me moving.

"Room 536 is next, Delaney. And stop being so hard to get along with. Mr. Vanderbilt is here to make the kids happy. Put your happy face on, Nurse Richards. It's about the kids, not you!" Sheila, my boss, tells me.

"Yes, it's about the kids, Delaney," he says with a low voice that's creamy and rich. "Not you. Now I know where you've been hiding from me. I've missed you as I've visited Sammy and his family every day. He's doing much better, you know."

"I do know. I've asked about him. And I heard that you ask where I am every day. How did you find me here? Who is the rat who told on me?"

"How sweet that you think I'd resort to stalking you," he says with a chuckle. "No one told on you. I had no idea you were working with the cancer patients. Just good luck, I guess. I filled out a form to come and visit the kids here and help make their holidays better. My background check cleared, and I started my work here just now. I think it's more than just a happy coincidence you're here too."

"I don't believe you," I let him know. "I'll find out who told you."

"Paranoid?" he asks as he opens the door to my next patient's room.

I give him a go-to-hell look, then step in past him as he holds the door open. "Hello, Terry, how are you doing today?" I ask the fifteen-year-old boy with stage-three cancer in his leg.

His eyes go straight to Blaine as he answers me, "Not too good. It really hurts today. Can I have more pain meds, boss?"

"Hello, Terry," Blaine walks past me to introduce himself. "I'm Blaine. I'm here to help get you kids into the spirit of the holidays." He reaches into one of the pockets of his scrubs and produces a pumpkin lollipop.

Terry smiles as he takes it from him. "Yum. So, about more pain meds."

Blaine looks at me, and I assume he notices my frown. This kid has asked for more pain medication every day. He takes the chair on the other side of the bed. "So, tell me what has you cooped up here."

Terry turns his attention to Blaine as I busy myself with checking his vital signs and tidying up his mess. "I was swimming at the end of the summer and felt a pain in my leg. I thought it was just a cramp, but it didn't go away. Four days later, I couldn't take the pain anymore and told my parents about it."

"You kept that to yourself all that time?" Blaine asks the kid.

"Yeah, I'm not some wimpy kid. I'm tough. I play football, ride motocross, and have even skydived. I'm not a crybaby."

"I'd say you're not!" Blaine agrees. "So, you have something in your leg, then?"

"Yeah, a big cluster of some cells that are overgrowing. And this crap hurts, man. The radiation isn't working. The chemo is terrible too," Terry says.

I have to intervene. "Terry, the radiation is working and the tumor is getting smaller. And the chemo is what's making the radiation work better. It takes time—the same way it took time for that tumor to grow."

Terry hooks his thumb at me and smiles at Blaine, "Nurse Hot Redhead, here, is the eternal optimist."

"She is one hot redhead, isn't she?" Blaine asks, then winks at me. "But, I think she must be right about your tumor and the treatment working." Blaine looks around the room. "I don't see any kind of gaming system in here. You don't like to play any video games?"

"I'm really more of an outdoor kind of kid. I don't even own any gaming systems," Terry says as he opens his lollipop and puts it in his mouth.

"Not yet," I say, pulling it right back out and handing it to him. "I have to take your temp."

He nods and looks grim as I bother him with taking his temperature. Blaine looks on and asks, "If I got you one and some cool games like football and motocross games, would you like that?" Terry nods enthusiastically. "Would you let me play with you too?"

Again, he nods, and I take the thermometer out of his mouth. "That would be freaking awesome! Are you rich or something?"

"I have a dollar or two in the bank. I'm going to take the hot redhead out for lunch to help me pick up some things, so you can look forward to playing some football with me after lunch. How does that sound?" Blaine asks him as I start to fume.

He's a fool if he thinks I'm going to lunch with him!

11

BLAINE

"Have you ever looked at yourself in a mirror when you get pissed off?" I ask Delaney, as she's fuming mad about having to go to lunch with me. The charge nurse told her to, so she could help me buy the things I'm going to give some of the patients. "Your cheeks get this rosy color to them and your green eyes sparkle like gems. The way your bottom lip is trembling is crazy good too."

"And you are infuriating!" she says as she presses the button on the elevator to take us down to the lobby.

I pull out my phone and call my driver. "Pick us up in front. We're on our way down now."

"Who's picking us up?" she asks as she crosses her arms in front of her.

"My driver." I look her up and down as I take the pilgrim hat off. "I really like that color on you. Pink isn't a color I'd say naturally goes with your hair color. I think it's the pink in your cheeks that lets you pull it off."

"Stop looking at me!" she says with a scowl, which only serves to make her even prettier. "And I don't want to ride around in a limo with you! I'll take my own car."

"First, it's not a limo. I'm not eighty. It's a Suburban. I brought it today so we'd have plenty of room to carry all the things I´ll buy the kids. Smart, huh?" I ask her.

"Well, I'll take my own car anyway." The elevator stops and she steps out first, hurrying to get ahead of me as she starts to pull her car keys out of her purse.

Casually, I reach around her, take the keys, and put them in my pocket. "No, you're riding with me. I'm not about to waste time having my driver go slowly so you can keep up."

"Give me the keys," she says through gritted teeth.

With a shake of my head, I say, "No. And stop gritting your teeth. That's very bad for them. Now, tell me where you want to eat."

"Home. My plan was to go home for lunch and eat a tuna fish sandwich."

Taking her elbow, I steer her out the door and see my driver holding the back door of the car open for us. "This is Mr. Green. Mr. Green, this is Delaney Richards."

"Nice to meet you, ma'am," he says as she slides into the car.

"We'll be eating at that Chinese place I like," I tell him, then get in and scoot on beside her. "They have tuna there."

The face she makes nearly makes me laugh, then she says, "I'm allergic to MSG."

"Fine," I say, then tap the control that lowers the glass between Mr. Green and the back of the car. "Instead of that place, take us to Dillon's Café."

"Of course," he says, then rolls the window back up.

Laying my arm on the back of the bench seat, I stretch my legs out. "Long day for you already?"

"I was up at four this morning," she says as she rubs her temples. "But I'm used to it."

"I was up at six. Only a couple of hours behind you. Now, I want to know if there are any kids up there who really need a boost today. I only met four kids. I figure I'll make a few kids happy each day," I tell her and play with her thick ponytail a little.

Her hair is so soft and silky, and I bet it looks gorgeous when it's down, falling over her shoulders, which I'm sure are the color of creamy porcelain.

Moving her hand, she quickly brushes my hand away. "There's this one girl I was planning on getting a long, blonde wig for. She's really down. Her mother is all she has and the poor woman is working so much overtime to pay her hospital bills, but it's not even making a dent in them. The poor little girl just wants her mom around more than anything else."

"Do you know where her mother works?" I ask, getting an idea.

"She's a waitress at Hasselbeck's. She's constantly working," she says.

I roll the window down again. "Sorry, Mr. Green. Another change of plans. Take us to Hasselbeck's instead."

"Yes, sir," he says and rolls the dark glass back up.

"And what do you plan on doing there?" she asks me as she frowns. "I shouldn't have told you where she works. I could get into trouble for that. It's confidential."

"Don't worry," I say and run my finger around her ponytail again. "She won't complain when I make her an offer."

Her green eyes roll. "And just what would that be?"

"You'll see." She moves her hair again and makes a huffing sound. "I really like the way your hair feels. What kind of shampoo do you use?"

"The cheapest stuff they make," she says. "I send any extra money I have to my parents so they can eat."

Like a punch to my midsection, her words take the wind out of me. "Ouch! About them. I'm working on making huge changes to my stores. I'm thinking about incorporating some of the businesses my stores shut down. I'd like to have your parents come to a meeting I'll be setting up with other owners I've shut out. My company will pay for everything. The flight to Houston, the hotel, their meals, everything."

"You're shitting me!" she says with wide eyes. "No way!"

"It's true. It's going to be scheduled for the first week in January. The invitations will be sent out just as soon as everything is made final. I'm changing the way we do business. I'm changing a lot about who I am, Delaney."

I watch her eyes go from wide open and accepting to a bit narrow and untrusting. "Well, when you get things finalized, then I'll believe you a little bit more. For now, you're pretty much all talk." The way her mouth quirks up into a crooked half-smile has me wanting to take those sweet lips and make them all mine.

I let out a sigh and wish she was into me the way I'm into her. But she's hard as a rock. "You will see. And just so you know, I'm doing this as much for myself as anyone else. It's me who decided to make these changes. With the death of my father, I found something opening inside of me for the first time in a long time. Since my mother died, I'd closed myself off."

"Your mother's dead too?" she asks and her eyes tilt a bit at the outer corners.

"She died twenty-five years ago, the day my brother was born. It took a lot for the five-year-old I was back then to understand why she never came back home after pops left us with his mother to take our mom to go have the baby. Pops came home alone, with Kent. He told Kate, who was three, and me that the Lord took our momma home with him. It kind of made me hate the guy."

"Your father?" she asks.

"No. The Lord."

12

DELANEY

I have to turn my head so Blaine doesn't catch me getting glassy-eyed with what he's told me. Swallowing back the lump that magically appeared in my throat, I manage to ask, "You don't hate God now, do you?"

With a shrug, he says, "I'm not exactly sure how I feel about him. I mean, pops is up there now too. If there really is a heaven. You see, he's been coming to me in my dreams."

"God?" I ask as I scoot over a bit. Because if he thinks God is coming to him in his dreams, he may be a little on the psychotic side.

"No, pops," he says with a light chuckle. "He's been talking to me and telling me what's right and what's wrong. He tried like hell to get me to listen to him when he was alive, but I wouldn't. Now he has my ear when I'm asleep and he talks and talks and it's beginning to sink in."

"So, you might really be changing," I say as I look out the window. "But, then again, you might revert right back to who you've always been after a year has passed. That's the typical mourning period after someone close to a person passes away. You might become the money-hungry vulture you've always been in a year's time."

"Wow, aren't you a little ray of sunshine!" he says with a sarcastic tone to his deep voice. "Thanks for the show of support."

"I'm not one of your supporters, so don't expect any from me." We pull up to the restaurant and stop at the front door. "I'm sorry if you don't like me."

"I happen to like you a lot. Your forthrightness is refreshing," he says with a smile.

"You've got to be kidding." The door opens and his driver is holding it open.

Blaine slides out and reaches back in for my hand. I take it only because the truck is tall and I don't want to fall when I get out of it. His arm runs around my waist as we walk up the walkway. He looks over his shoulder and says, "I'll bring you something delicious, Mr. Green, and a sweet tea too."

"Oh, thank you, sir!" his driver says, sounding genuinely glad to be getting some lousy take out while we go inside and eat and he has to wait in the car.

"Invite him in," I say.

"Huh?" he asks as he stops.

"You should invite him to join us," I tell him and find him smiling at me.

"Hey, Mr. Green," he turns around and calls out. "Park the car, come in, and join us, please. We'll wait right here for you."

"Oh, that's too much, sir," the older man argues. "The meal is more than enough."

"Insist," I whisper.

"I have to insist, Mr. Green. Please," he says.

"All right, sir. I'll just park, then, and be right up."

I let out a sigh and smile. "Now, that's a nice thing to do."

"See, you're good for me, Delaney." His hand moves up my back. "I need some good influences in my life right now. I've had them all along. I just ignored them. I'm not about to ignore you."

I find myself looking into his light-brown eyes and I want to believe him. "I'm more of a show-me kind of person, Blaine. I don't fall for words."

His hand creeps all the way up to rest on my shoulder and he pulls me closer to him as he whispers, "I'd love to show you, Delaney. I'm glad you don't fall for mere words. You're the kind of woman a man needs around him on a regular basis to keep him on the straight and narrow."

And just like that, I see he's looking at me to be his mother—someone I'm not about to become. But with his father's death still so fresh, I'm also not about to go on a rampage and tell him anything just yet.

Mr. Green makes his way to us, hobbling a little bit, and I notice he's giving in to his right knee. "Knee problems, Mr. Green?" I ask.

"Well, last month this one started giving out on me. I probably will have to have a knee replacement. My older brother had to have that done two years ago when he was my age."

We head into the restaurant, Blaine's arm still around my shoulders and me still wondering how I'm going to avoid falling for the handsome man with a troubled soul.

I spot Tammy's mother right away as she hustles around a table, picking up the empty plates. The hostess asks us if we want a booth or a table. Blaine answers quickly, "A booth. And I want one in," he looks at me. "What's her name?"

"We want a table in Patsy's section," I say.

"Oh, friends of hers," the hostess asks as she leads us away.

"Not yet," Blaine says. "But I hope we will be soon. You see, I'm about to make an attempt to steal her away from here."

"How romantic," the hostess says, then looks back at us. She takes notice of Blaine's arm around me, then frowns. "Oh, sorry. I guess I misunderstood."

Blaine laughs, and I nearly pass out as his lips touch the side of my head. "Not romantically. I'm going to offer her a job at my company."

"Now I get it. Well, she's one hell of a worker," she tells us, then gestures to a booth. Obviously, she ignored my words when I said we wanted a table instead of booth.

Blaine moves me into the booth and sits next to me, moving in so close that our legs touch. I lean against the wall and find him leaning too, so our bodies stay touching. "How about a little cocktail with lunch? I won't tell on you, Delaney."

"No," I say quickly. "No drinking when in charge of people's health. It's a hard and fast rule I have."

"I was just testing you," he says with a laugh. "You passed."

Patsy makes her way to us and nods when she sees me. "Nurse Richards, how's my girl doing today?"

"She's blue," I tell her. "But I think I have found something or someone to help."

Blaine extends his hand, and she shakes it with a confused expression. "Hello?"

"Hi, I'm Blaine Vanderbilt and I think I'm about to help your life become a bit easier for you. When can you take a break to talk to me?"

"Blaine Vanderbilt? The man who owns that chain of stores called Bargain Bin?" she asks.

"That is me," he says with a big, old smile.

"I'm sorry, sir. I don't see how you could make my life easier," she says. "Now, what can I get you all to drink?"

"Sweet teas all around," Blaine says. "Please give me a chance to tell you my offer. I think you'll like it very much."

She looks at him for a moment, then at me. "Can you vouch for him?"

I don't want to vouch for him. He hasn't even told me what he's going to offer her. But I find myself nodding anyway. "I can."

"Okay," she says. "I'll be back with your drinks, then place your order and take ten minutes to talk to you."

"Great!" Blaine says. "You will not be disappointed."

She leaves us and I ask, "So, what are you going to offer her?" His hand moves over my leg, and I nearly slap it away until I realize my keys he took from me back at the hospital are in it. I bite my lip with how hot his touch is making me and have to clear my throat before I say, "Oh, my keys. Thanks."

"I thought you might want them back. I forgot I had them until I sat down. They were making me uncomfortable."

Our hands touch under the table as I take the keys, and I hate the way my heart is pounding in my chest. *I hope he can't hear it!*

13

BLAINE

She smells like sterile alcohol and mint and it's driving me crazy. "What made you become a nurse, Delaney?"

"Um, the need for money. Nursing school was a shorter program and the need for nurses had me knowing I'd get a job as soon as I graduated," she answers as she looks at the menu. "Do you think the chicken-fried steak is good here?"

"I have no clue. You should ask our waitress, Patsy," I say as I look over her shoulder at the menu. Her hair smells like apples, and I take a deep breath. "Man, I love that shampoo."

She makes a little huffing sound as if I'm bothering her, and I know it's not in the way she's trying to make me think. When our hands had touched, hers had trembled. That only happens when you find the other person attractive. Her body is telling me more than she realizes.

"The picture on the menu looks good, so I'm going to go for it," she says, then hands me the menu. "You seem to be looking at mine instead of yours, so here you go."

"I'll have what you're having. It does sound good."

"Me too," Mr. Green says. "Thanks for inviting me. This place is pretty nice and the prices are reasonable. I think I might bring Mrs. Green here for dinner."

"That's so nice," Delaney says as she smiles at him. "How long have you been married?"

"Thirty-seven years. We've got three grown kids and five grand-kids. Life didn't start out too great for me. I was nineteen and in prison when I met my wife. She came into the prison on a missionary project with her church. I fell in love with her the minute I saw her."

"Aww," Delaney says, then looks at me. "Did you know that?"

I shake my head. "I've never taken the time to ask." My eyes move to Mr. Green, the man who's been my driver since the very beginning. "I'm sorry about that. It's just that I thought of employees as just another part of business. I made sure to keep emotions out of every aspect of it."

"You won't ever hear me complaining, Mr. Vanderbilt. I know many drivers who get caught up in the personal affairs of their employers. I've never had to worry about that with you."

"Well, nevertheless, I am sorry and I hope you know you can talk to me about anything you need. I know I've never been approachable in the past, but I'm changing that. If you have something, you let me know."

Patsy comes back to the table with a smile on her face. "Here are your drinks and what can I get you all to eat?"

"We've made it super easy for you. And take note, this is the last order you will ever have to take if you take me up on my offer, Patsy," I tell her. "We're all having the chicken-fried steak."

"You did make that easy," she says, then turns to leave.

"Hurry back," I say. "I can't wait to ask you."

She nods as she leaves, and I find it hard to believe she's not excited in the least. Delaney looks at me and says, "I can see you're not getting her calm demeanor, are you?"

"Not at all," I say as I watch her walking slowly to turn the order in. "If I was her, I'd be jumping around with the want to hear what the offer is. She seems somewhat distracted."

"She's having a hard time believing you can offer her anything that will actually help her. Her daughter is dying, Blaine. The only thing you can give her to make her happy or excited is to take the cancer away from her baby girl."

"Oh," I say, as I can't comprehend what she must feel like. I lost my parents, but to face the loss of a child would be devastating. "I can see I shouldn't expect much of a reaction. And you know what?"

She shakes her head as she looks into my eyes. "What?"

"That's okay. I'm not doing this to get great reactions out of anyone. I'm doing this to help. That's all. I don't need to get a damn thing out of this. I just need to help where I can. Thanks for explaining that to me, Delaney. You really are a Godsend."

Her eyes cut away, and I take her hand under the table. When she looks back at me, she has glassy eyes. "I'm not anything like that."

Pulling her hand up, I kiss the top of it. "Yes, you are."

My attention is taken as Patsy pulls up a chair and sits at the end of the table. "Okay, tell me what you have, Mr. Vanderbilt."

I don't really want to let Delaney's hand go, but I do as I turn my full attention to this woman who is having to live and work. Meanwhile her daughter might be living her last days or needing her more than she ever has since she was a baby.

My soul fills with something it has never experienced before. I don't even know what the hell to call it. Maybe empathy. I don't know. I just know it kind of hurts.

"Patsy, I want you to know I have no idea how hard things are for you right now. I do know that I can't fix anything for you or your daughter. I can, however, give you time to be with her. I can give you the money you need. I can give you a job that will pay you until you can come do it. I'm offering you a job at the headquarters of my company. The position is as a consultant. The salary is six figures and it comes with immediate insurance benefits. I will personally pay the co-pays. You don't have to worry about a thing. Just be there for your daughter during the time she needs you the most." I take my wallet, pull out three thousand dollars, and place it on the table in front of her. "This is your first bonus. If you take my offer, you'll be paid every Friday, starting this coming Friday. Do you need a minute to decide?"

"A minute?" she asks. "No, I don't need a minute." Tears start flowing in rivers down her pale cheeks. Her dirty-blond hair hangs in limp strands around a face I bet was pretty before this fell on her.

I hand her a napkin, and she wipes her tears, then breaks down completely. Delaney pushes me and whispers, "Give her a hug."

Getting up, I pull the poor woman up and hug her. Shushing her, I whisper, "I'll take that as a yes."

She can only nod as she cries, and I rock her back and forth as I hold her quivering body that's much too thin in my arms. Her reaction is nothing like I thought it'd be. I envisioned happiness, pure joy, some jumping up and down, and maybe a high five. Never this.

I don't know what kind of road I've stumbled upon, but it's certainly a lot more emotional than I ever thought it'd be.

14

DELANEY

The day hasn't gone the way I expected it would once I found out I had to spend it with Blaine Vanderbilt. Watching him hand out the gifts he'd brought to the four kids he met today is more than heartwarming.

The best part about it is watching Blaine, as something inside of him seems to be growing with each interaction. He seems to be gaining an understanding of the human spirit. It's kind of like watching a baby start walking and seeing how amazed and scared they find themselves.

"I'll let you practice today, but come tomorrow, I'm bringing my A-game, Terry," Blaine tells him, then gets out of the chair and hands him one more pumpkin lollipop. He turns back just before we walk out. "Hey, bro, do you want me to bring you anything when I come back in the morning?"

"No way," the teenage boy says. "Dude, you've given me enough. But I tell you what. There's this guy a little older than I am. He's major bummed about losing his golden locks. Go visit him tomorrow, will you? His name's Colby."

"Will do," Blaine says. "And let me tell you that I think you're one great guy. I think you'll go far in this life."

"If I live," he says.

Blaine looks back at me, and I can see he's upset with what the kid said. I shake my head and hold out my hand for him to come with me. "Time to go see Tammy."

He nods. "Bye, Terry. I'll see you tomorrow."

Once we're out the door, Blaine falls back on the wall. "Shit! This is hard!"

I still have his hand and find him tugging me to him. "Come on, Blaine. Around here, we suck things up. If you want to fall apart, you do that away from here. While we're here, we are nothing but a tower of strength."

He pulls himself together and stands up straight. "You're right. Okay, let's go visit Tammy now. I hope she likes the wig you picked out. Is her mom here yet?"

"I doubt it. You sent her to the salon to get all gorgeous. But she should be here soon, I'd think." She gives the door a quick two-tap knock. "Tammy, can I come in? I have a male visitor with me."

"Wait!" she shouts.

We wait, and then Delaney holds her hand up. "Wait here."

As I wait while she goes inside, I lean on the wall again and try to steady myself. I thought this would be like a walk in the park—an easy thing to do. Come to the hospital …give some gifts. Then I'd simply stand back and watch the kids smile about it. The huge waves of emotion are like a shot out of the dark.

The door opens and Delaney looks around, then over at me. "Again?" She holds out her hand. "Come on."

I take her hand and pull her out into the hallway. "Can you do me a favor and give me a purely platonic hug?"

Her eyes go soft and she pulls me into her arms. "I know how rough it is. But I can see things are working inside of you, Blaine. Don't let this give you a big head or anything, but I'm growing proud of you."

The way she's holding me tells me she's great at making people feel better. "You have a gift, Delaney. You really know how to help people."

She lets me go and gives me a smile. "Hmm. Now, maybe that's why I was sent in the direction to become a nurse. Maybe there was a bit of divine intervention that directed me to this place."

"Maybe so." The click-clack of high heels draws my attention, and I look down the hallway to see a tall, very pretty lady coming down it.

"Would you look at her?" Delaney says, then lets out a wolf-whistle.

"Is that Patsy?" I ask as I take a harder look.

"It is," Patsy says as she gets to us. "Thank you for the much-needed pampering, Mr. Vanderbilt. And the job. I feel better than I have in a long time."

"You are welcome," I say. "And may I say you clean up very nicely?"

"You may," she says with a bright smile. "And, now, to be with my daughter and try to rub some of this new, hope-filled attitude off on her."

"I'd say you have enough for that," I say, then we follow her into the dimly lit room.

"Mom?" the little girl in the bed asks.

Her eyes have deep, dark half-circles under them. She has a blue scarf around her head to cover her hairless, little head. I want to cry, but I know I can't do that. So I look at Delaney and reach out for her hand.

She looks at me with understanding and takes my hand as we stop and let the two of them have a moment.

Patsy runs her hand with a nice, pink manicure over her daughter's cheek. "Hey you. I have the best news ever. I'm going to be able to stay here with you for as long as you want me to."

"How's that?" the little girl asks. "You have to work. You didn't get fired, did you?"

Patsy laughs and looks back at me. "No, I quit my job at the restaurant. I'm now a consultant for the Bargain Bin chain of stores."

"What?" the little girl asks.

"Tell her, Mr. Vanderbilt," Patsy says.

"I gave your mother a job so she doesn't have to worry about bills.

She doesn't have to come to work until you're better. She's all yours, Tammy."

Tammy's light-blue eyes go to Delaney. "Did you have a hand in this, Nurse Richards?"

"Maybe," she answers. "You see, when you tell someone what you really want, sometimes it happens. You should do that more often."

Tammy's eyes fill up with tears and my stomach knots as she says, "Then I better get this said. I want to get better. I want to feel healthy again. I want to go home. And I want my hair back!"

Delaney laughs, pulls the wig she had stashed in her large pocket out, and holds up the long, blond hair. "Well, it's not yours, but will this do for now?"

She can only nod as she starts crying. All I can do is stand back and try my best to hold onto myself. I can't run out of here, bawling like a baby. But I also can't trust myself to say a damn word as emotion is filling me up.

Another nurse wheels a roll-away bed into the room, and I step out of her way. "Here we go. Seems mom's coming in full time, I've been told. Nurse Richards, you're officially relieved of your duty for the day. I'll see you back here in the a.m. I have them under my watchful eye for the night."

"See you guys in the morning. Have a good night, Tammy and Patsy."

"We will now," Patsy says. "And thank you again, Mr. Vanderbilt."

I nod and open the door, letting Delaney walk out in front of me. Instead of hurrying away, like I half-expected her to, she lingers in the hallway for me. "Are you okay, Blaine?"

Shaking my head, I look down as I walk toward the elevator. I still can't manage to talk with the knot that's formed in my throat. *This is terrible!*

"Want to go out for a drink?" she asks, shocking me.

15

DELANEY

With a nod, Blaine takes my hand, and we make our way to the nurses' station, where I pick up my purse, and then go to the elevator. I can see he's upset and trying hard to hold on.

Stepping into the elevator, I wait for the doors to close before I say, "I cried every day when we had clinicals in the nursing home. For three weeks, I left that place and cried for just about an hour the first few days, then it slowly dwindled down to nothing. Not that my heart got hard or anything like that. I just began to gain an understanding of life."

His Adam's apple bulges as he swallows, and the elevator doors open as we reached the lobby. "Ride with me. I'll pick you up in the morning, too. You can leave your car here."

"I can have a couple of drinks. It won't affect me for driving," I tell him, then stop as he makes an abrupt stop.

"No. I have a driver. If you want to get a drink with me, you have to do it this way."

I find myself a little taken aback. Honestly, I thought he'd jump through hoops to have a drink with me. So I test the waters a bit. "No, I want to drive, or I'm not going."

"Suit yourself." He lets my hand go and walks away. "I'll be in my car if you change your mind in the next two minutes."

I'm stunned and a little shocked. Then I'm really shocked to find my feet taking me as fast as they can up behind the man. "Wait!"

He stops, but doesn't turn around. "Yes?"

"What's the big deal?" I ask as I get in front of him.

"The big deal is that I don't let my friends drink and drive. After what we shared today, I consider you a friend."

"You do?" I ask and start walking backward as he begins to move forward.

"Yes. So, are we on for drinks or not?" he asks, and I find myself in the wrong position.

I thought I was calling the shots here!

His driver pulls up and jumps out, opening the door as I stand there looking at Blaine and not completely understanding where I stand with him. I thought he wanted me and would do anything to have me. I might have been very wrong.

He gestures to the back seat, and I find myself getting into his car. Without a word, I move over, put my seatbelt on, and find him sliding in. "Thank you," he says as he puts his seatbelt on too. "I really could use your company after this trying day. I can't think of a better person to wind down with after all I've seen and heard today."

"Glad to be of help to you," I say.

He's holding himself in a tense posture and his eyes look tired. I recall that look. We all had it when we started the training to become nurses. My first stint in the terminal ward nearly killed me.

"It gets easier. I know it's hard to believe, but it does. You aren't thinking of bailing out now, are you?" I ask him as he looks vacantly out the window at the streetlights that flash as we go underneath them.

"I will not be bailing. I made a commitment and I intend to keep it. I always fulfill my commitments. I think I need to learn how to reign in these emotions. I can do it in business. I just have to figure out how to do it with poor, little, sick kids too."

"I think it's important to feel things. And, with time, it gets easier.

You still feel empathy, but you gain an understanding and can control the crying, or in your case the complete sadness. I know men don't cry," I say and giggle.

"Men cry," he says. "I should probably just break down and do that, huh?"

My heart stops as he admits this to me. I've never known a man who would let me see that deeply into them. I'm not sure if I can handle it. It might be too much to take.

I watch as he takes off his seatbelt, then gets off the seat and onto his knees in front of me. His hands move up the sides of my thighs as he looks up at me. I run my hands through his dark-blond waves and look back into his eyes.

"Or I could kiss you," I say without thinking.

"That might help too," he says, then moves up until our lips are so close I can feel the warmth of his breath on mine.

He waits with them that close, then I realize I said I could kiss him. He's waiting for me to come to him!

I can't believe I am going to do this!

My hands come around to cup his face in them without me thinking about what I'm doing, and I pull him the rest of the very short distance to press my lips to his. His lips are soft and supple, and I want to feel more.

I feel his hands moving back and forth along my outer thighs, stirring heat inside of me. I've gone this far. I might as well go a little further.

My tongue moves over his lower lip, and he parts them. Slowly, I move mine past his lips and find his. His hands move up my sides until he's gripping my waist as his mouth goes soft and yielding to mine.

I cannot believe I initiated this. But, damn, I'm glad I did!

When he pulls back, slowly ending the kiss, I find myself breathing a bit on the hard side. "Thank you," he whispers with a throaty voice.

"Thank you," I say as my head is so light it feels as if I'm drunk.

Who needs alcohol when one kiss from the man on his knees in front of you can intoxicate you. *And there's no fear of a hangover!*

"Did that help?" I ask, running my hand under his chin as he gazes at me.

He nods. "Wanna help me some more?"

I nod and find his mouth back on mine. Now he's taking control of the kiss, unbuckling my seatbelt, and pulling me to him. We end up on the floor, me on top of him. His manhood is swelling under my crotch, making me go wet for him.

This is by far the fastest any man has ever made me this horny and hot!

Rolling over, he pins me underneath him and pulls his mouth away only a little as he says, "How about drinks at my place, then we can take a quick dip in the indoor swimming pool? My cook can make us something great for dinner."

"That's probably a bad idea," I say with a hoarseness to my voice I don't ever recall having before.

"Why is it a bad idea?" he says, then kisses my neck as he grinds into me.

"I think we both know why it's a bad idea."

"I won't do anything you don't want to, Delaney," he says, then my earlobe is between his teeth, sending a shot of pure ecstasy through me.

The only problem with that is that I think it would be damn hard to say no to this man. I can't be that girl—that slutty chick who has sex right off the bat with a man. I barely know him!

And he is my family's mortal enemy. *What am I doing?*

16

BLAINE

I knew it was a long shot that she'd accept my offer to take her to my place, but I had to ask. So I get off her and pull her up with me to take our seats. "Sorry. I had to ask." I buckle her in as she looks a little discombobulated.

Her ponytail has gotten messed up, so I pull the rubber band all the way out and use my hands to fan out her hair and fix it a little. It looks great, just like I knew it would.

She blinks a few times in rapid succession. "Sorry, that's not like me."

"Don't be sorry. I can see you're not a tramp. So what bar do you like to go to?" I ask her as I put my seatbelt on. I can see I've affected the hell out of her and it has me on cloud nine.

I would jump up and down if she wasn't around to see it!

Her head falls back on the headrest and she looks at me with shining green eyes. "That really isn't like me, Blaine. I want you to know that, and I want you to know I won't ever do that again."

"Well, that's some really bad news. I liked that a lot and I am going to want to do that a lot more." I reach over to adjust her shirt, as half her bra is showing. "Nice bra!"

Her head snaps forward as she finally notices what I'm doing and bats at my hands. "I can do it!"

"Where did you get that?" I ask her as she puts herself back into place.

"What?" she asks.

"The pink, lacey bra? Fredrick's? It's sexy," I say and lean toward her, then take her hands to stop her from messing around with her shirt. "You're sexy."

"Ha! I really fucked up!" she says as she looks at me with scared, little, rabbit eyes.

"I can see you're scared."

Before I can finish, she laughs. "I'm not scared. I am smart! You are a rich, rich man, and my family's sworn enemy! I can't get into bed with you!"

"Sworn enemy? Well, that's not cool, is it? But I have a plan that will completely fix that. I don't like being the sworn enemy of anyone. That was never my intention when I started my business. And what's this talk about getting into bed with me?" I wait for her response and smile when her cheeks go nearly as red as her hair.

"Don't act like that wasn't your intention," she says. "You asked me to come to your house. You know what you wanted. I'm just saying it out loud."

"I think I said I wouldn't do anything you didn't want me to. I don't recall asking you to sleep over. It seems to me your inner mind is telling you that it's something you want to do. If that's the case I need you to know that I am all for that idea. You can sleep over if you want. I'll lend you a T-shirt, or better yet, you can sleep naked. I think that's an even better idea. Should I tell Mr. Green to take us home, then?"

"You're making me dizzy with all of your intellect, Blaine. Let's go to that club over there. It's all lit up and seems to be hopping. No going to your home to swim, eat, and have sex," she says, then gestures for me to roll the window down to let my driver know I want to stop there.

I roll the window down. "Can you drop us at the club, Mr. Green? We'll hang out there while you go take your wife to dinner. My treat."

I just thought of that brilliant plan. That way I'll have her to myself for the next couple of hours.

"Oh, how nice of you, sir. Thanks so much!" he says, then rolls the window back up.

"That'll take a couple of hours, Blaine. I meant a drink or two," she says.

"I'm not going to be pouring them down your throat, Delaney. We can dance, talk, and kiss some more. There's more to do than just drink in these kinds of places."

"We can't kiss anymore. That was a mistake," she says as we pull to a stop in front of the club.

Grabbing her hand, I get out, meet my driver at the door, and slide a couple of hundreds into his palm. "Give us at least two hours, please."

He nods and smiles. "I like you two together. You balance each other out very well. Mrs. Green is going to love to meet you, Nurse Richards. I'll have her with me when I come back for you two."

"That sounds nice, Mr. Green," she says, then I pull her away to go to the door with the loud music rocking behind it.

"I feel weird going out in scrubs," she says as we go inside.

"Tomorrow we can go home first and change, then go out, if you want to."

She looks at me kind of funny as I pay the guy at the door, and he stamps our hands then we head into the crowd of people. Her hand is tight in mine as the sea of people make us stay close together. Pulling her through the people like this is slow going to get across the dance floor to the bar. So I pull her around in front of me and hold her tightly as I dance across the floor with her in my arms.

The surprised look on her face is priceless, then her arms go around my neck as she gets what I'm doing. "You're very smart."

"I know," I say, then kiss the tip of her nose. "You're very beautiful."

"I know," she says with no hesitation.

It's pretty obvious she knows how beautiful she is. She knows she's smart and talented too. She hasn't got an insecure bone in her body, and her sweet, kind, giving soul pulls all of Delaney Richards together into one tight, little package.

Picking her up when I reach the outer edge of the dance floor, I carry her to the bar as she smiles at me. "Name your poison, sugar."

"I'll have whatever you're having," she says as I place her feet on the ground.

Pressing my lips to her ear, I say, "What I really want, they don't serve here."

She shakes her head and laughs. "I get it. Give me a gin and tonic."

Wiggling my finger at the young bartender who can't keep her eyes off me, I ask her, "Do you make a good gin and tonic?"

"I can make you a good anything, handsome," she says, and I see my little redhead's cheeks go red.

She holds her tongue, though, so I decide I'll press it a bit. "Hey, honey, can you tell me what your specialty is?"

The bartender, who I can tell is a really easy woman, is quick to say, "My specialty is the cock and balls. I can administer pleasure to them for hours." She laughs a high-pitched laugh, then puts two fingers over her mouth. "Oh, you meant what drinks, didn't you?"

I barely catch Delaney as she cracks her neck, then leans over the bar. "Hey, bitch! Ease up there, honey. I guess you can't see—he's with me!"

"So?" the poor fool says, and I barely catch the empty shot glass that was sitting on the bar. Delaney snatches it up and throws it right at the other woman's head.

"Whoa," I say and take Delaney's hands into mine. "Where did that come from?"

"Let's go to your place. This place is making me sick!" she says.

I find myself hurrying to leave as I hold her close to me again and dance her back across the dance floor. "I'll get us a cab and call my driver to let him know he has the rest of the night off."

"You do that," she says as she looks into my eyes. "I want to have a sleepover."

Holy shit!

A FALL FEAST BOOK THREE

A Holiday Romance

By Michelle Love

Blurb: Secrets. Desire. Passion.

Delaney and Blaine have one very steamy night and with it comes a little agreement. She agrees to be his, but only sexually, and they have to keep their little secret from getting out to the hospital staff.
Both find jealousy comes along with keeping their relationship private.
After a week of staying together every night, Thanksgiving comes along, and they throw a party for their cancer kids.
One of the parents puts a damper on one of Blaine's good deeds, reminding Blaine that life isn't always great. The shininess of his new path is wearing off fast, leaving Delaney to watch him retreat into his former self.
Or can she stop him from going that direction?

17

DELANEY

November 15th:
   The whole cab ride to Blaine's estate is a blur of his hands all over me, his mouth all over mine, and so much heat that I had to stop myself from pulling my clothes off.

I don't know what's come over me. That bitch bartender set something off inside of me with her blatant remarks to Blaine that sent me into a red-hot anger instantly.

I can't believe I threw a shot glass at her!

It's hard to imagine, but I was actually reining myself in when I threw that little empty glass at the brunette bitch from hell. I wanted to jump over that bar and completely kick her ass.

And that is not like me!

Not at all. So I made a snap decision to have sex with Blaine Vanderbilt. I figure such a rash reaction to a woman coming on to him means there's just way too much sexual tension between us and the best way to get that over with is, quite obviously, to have sex.

With this out of the way, I can go on and be more normal. He might be around the hospital the whole holiday period and I can't be getting insanely jealous when women talk to him. It's not professional!

So, in the name of staying professional, I am about to walk out of this very nice bathroom and into Blaine Vanderbilt's master bedroom, where he's waiting for me on his large, king-size bed.

My heart is racing and I take one last look in the mirror to see if this is really something I want to do. I find my eyes shining back at me and a grin that won't go away.

Yeah, it's something I want to do!

Need to do, really. It's been a month or so since I've had sex. It was with Paul and it was not spectacular—something he said was my doing. It seems I'm bossy in bed. Or so he said, anyway.

I was just trying to get him to do things that were pleasing to me. I don't think of that as bossy so much as necessary, at least where he was concerned.

Stepping back from the vanity with globe lights all across the top of the mirror, I shake my hair out a little so it'll look a bit wild. I want tonight to be over-the-top hot.

I need it to be!

Blaine is a one-shot deal. I'll take all I can from this because I can't allow myself any more than that. He is the enemy of my family, and I just know he'll go back to his ways once his mourning over his father's death passes.

I take one shot of mouthwash to make sure my breath is minty fresh, then I spit it out, rinse the sink, and ...

"Hey, you okay in there?" I hear Blaine call out.

My body has frozen for some reason. I can't seem to talk or move. Then a knock comes at the door and I feel as if I might pass out. "I'm fine," I manage to say.

"You want to talk?" he asks me.

I just about melt with his words. He'd talk to me instead of screwing me—awww!

Taking a step toward the door, I open it and find him standing there in a pair of pajama bottoms and nothing else. They're black with gray fleur-de-lis all over them. "Nice jammies," I say as I look at them instead of his chiseled upper body.

Out of the corner of my eye, I can see some massive hills and valleys, and I'm afraid to look at it all head-on. He is very impressive in the muscle department.

One of his fingers hooks my bra strap. "Nice bra and panty set. But I think I've told you something about your bra being sexy before. Are you feeling nervous?"

"Me?" I ask with a really high voice.

"Yes, you, Delaney," he says with a smile I can hear in his voice, as I won't look up at him. Then his hand is on my chin, lifting my face up. My eyes graze over his abs, which are ladder-like in structure. They go up and over his pecs that move as he breathes. Then they land on his very handsome face. His light-brown eyes are glittery as he looks at me.

"I suppose you think I'm nervous because I've taken some time to freshen myself up for this."

"For me," he says, then his hand leaves my chin. One fingertip runs over my lips, outlining them. "You were taking some time getting ready for me. Isn't that what you meant?"

"Kind of, I guess. It's been over a month. I wanted to be sure everything was neat and tidy," I say, then find him moving that finger past my lips, into my mouth, and I suck it quite involuntarily.

"I want you to know I think you're very special. A one-of-a-kind woman. I want you to know this isn't something cheap to me. You can trust me, Delaney."

He pulls his finger out of my mouth and runs his hand over my shoulder, then all of a sudden, he has me in his arms, picking me up. "I can walk."

"I want to carry you. I want you to know I respect you. I want you to know you are safe with me. Do you understand that?" he asks me, then places me on his bed with the black comforter turned down so the white sheets show.

My head rests on a fluffy, black pillow, and I watch him look at my hair that's splayed out over the pillow case. "Are you thinking about joining me on the bed, Blaine?"

He nods, but stays standing. "I love the way your hair looks against the black pillow. I love the way your body looks, lying in my bed. I think I could get used to this."

And now he's gone and made it all weird!

18

BLAINE

The contrast of the colors of her hair and the black color of my bed's pillows and blanket make my heart beat a little harder. She is gorgeous and she is here in my home and in my bed.

I can't believe it!

"Can you turn the lights off?" she asks me as she points at the lamp that's on the bedside table.

"I think I'd like to look at you for a while, if that's okay."

"Blaine, you're making this weird," she says, then sighs. "Can't we just get right back to the heavy making out we were doing on the ride here? I think things will progress on their own."

Lying on the bed beside her, I get on my side, rest my head in one hand, and run the other hand over her stomach as I look down at her. "No need to rush things. Tell me more about yourself, Delaney Richards. Tell me what your favorite color is."

Her green eyes roll as she says, "Green. So we're going to get to know each other some more, huh? Then tell me what your favorite color is, Blaine."

"It's blue. I like that deep, cerulean blue. What kind of car do you drive?"

"A Honda."

"What kind of car would you like to drive?" I ask as I take my fingertips and barely touch the exposed part of her breast above her pink bra.

"I'd like to drive a Mercedes. But that's a few light years away for me. I suppose you have every vehicle you've ever even half-way wanted to drive." Her hand moves up my arm and rests on my bicep.

"Yes," I say and let my finger dip down into the valley between her plump breasts. "What is your absolute favorite meal? Like, if you were on death row and it was your last meal, what would you pick?"

"Easy—pizza," she says. "From Dominick's—the thin crust with Italian sausage, mushrooms, peppers, and a ton of mozzarella cheese. And you?" She gives my bicep a nice squeeze, indicating she likes the way it feels in her hand.

"Promise not to laugh?" I ask her as I stroke her hair.

"Promise, unless it's really crazy," she says.

"At least you're honest," I say, then kiss her forehead. "My favorite food is chicken noodle soup with saltine crackers."

"I have a feeling there's a reason behind that." Her hand is soft as she moves it over my cheek and gazes into my eyes as if she can almost see the reason, but can't quite make it out.

"That's the only food I remember my mother making for me. I guess it was one of the last things she made before she left us to go to the hospital. I recall one of the first things I thought when pops told us mom wasn't coming home again was that I'd never taste her soup again."

"I'll make you some," she says, then pulls me to her and hugs me tightly in her small arms.

I hear her heart beating under my ear and feel myself falling. *I'm falling so damn fast for her, it's insane!*

Moving my hands up and down her arms, I move them behind her and unclasp her bra. I hear her heart beat faster and smile against her skin. Moving back, I pull her bra away and find myself looking at a very nice set of tits. "Those are nice."

"Thanks," she says, then pushes at the waist of my pajama bottoms. "How about you get rid of these?"

Rolling off the bed, I get up and take her panties off first. My cock goes even harder with the sight of her naked body on my bed, and I know I could get used to this in a hurry. "I have to tell you once again, Delaney, you are gorgeous."

Reaching over to turn off the light like she requested a while ago, I stop as she says, "Leave that on. I'd like to see what you're working with."

"You would, huh?" I slide the pajamas down and watch her as she takes me all in with wide eyes. She pulls her bottom lip in and holds it with her teeth. She makes a gesture for me to turn around, and I do as she's asked.

"Oh, Lord help me, Blaine," she says with a moan. "I have to let you know you are a work of art."

"Aww, come on now. I'm not that great," I say and fall onto the bed beside her.

"You know you are," she says with a smile. "I can see it in your eyes. You're hot as hell and you are well aware of the fact."

"I might be a little aware of it," I tell her, then lean over her and kiss her the way I've wanted to for a while now.

Her hands feel like satin as they move over my arms, then around my neck as she pulls me to move over her. I only lay half of my body on hers as I take her in my arms and kiss her like she's the most special person on this planet.

Her body feels perfect against mine. Her lips form so completely to mine. It's as if she was made with me in mind. Everything about her intrigues or excites me. From the curve just above her plump ass to the bow in her top lip. Everything about her draws my attention and admiration.

One of her hands touches my stomach in a downward caress. Needles of anticipation pepper my skin as she goes down until she has my cock in her hand, moaning as she runs her hand up and down it.

She has no idea how badly I want to be inside of her right now.

But I want her to feel special. She's the kind of woman who remembers every little word you say. I will show her I mean it—not just tell her.

As she moves her hand up and down my length, making it harder and longer, I move my hand down to dip my finger into her only a bit, to wet it, then I move up her folds and find her little button.

She arches up to me slightly as she moans, and I feel the vibration in my mouth, making my tongue tingle. She is the sexiest thing I've ever had in my bed. And I've had many women in this bed.

Women I thought nothing of. Women who were there to give me pleasure and that was it. Women who meant nothing to me.

Delaney Richards is the first women I've ever felt anything for. From the moment I saw her, I knew I'd have her someday. But I want more than just this night from her.

So I'm going to show her why she's going to want to come home with me every day after work. I'm going to make her scream for mercy that I will not give until I have pleasured her in every way imaginable.

Her nipples are hard against my chest. I have her ready and primed, but I'm not about to give her all she wants just yet. My mouth leaves hers as I kiss along her neck. She moves her hand on my cock a little faster, then I move my hand to take hers away from me. I'm about to show her what it feels like to be mine.

I will make her beg to become mine and mine alone.

19

DELANEY

I can tell I should not be doing this!

Everywhere the man touches me leaves me tingling. And now that he's making a trail of kisses down my body, I know I'm in for it. If his mouth feels as good as it does everywhere else, I know he's going to be amazing in that area too.

"Ah!" I shout as his lips touch my throbbing clit. I grip the sheet in my hands and hang on so I don't end up on the ceiling. I'm arching up to him so high.

I'm a wanting slut!

He's making a fantastic groan as he kisses me in my most intimate of areas. It's as if it's actually pleasing him to do this to me. Most men have seen this as a chore and something to hurry me along, rather than how he's acting.

His fingers are gripping my ass as he lifts me and kisses me hard. His tongue is moving up and down my folds and every third or fourth time he lets it slip inside of me.

Already my legs are shaking, as I've never felt anything like this. Not anything!

I'm beginning to think all the other men I've been with didn't know what the hell they were doing when they did this to me. I certainly never felt my body coming undone the way it is right now.

His teeth nip me just a little and it brings a scream out of my mouth. "Blaine! God!"

He goes right back to making a meal out of me, and I can't stop moaning as he does. I've never been so completely devoured before. I'm hating that I can only allow this to happen one time.

Damn! Why does he have to be the enemy?

I suppose this is what they mean when they talk about the devil tempting you. This man is tempting me more than any other ever has.

His hands move on my ass. One grinds hard, then I feel the other inching it's way lower. *What the hell does he think he's doing?*

I feel his teeth on my clit, then his tongue goes over it again and again. I'm on the edge, teetering, then I feel something new. Something foreign. Something is pulsing in my ass, and I think his finger is what's doing that.

It sends a heat through me like an eruption and I scream as I climax, "Yes! God! Blaine! Yes!"

I cannot believe how amazing this feels. It's like a dream. A marvelous dream I never want to end!

His kiss slows, his finger leaves me, and my body is still shaking with tremors from the insane orgasm. I shudder as he blows warm air over my vagina. It makes it quake some more and I find myself near tears.

Soft kisses cover me, then his mouth is gone and I open my eyes to find him looking at me. His hair is damp and his face is glowing. "You liked that, did you?"

I can only nod and hold my arms out for him to come to me. He shakes his head and gets off the bed, standing to one side of it. "On your knees. Ass right here," he says as he points to the place in front of him.

I smile at him and do as he says. I've never had a man boss me around in bed. Or boss me around at all, really. *It's kind of exciting!*

His hand comes down on my ass just as I turn around in front of him and it completely stuns me. Not so much because it hurt, but because it sent a sensation through me I've never felt before.

He does it again, and I feel even wetter than I did before. One more time he smacks my ass, then I hear the sound of a vibrator. "No!" I shout and look back to see something glowing pink in his hand. "I want you!"

"Do you now?" he asks, then shakes his head. "Turn that pretty little head around and let me take care of you. You will get me. When the time is right."

"Damn it! Blaine! I want you! I want to feel you!"

His laugh makes me see red, then I feel the tip of the vibrator touch the outer edge of my asshole, and I'm shocked to find my body wanting it. I'm actually moving back so he can use it on me there.

I moan as the warm vibrating thing goes into my ass. I cannot believe how good it feels. No one has ever even tried to do such a thing to me. If he would've asked me if he could do this, I would've told him no way. Not in a million years. But he didn't ask. He just did it.

Am I am damn glad he did!

Slowly, he moves it inside of me as his other hand rubs my ass cheek. I find myself moaning along with the sound of the vibrator as it does some magic on me.

My eyes close as my body is massaged in a way it's never been before and I drift off to another world—a world I've never been in before. Pure bliss surrounds me, then a hard slap on my ass brings me back, and then I feel teeth on my ass, biting me pretty hard.

That's going to leave a mark!

The vibrator goes faster, as he must be turning it up a notch or two. It's getting hot and jerking inside of me. I feel him moving around behind me, then his head slips underneath me. He is face up, I can tell, as his tongue goes inside me, moving in and out as the vibration goes up another notch in my ass.

"Ahh!" I scream as another orgasm rips through me. "Blaine! Damn it!"

He doesn't ease up on me. The vibrator is turned up another

notch and his tongue is lapping up everything I'm putting out. It's animalistic, and I've never experienced anything like it in my life.

I can't stop the orgasm. It goes on and on until he turns the machine off, but he continues to eat me out like I'm the best-tasting thing on the planet. His fingers press into the now tender flesh of my ass as he pulls himself up to go deeper into me with his tongue. He's making the best groaning sounds I've ever heard.

Deep, guttural, and hot as shit!

Suddenly, his mouth is gone, he's not under me anymore, and I'm flipped onto my back, panting like a marathon runner at the end of a five hundred mile run.

He's standing at the end of the bed, also panting very heavily. "Do I need to show you some more of what I can do to make you happy?"

Moving up the bed, I keep going until my head hits a pillow, and I rest it there. I wiggle my finger at him and find my voice harsh and gravelly as I say, "I want you, Blaine. I want you inside of me. And I want it now."

I take a sharp breath as he strokes his cock, which has grown even larger. Veins are rippling through it that weren't there when I first laid eyes on the magnificent piece of male anatomy. He should have pictures of that thing in a museum of art, it's so large, fat, and juicy.

So juicy, in fact, that small amounts of creamy juice are coming out of the tip, and I find my mouth watering to taste it. I roll over and get on my hands and knees and crawl over the bed to him.

"Well, maybe just a little taste, then I want you inside me. I want to feel you stretch me to fit your huge dick, Blaine."

My mouth covers his cock, and his hands go straight for my head, moving it to make sure I take him all the way in as he makes the best sound I've ever heard in my life!

20

BLAINE

W atching Delaney's head move back and forth as she takes me in is by far the best thing I've ever seen in my life. And her mouth is perfect. Her lips sheath her teeth and flow back and forth over me like hot, silky perfection.

I rock a little to aid her in her endeavors and can't believe she's doing this. It wasn't in my plans. I was planning on totally concentrating on her tonight, and showing her some of the things I can do to make her sex life a lot better than she thought it could be.

But she really looked like she wanted to do this, so who am I to stop her?

I feel a bit of jerk as I release a little juice for her, then pull her hair to make her stop before I really make a splash. Only she doesn't want to stop. She's grabbing my legs and going at me harder. "Baby, I'm about to drown you."

She moans and keeps going. So I guess she wants the whole enchilada, and I'm feeling very happy about that. Closing my eyes, I let her take me away until I'm growling with one of the hardest orgasms I've ever had.

I can feel her gulping it all down and it makes me so fucking hot for her. With the last jerk taking what I had left in me, I pull her hair back and pick her up until she's on her knees in front of me. Then I kiss her hard, tasting me on her lips.

She grabs the back of my head, holding me to her as we taste ourselves inside the other's mouth. It's barbaric, and I have to admit, it's the sexiest thing I've ever felt.

Pushing her back onto the bed, I press my still-hard cock against her hot wet folds. Her legs wrap around me as she tries to wiggle in a way that will let my cock will go inside of her.

I'm not about to let her have me until I know I have her. Pinning her shoulders to the bed, I pull my mouth away from her and feel her protesting as I do. "Blaine, what are you doing? I'm aching for you."

"Are you? Are you ready to know what it feels like to belong to me?"

"Belong to you? Stop being so damn dominating. I will never belong to anyone." Her eyes roll, and I see she's not nearly as close as I thought she was.

"You're mine already. Your body knows it. Let your mouth say it to me." I press my dick to her, but don't put it in. She's struggling to make it happen, but I won't let her move.

"No! Come on!"

"I need to know that you won't be with anyone else. This is for the protection of others, because I will kick ass over you, Delaney. It's essential to let you know that before anything like that happens. That Doctor Paul guy, for instance. If he lays a hand on you, I will have to kick his ass. And I already know you feel the same about me after that bartender had you throwing a glass at her. So do us both a favor and say what I want to hear. Tell me who you belong to."

"No! I won't do it!" she says with stubborn pride.

"Then neither will I. But I will hold you just like this and kiss you until you are so frustrated it will drive you insane," I tell her then lean over and give her a kiss to let her know what I mean.

Her mouth is ready and accepting and so is her body. It's only her brain that's holding her back. But I think soon her body will win out over her brain and we can get this relationship on track.

After a few minutes of kissing torture, I ease up and look at her, finding her eyes closed and her jaw slack. "Damn it, Blaine."

I give her a little jab with my cock, putting it in only about an inch, making her groan and truthfully, it's getting harder to hold this back. *But I'm stubborn too.*

"I want to be the only man who gets to do this with you. Is it too much to ask, Delaney? I want you to myself. And you get to have me to yourself. It's a win, win."

Her eyes open and she looks a little worried. "I would like that, I think. I can do that. If I saw a woman after you, I think I might claw her eyes out. So, yeah. We can be exclusive."

"So let me here you say it."

"Now don't be a Neanderthal about it. I said we could be exclusive. I'm not going to say I belong to you."

I sigh, as I see I may have met my match. "Can you say your pussy belongs to me?"

A smile stretches over her red, kiss-swollen lips. "I'm pretty sure that is something I can say. It's pretty impressed with your work thus far."

"So tell me, baby. Who does that pussy belong to?"

"It belongs to you," she says, and it's like music to my ears.

"That's right. It belongs to me. Now let me show you why, because I'm about to ruin you for any other man. None will ever compare to me."

Her eyes go wide and light up as I press myself into her. A tear slips out of her right eye and runs down her cheek. "Blaine, this feels amazing. It feels like nothing ever has."

"It does, doesn't it?" I agree as I make a long, slow stroke, finding her to fit me like a glove. Her leg moves up, and she rests her heel in the small of my back as I rock our bodies together and feel as close to being one person with someone as I have ever felt.

We look into each other's eyes as I move inside of her, and I see something in hers that wasn't there before. I've broken that hard shell she had to prevent me from getting close.

I've made it inside of her heart too!

Moving slowly and easily, I take the time she deserves. Her body is quivering and another tear falls down her face. Her lips part as if she's about to say something, then she bites her lip, stopping herself.

I can't stop myself, though. "I think I'm falling in love with you, Delaney Richards."

Three more tears fall, one right after the other. But she doesn't say anything back. I make a deep stroke, her breath comes puffing out of her mouth, then I kiss her softly and sweetly.

Her hand moves through my hair as she kisses me back. I have no idea how this will turn out, but I'll be damned if I let one day go by without letting this woman know my true feelings for her.

Not one damn day!

Releasing her mouth, I kiss all the way across her cheek, tasting the salt her tears have left. Her earlobe is soft between my lips, then I press them against her ear. "You feel like home to me."

"Oh, Blaine," she moans. "You feel like that to me too."

Great, looks like we are on the same page!

21

DELANEY

November 16th:

Falling asleep in Blaine's arms is the safest I've ever felt. And it's going to be so damn hard for me to tell him that, while my female anatomy may belong to him because, let's face it, he was the best I've ever had and I'm pretty sure ever will have, I have to guard my heart. He will go back to his original ways. I have no doubt about that.

Until that happens, though, we can keep hitting the sheets. Just nothing more than that. *Sex only!*

The alarm on my cell phone goes off inside of my purse, which is in the bathroom along with my clothes. The sound has him moving, and I ease out from under his tree trunk of an arm and out of the bed.

My first step lets me know he has screwed the hell out of me. *I can barely walk!*

With little winces, I take each step slowly and make it to the bathroom. Pulling my phone out of my purse, I silence the small noise it was making that usually wakes me up each morning.

My bra and panties are in the bedroom, and I need to get home to get ready for my day. Only, I don't have my car here, or any clue where here is at all. Blaine occupied me completely on the cab ride over here.

I don't even really know what his house looks like, as he kissed me all the way until we got into his bedroom. I bet he has a huge house, like all super-rich people have.

"Shit! I'm going to have to wake him up." Starting the shower, I decide I may as well get cleaned up so that all I have to do is run into my house, put on fresh scrubs, and pull my hair into a ponytail, as he's lost my rubber band.

The hot water is helping with my soreness, and when I pour some of his shampoo into my palm, I find the smell so much better than any I've ever used. "What have I been missing by buying that cheap crap?"

"A hell of a lot," I hear Blaine say.

Wiping the steam off the clear shower door, I see he's found me and is opening the door to join me. "Won't you come right in?" I laugh and rinse the shampoo out of my hair.

"I'll drive you home so you can get ready for work, then I'll take you. We can go in together this morning. I'll call my office and let them know," he says.

"That might look kind of bad, Blaine. Why don't you come a little later? I don't want to get the gossip started already," I tell him as I pick up the conditioner.

He takes it out of my hand, fills his with it, then rubs it into my hair. "So I'm assuming you don't plan on putting it out there that you and I are together now."

"Well, it's so quick. I don't want anyone to think I'm a gold-digging slut. It's nothing personal—just that this is where I have to work," I tell him and watch his frown ease up a bit.

"Well, I get to be with you all day, and I guess I can see where you're coming from. But you're still untouchable, right?" he asks.

"Untouchable?"

"Yes," he says, then his hand moves between my legs. "That still belongs to me."

I know I'm blushing as I stutter, "Uh, yeah, if you want."

He moves forward, pressing me between him and the wall. His lips touch my ear. "I want you. So tell me what I want to hear, baby." His mouth is hot on my neck, and I can't believe how quickly he's made my insides get all shaky. I'm soaking wet for him.

"It's your pussy, Blaine," I whisper as my arms go around his neck, and then he's kissing me.

His cock is swelling against my stomach, and my vagina is pulsing with need for him. I wrap my legs around him and he takes my hips and moves me until he sinks his hot, throbbing cock into me.

I groan with pain, as I am so damn sore, it's not even funny. But with only a few strokes, he has me feeling only pleasure as he moves back and forth.

His mouth leaves mine and moves around to my neck where he nibbles, licks, teases, and sucks until I'm coming undone and shrieking his name.

I feel the tears again, and I've never been moved to tears by any man before. I don't even know why the hell it keeps happening. His soft kisses pepper my face as he keeps stroking. My orgasm keeps going, then, and when his heat fills me, my body goes into deeper quakes of desire and ecstasy.

I can't believe how amazing the sex is with this man!

22

BLAINE

S he is taking my breath away as I watch her comb her hair out. "Let me braid it for you," I say as I walk up behind her, dressed in my scrubs already. "I kind of made some pretty great marks on this side of your neck, but I think a nice braid falling over your shoulder will keep them under wraps."

She stretches her long neck out as she looks in the mirror. "Blaine! Damn it!"

"Shh, I can fix this. That's not nearly as bad as the marks I left on your ass," I say, then pull up the towel she's wrapped around herself and turn her so she can see them in the mirror. "Better keep that thing covered up too if you don't want anyone to know what we did last night."

She bats at my shoulder. "You rogue!"

"Rogue, huh?" I ask, then run my hand over her ass. "You weren't bitching when I was making those marks, baby."

"Stop messing around. I have to get to the hospital to relieve the night nurse. And we still have to stop at my place so I can change." She pushes me away and grabs up her dirty clothes.

"No, here. I have some sweats you can put on for me to take you home. Just leave those there. My maid will clean them and they'll be hanging in my closet for you. You can leave them here along with that bra and panty set. I think you should bring some of your clothes over here so we don't have to do this every morning."

"I think you think I'm going to be doing this most nights, and I am not. Maybe two times a week," she says as she pulls the clothes on.

"We'll see," I say, knowing full well she's going to get a lot hornier than she thinks she is. *I'm going to see to that.*

Taking her by the hand once she's dressed, I lead her through the house to the garage. "Damn, Blaine, this place is enormous."

I open the door off the mudroom to the garage and watch her reaction as I turn the overhead lights on. "Pick your chariot, princess."

"Blaine! I can't even count all the cars in here. This is way too many cars!" She points at the one that's three cars away from us. "Is that the Bat Mobile?"

"One of them, yes. You don't want to take that one, do you? It will get us noticed for sure. But I'm game if you are."

"No, I want to go in that demure, somewhat normal, black BMW. Lots of doctors have cars like that one. We won't stand out at all. You can take me to the parking lot where I parked and discreetly let me out," she says as we make our way to her choice.

"Okay," I say as I open her door. "We sure don't want anyone getting wind about us." A chuckle follows my words and I see a frown on her pretty face as she looks up at me from her seat inside of the car.

"You will act appropriately, won't you?"

I nod and don't say a word about my plan to fuck around with her all day today. *This should be fun!*

23

DELANEY

"Did you strain something, Nurse Richards?" the charge nurse, Becky, asks me as I put my purse behind the desk and moan as I have to squat to put it behind another one that's already there.

"My back," I lie. "Moving furniture in my apartment. I don't know what got into me last night. I rearranged my living room."

"Maybe you were trying to get rid of some of the pent up sexual frustration after spending the whole day with that sexy hunk of man yesterday," she says, making me freeze. "Is he coming back today or was it all too much for him?"

"I think he's coming back. That's what he said, anyway." I turn away from her to start making the rounds.

She stops me as she asks, "Didn't you leave with him? That's what Matilda in the gift shop said. She saw you leave with him and get into his Suburban."

Fuck!

I turn and think quick. "He insisted on having his driver take me to my car in the back parking lot. He's a gentleman, through and through." *Except when he's an animal in the bedroom!*

A rush moves through me as I remember the way he smacked my ass, which aches in the best way.

"Oh, I see. I thought it was kind of odd. You aren't that girl, after all," she says.

"Not me," I say and get the hell away from her area before I break into a sweat.

Checking on Tammy first, I find her and her mother up and am happy to see a smile greet me as I come into the room. It's been a long time since I've seen this kid smiling. "Good morning. You look amazing, Tammy."

"Thanks, Nurse Richards. Mom helped me take a shower this morning and she put a little makeup on me too. Do you like my new sweats? Mom bought them for me. I think they're cute."

"I do too. I love pink. You look precious, Tammy. Let me check your vitals really quickly before your breakfast gets here this morning." I notice Patsy looking a little tired. "How did you sleep, Patsy?"

"This place gets busy pretty early. I'll get used to it, though." She pushes a strand of her hair back and it makes me think.

"You know, now is the best time for you to run home and get yourself bathed and all cleaned up so you can come back up here before lunch. I'll take good care of our girl while you're gone. Don't worry."

The way she looks at me lets me know she's thankful and she nods, then asks Tammy, "Would that be okay with you, baby girl?"

"Yeah, Mom. Please, go take a bath and a nap if you need one. I'm just so happy that you're going to be here so much more and will be spending the nights with me. But I understand you need time to get your act together each day. Go. I'll be fine."

"You are an amazing girl," her mother tells her as she runs her hand over her shoulder. "I'll be back in a couple of hours." She looks at me. "Thanks for everything, Nurse Richards. You are a gift straight from God."

"No, Mr. Vanderbilt is. I let it slip about Tammy and he took the initiative on his own to do what he did. You can't give me that credit."

"I'll be sure to thank him. He is such a nice man. Is he married?" she asks, making my hackles raise.

"No," I say and act like I don't care that she asked that, but I do care. I care a lot. "Why do you ask that?"

"Oh, no reason. I mean, he's just so nice and sweet. A very handsome man, to boot. He's a catch, is all."

"Yes, I'm sure he is. But you work for him now, so you know any flirting would constitute sexual harassment and might cost you your brand-new job, so make sure you keep that in mind," I say, trying my best to make sure she doesn't make my insane jealousy over him come to the surface.

"I didn't think about that," she says. "Thanks for bringing that up before I messed myself up good. Well, see you later. Love you, baby."

She leaves, and I find Tammy watching her go. "You know, mom's been alone for a couple of years. Her last boyfriend was a terrible man. He hit her at least two times that I saw. She could use a nice man. And Mr. Vanderbilt is very nice."

Not her too!

"But your mother has to keep her new job. Now that she's working in a new line of work instead of waitressing she'll find a great man. I'm sure she will. You'll see. Her self-esteem will go up, and along with that, good men will look her way. Don't worry."

"Mr. Vanderbilt, I can let you come with me today." I hear a woman's voice coming from the hallway.

"Gotta go," I say and hurry out of the room to see who the hell is trying to grab him up now.

As I open the door and step into the hallway, I see Blaine with his back to me as Nurse Amanda 'Slut from hell' Jones walks up to him, swaying her hips as she does. "I heard you needed an aid. Nurse Richards must have expressed her disinterest in helping you. So I'm here to take you around today."

"Who the hell said that?" I ask as I come up behind them, making Blaine spin around with a surprised expression on his handsome face.

"Did you say you weren't interested in helping me?" he asks.

"Not at all," I say as I look around him at Amanda. "I have him, Nurse Jones. Go on about your business. We made plans yesterday for the children he wants to see today. I'll be aiding him the entire time he's visiting our kids here."

"Do you really want that?" she asks Blaine.

He turns back to her and asks, "Sure. Why wouldn't I?"

She shakes her head. "Because she's kind of bitchy."

"Hey!" I say and try to step around Blaine, who grabs my arm.

"Well, you are," she says as she steps back. "Even I overheard you being mad you had to let him tag around after you yesterday. I thought I was doing you both a favor. Excuse me." She turns away and starts walking.

"Well, you're not. I'll be his aid," I shout after her.

Blaine smiles as he looks at me. "You need to chill out, Nurse Richards. People might get the wrong idea about us."

Damn my temper! He's right.

"Okay," I say, then take a breath. "Let's go see Colby first since Terry asked you to do that."

"Have you seen anyone yet?" he asks me as we walk side by side down the hallway. He takes something out of his pocket and holds it out to me. "I thought you could use these. You're walking kind of funny."

I hold out my hand and find a couple of menstrual cramp pills being put into it. "You stopped and bought me some of these?"

"Yeah, you won't be as sore and stiff once you take them. We can stop off at the cafeteria really quick and grab a donut and apple juice for you to eat with them."

I stifle an *aww*, as this is one of the sweetest things any man has ever done for me. "This was nice of you."

"I know. I'm learning how to be a nice guy. You make it easy."

His fingers move across my thigh for only a moment, then they're gone, and I find I miss them already.

This isn't going to be very easy to hide today!

24

BLAINE

Leaving Colby's room after finding out what would help him feel and deal better with his leukemia, I have the first item on my list for today's gifts for the kids. It's an electric guitar, and I have to get headphones to go along with that so he doesn't get thrown out of the hospital for shredding too loudly.

Delaney is only a step ahead of me as we hurry away to see the next kid. I'm checking where I can get what he's asked for on my cell phone. "I need you, Delaney," I hear a man say and stop searching for guitars to look up and see Doctor Paul taking my woman by her arm, stopping her.

I stop, too, and wait to see what they say to one another. Delaney looks over her shoulder at me with a deer-in-the-headlights kind of look, which I find kind of amusing.

Let's see how she handles this little situation!

"Why?" she asks him.

"I need a date for Thanksgiving. My parents are insisting I bring someone and mom likes you," he says, then gives me a nod. "How are you doing today, Mr. Vanderbilt?"

"I'm great. I had a good day here yesterday, followed by a great night. Cannot complain, not one bit," I say as I wait to see how Delaney gets out of this.

"Is it in the afternoon or evening?" she asks, making my insides get a bit on the jittery side. If she thinks she's going to go with him to his family's house, she has another think coming!

"Evening," he says, then he moves his hand up to stroke her cheek with his knuckles, and I get very jittery insides.

She steps back and shakes her head. "Can't do it then, sorry. You see, I'm Mr. Vanderbilt's aid and he wants to throw the kids a Thanksgiving dinner in the evening. During the day, he'll be with his brother and sister to eat with them."

Then the monkey is on my back and Paul looks at me. "Can't you switch things around, Mr. Vanderbilt? You can do lunch with the kids here and eat a nice Thanksgiving dinner with your family in the evening. Then she could come with me."

No way in hell, buddy!

"No can do. My sister has invited someone and they have to work in the evening. Sorry. Maybe next year," I say and watch him frown.

"Surely another nurse can help him for that day. Find him someone else, Delaney," he says, then reaches out for her again. "I need you. You know I wouldn't be begging like this if I didn't."

She takes another step back to avoid his touch. "Paul, I can't do that. End of discussion. We have a ton of things to do today and this is slowing us down and putting us behind. Ask someone else to go with you. I already told you we were done anyway." She reaches back and grabs my hand. "Come on, Mr. Vanderbilt. We have three more patients to get to before lunch." She tugs me along behind her as Paul watches her with his lips held tightly together.

I wait until he's out of earshot, then whisper, "He is not a happy man."

"I know. He'll move on. I'm sure of it," she says, then turns abruptly and knocks on another door, "Meagan, are you decent?"

"Yes, ma'am," a young girl answers her.

As we walk in, I am struck by the many lines that are going into the young girl. "Hi," I say as I make my way to her bed, which she obviously can't get out of. "I'm Blaine. I'm here to make some of your dreams come true, princess."

She has a tiny, pink bow taped to the top of her bald head. Her green eyes are so light, they're nearly transparent. She has to be all of six years old, I bet.

"My dreams?" she asks as she peers up at me from her flat position on the bed.

"Yes, your dreams," I tell her and sit on the side of the bed. Gently, I stroke her shoulder, then run my hand over her forehead. "How are you feeling?" Her head is warm and her cheeks are red, while the rest of her is so pale it seems unreal.

"Not good," she says.

I turn back to find Delaney busily checking the machines. "She's kind of warm, Nurse Richards."

"Let me get her temp," she says and hurries to place a thermometer in her mouth.

It doesn't take but a moment for it to start beeping. "You have a fever, precious," I tell her as Delaney pulls the thermometer out and checks it.

"One hundred and one. Let me have Dr. Jensen paged. She's here today." Pressing the nurses' station call button on the side of the bed, she sets things in motion for the doctor to make this very sick little girl a top priority.

I sit on the bed and run my hand back and forth along her thin arm. Never have I seen someone so small and frail. It hurts me to know children can get this sick.

The memory of the first few weeks when mom didn't come home linger in the back of my mind. I recall asking Pops if there was any way possible that she might get to come back home. I asked him nearly every day, and I prayed she'd walk through our front door on many occasions.

It was all the way back then that I started questioning if there was a God at all. And if there was, why would he take away three little kids' mother? We needed her and he took her away from us.

I look at this poor, sweet little girl and have to ask, what did she do to deserve this? Why was this put on her tiny shoulders to bare? What kind of a God would do that?

After I swallow back the knot in my throat, I say, "I'd like to bring you something to make things better for you. What kind of toy would you like? Anything in the world is yours for the asking."

"I have been wanting a tablet. I can't sit up and watch television. I could use that to watch cartoons. I used to like to watch cartoons before I got sick and had to come here." The door opens and her little eyes go to it. "Hi, Daddy."

"Hey there, darlin'. How's my baby?" he asks as he looks at Delaney.

"She's got a fever. I have a doctor coming to check her out."

"This is Blaine, Daddy," Meagan says as she points at me. "He's going to buy me a tablet."

"And why is that?" he asks me with a frown on his face.

I get up and shake his hand. "Hello, I'm Blaine Vanderbilt. I'm spending the holidays here with the kids on this ward and trying to make their stay here a little bit happier by giving them gifts."

"Well, we don't allow our kids to have electronics," he tells me.

"Daddy, please. I'm so tired of lying in this bed with nothing to do," she whines at him.

His words are sharp. "I said no!"

What an asshole!

25

DELANEY

November 24th:

Standing in the hallway, waiting for Blaine to meet me in front of the cafeteria where he has a full staff from one of the local restaurants here to prepare and serve the Thanksgiving feast to the kids and their families, I feel like a damn fool.

He decided costumes for us were in order for this festive occasion. He found me a turkey costume, and I feel ridiculous. I have no idea what he's dressing up as. It's a surprise.

We've spent every night together since the first one. I start out each morning by telling him I won't be staying the night. By the end of the day, though, I find myself craving the man.

But I can tell he's getting impatient with me. I still think it's a bad idea for our relationship to be out in the open. I already hear little bits and pieces of gossip about us as it is.

The sound of a man clearing his throat has me looking back, and I see Blaine looking like a very handsome pilgrim while I look like an idiot. "Blaine! That's not fair! I look like a fool. Why do you get to be that and I have to be this?"

"I think you look adorable," he says. "Give me your wing and let's greet our guests, my turkey lady."

With a huff, I walk away from him. *Or waddle!*

He's quick to get to my side as he chuckles.

"Shut up!" I hiss at him.

"Good evening, ladies and gentlemen," he greets the room full of people. "I'm happy to have you all here today for this feast. And with no further ado, let the food be served!"

The guests cheer as the waitstaff begins to bring out the food. Blaine and I split up to hobnob with the patients and their families. I watch him pass by the table where Meagan's family sits. He hates her father, Mr. Sanders.

The poor girl can't even be with them, as she's stuck in her bed. Blaine offered to have a table set up in there so they could be served in her room. It was her father who said not to do that. He's a strict man.

I had to take Blaine out of the room when he turned down his offer. His reason was that he doesn't believe in spoiling his children. No one gets special treatment at any time. If they were to alter things for Meagan, then he called that spoiling her.

I've noticed Blaine's progress slowing. What was going quickly has slowed to the speed of molasses on a cold day. He's spoken to me several times about why kids would be put through these horrible things.

I have no words to tell him. There is no explaining things of this nature. I never say it's God's plan. I can see he already has an issue where God is concerned.

As a matter of fact, he was asked if he wanted to say a blessing over the food this evening and he declined. I don't know if seeing all this tragedy is something his poor spirit can handle. It seems to be cementing his feelings about things. It seems to be showing him we live in a world that is either without a divine presence or at least without one he cares for.

As I turn around after telling Tammy and her mother hello, I see Blaine with a plate in hand, heading toward the door. Then I see Meagan's father get up and go in the same direction. I smell an argument and hurry to intervene as fast as my damn costume will let me.

"Where are you going with that?" I hear her father shout.

Crap!

Blaine stops and turns around. "To your daughter's room."

"I don't think so," her father says. I can see the look in Blaine's eyes and it's bad.

I manage to get to where they are and maneuver them the rest of the way out of the cafeteria and into the hallway before anyone pays any attention to them. "Shh," I hiss at them. Tugging them both by their arms, I pull them around the corner. "What's the problem here?"

"He's taking that to Meagan. I don't think this food is good for her. She's on a strict diet. This man doesn't seem to understand that," he says.

"This was made just for her by the nutritionist, Mr. Sanders," Blaine tells him, then lifts the silver dome off the plate, revealing the single slice of white turkey meat, green beans, and a small amount of white rice.

"That plate will be fine for her to eat," I say, then give Blaine a nod, and he covers it back up.

"But that would mean she's getting special treatment. We don't want her thinking she's any more special than any one of our other four children. So, I am telling you, I don't want her to have that. As a matter of fact, take her off your list of kids you want to spoil with material things, Mr. Vanderbilt."

"How about if I give her only my company?" Blaine asks.

"I'd rather you stay away from her. As a matter of fact, I demand that you do," Mr. Sanders says and looks at me. "See to that, or I will. If I do, it won't be pretty." Then he turns and walks away from us.

Blaine doesn't wait for the man to get out of hearing range before he says, "That man is a complete jackoff."

Thankfully, the man keeps walking. I'm pretty sure that, given how he has such a strict way of doing things, he's used to being called names. He is a jackoff, after all.

"Come on, Blaine. There's nothing we can do. Let's just enjoy the kids who we can." I try to take his hand, but my feathers get in the way and I just huff and start walking. "Come on. Man, I hate this suit."

"I hate that asshole. I think he needs an adjustment," he mumbles as he follows me. "I think I might just have to make that happen."

I spin around and look at him to see if he's being serious. "Blaine, what does that mean?"

"Nothing. Don't worry about it. I should just leave it alone. Like you've told me about thousand times since I came here, there isn't a thing I can do to change any of this. I don't really know why I'm even here, continuing to pretend that life can be great. For some, I assume it can, but not for all of us."

Just like I was worried about, it seems the old Blaine with his shielded heart and dim views of humanity is coming back to the surface. "Blaine, let's just have fun. Then we can go back to your place and have some naked swim time. What do you say to that?"

"No, thanks. I think I'd like to be alone this evening. I don't really feel up to company," he says as he looks past me into the cafeteria. "Let's get this shit over with. I can put this fake smile on my face only a little longer."

This is not good!

A TREE FOR ALL BOOK FOUR

A Holiday Romance

By Michelle Love

Trust. Passion. Decisions

Blaine won't go back to the hospital. He's avoiding the bad feelings that come along with seeing the children in such bad conditions.

That has him asking Delaney to move in with him, so he can see her more. She has her misgivings about taking such a big step so early in their relationship, but finds he really does need her, and she wants to be there for him.
When she gets him back to the hospital to visit a few of the kids and take them Christmas trees, all does not go well.
Can one man really ruin the holidays for all the children in the hospital and Blaine and Delaney?

26

DELANEY

December 2nd:

"When's Mr. Vanderbilt coming for a visit?" Colby asks as I check his vital signs. "I made up this rad tune. I want to let him hear it."

"I'll be sure to let him know that, Colby. He's just been really busy at his job with the holidays. His stores sell a lot of things. I'll be back after lunch," I tell him, then leave the room to make my way to the next patient.

A week has passed since Blaine was here last, on Thanksgiving evening. He's made excuses every day for why he can't come to the hospital. I know what the real reason is, though. He can't handle the sadness—the utter helplessness of being a human and watching other humans struggle. It's just too hard for him to do.

Instead of bringing something out in him, all that surfaced was his original outlook on life—the outlook that says, fuck doing things the right and fair way. Look out for number one because no one else will look out for you.

Taking a break, I go to the break room and take my cell phone out of my pocket. I haven't stayed a night at his place this last week either.

He says he's not in the mood to be around anyone and would make bad company.

I think it's time to force him to see me. Maybe if he does, it will stir some kind of want in him again. I make the call and find his secretary answering his phone. "Hello, Miss Richards. Mr. Vanderbilt is in a video conference. Can he call you later?"

"Can you tell me what time he'll be done with that and if he has anything else scheduled after that?"

"These things usually last about an hour. He has something at four, but he'll be free here in the next thirty minutes for a couple of hours. You should come by and see him. I think that would help him," she says in a hushed voice. "He's pretty Grinchy."

"Grinchy, huh? Well, we cannot have that. I will come see him. I'll be there soon. Thank you. I believe he told me your name is Blanch, right?"

"Yes, Miss Richards, I'm Blanch. I went to school with his mother. She was one of my best friends. And I saw a light in the man when he was hanging around with you and those kids at the hospital—a light I hadn't seen since he was a kid, before she passed away. He's lost it again, and I hate that. I love the man. I wish I could do more to help him, but he never lets me get very close."

"I see. Thanks for telling me. I'll show up with lunch. He and I can have an office picnic and perhaps I can rekindle that light that's left him," I say and end the call.

Now to find someone to cover for me for the next little while so I can go find out if there's anything left of the Blaine I found myself falling for.

27

BLAINE

"Why would you make a deal with that crappy company, Blaine?" my brother asks me after I end the video conference meeting we had with a toy company from Taiwan.

"The items were dirt cheap, Kent. How do you not understand that? The toys can be here on our shelves within one week. We need something filling up the toy shelves. With Christmas fast approaching, the toys are flying off the shelves. Manufacturers know there's a high demand and most of them are making their prices higher than normal. This is always how I do business at this time of year."

"But I thought we were going to look for better products for our customers. Those toys will all be broken the same day they open them. Think about the poor kids who get these cheap things," Kent says as we get up to leave the video conference room.

Kate finds us in the hallway. "Hey, Blaine, we need to talk." She steps in next to Kent and walks with us down the long hallway. "You haven't signed off on the new return policy. I have everything together to start the training of the customer service staff. I have even made a video that can be shown to them so I don't have to go from store to store."

"About that," I say as I recall the document she gave me. "You have our policy so very different. You have in there that we will exchange things and accept all returns without any exceptions. Now, how are we going to make money when we take back broken things the manufacturers will not accept back from us for credit with them? You're not looking at the big picture. Only the manufacturers who accept returns are the ones we can do that with."

"You don't use ones who accept that," Kate says as we stop at my office door. Her hands go to her hips and she looks at me like I'm the one who's annoying.

"You need to go to the files and pull the companies we do business with. If you find one that takes returns for credit, you can accept returns on their merchandise. You'll have to make a whole new return policy. Sorry. It's just business, Kate."

"But I thought we were going to try to make this store better," Kent says as he also is looking annoyed at me.

"Well, we are. But you two have to understand what it is my stores do for people. They provide the cheapest versions of things they want or need. When you pay the cheapest price, you cannot expect top quality. If they want that, they need to shop elsewhere. It's not so hard to understand," I say as I put my hand on the door knob.

"But you ran the places of business where they could get quality products out of their towns. What do you expect them to do?" Kent asks me.

"Not my problem," I say as I shake my head. "Are you telling me these people don't have a way to get to a large city to make higher quality purchases? Because that's also not my problem."

"You know what your problem is, Blaine?" Kate asks as she looks at me with eyes that tell me she's disappointed in me for some reason. "You don't really think about other people."

"I do think about them. I think about them a lot more than I used to. And you know what I found out? I can't really do anything to help any of them. So why try? I've found out a way to make money. Lots of money. Money that's paying you both more than you could ever make on your own. So let that sink in."

Then I open the door to my office and find a half-naked elf lying on top of my desk.

28

DELANEY

"Finally!" I say as the door opens and Blaine steps inside.

"Delaney, what in the world are you doing?" he asks as surprise moves over his face—a face that had been void of any emotion when I first saw it as he came in.

I sit up, getting out of the sexy position on my side, as he comes to me. "I came to see you. I missed you. Don't you miss me at all?"

"Now that I see you, the answer to that is yes." His hands move over my shoulders as he looks into my eyes. "I have missed you very much, and now I'm trying to figure out why the hell I've been putting you off."

"Because I would get in the way of you being Grinchy," I tell him as I wrap my arms around him. "I love the business suit on you. Now you really look like a billionaire. So hot!" I press my lips to his neck and hear him make a little moaning sound.

"Delaney, my God, I've missed how you feel in my arms. Don't let me go this long without being with you again," he says, then his lips graze my neck as he moves them to mine.

My heart fills with desire as our mouths mingle. It's only been a week, but it's felt so much longer. He ends the kiss, resting his forehead against mine. "You have a bunch of kids at the hospital who miss you too."

His body goes tense and he lets me go. "I don't know if I can do that anymore, Delaney."

"Okay, I won't push you about it," I say as I get off the desk and follow him. I'm not about to let him shut down. Running my arms around him from behind, I hug him. "Why don't you just sit down and let me help you relax?"

His deep chuckle shakes me as I hug him, and he pulls me around in front of him. "First, you have to tell me where you found this naughty, little elf outfit," he says of the tight teddy that looks like an elf costume.

"The internet," I tell him. "I ordered it a couple of weeks ago. I thought it might be fun to role play. You were going to be Santa."

"Ho, ho, ho," he says, then picks me up and plants another kiss on my lips.

I run my hands through his silky, dark-blonde hair as he carries me back to his desk and sets me down on top of it. His hands move over my shoulders, then down to my waist. Then I feel his fingers moving under the short hem of my tiny outfit. He finds that I have no panties on and he groans, then his lips leave mine.

Pushing me back onto the desk, he looks at me with an evil grin. "You're going to have to be quiet, baby. We don't need an audience gathering outside my office door, listening to you moan.

My body instantly fills to the top with heat as I watch him lick his lips and push the crotch of my outfit over to one side. I grab the sides of the desk in anticipation of his mouth touching me.

His growl vibrates his mouth as he kisses me softly. I want to moan so badly it's not even funny, but I hold it in. I know all too well how sound travels in buildings.

The hospital has shown me that many times as I've passed janitors closets or empty rooms and heard a couple going at it more than once. It does draw a crowd.

His tongue works some much-needed magic on me as I writhe with the sensations he's giving me. I hope like hell he asks me to stay the night with him tonight. I feel the need for an all-night session with him.

With several licks directly to my love lump, he has me falling over the edge, and just as it begins, he stops what he's doing, and I hear him unzipping his pants.

Lifting me up, he stands me up in front of him, then turns me around and presses my shoulders until I have my upper body laid out on his desk. I'm shaking with the climax that's still pulsing around my insides as he thrusts his erection into me from behind.

I have to bite my lip so I don't cry out with the pleasure I feel with him inside of me. He fills me up completely, stretching me in the best of ways. He makes little puffing sounds that are quiet, but I love the way it sounds.

Our flesh smacks quietly, as he's not making deep enough to be so loud that someone might hear. But I ache for him to go in deeper. He leans over me, his front on my back, and goes in deeper, as if he needed to feel that too.

His lips rest on my ear. "My God, I've missed you, baby." Then his mouth is hot on my neck as he bites me, then sucks at the tender flesh.

He has me quivering throughout my entire body with how he handles me. The way he's pumping himself into me as he sucks on my neck is too much. I make a quiet moan as my body gives into him.

I hear a soft moan coming from him. "Baby, that feels insanely good. Come all over me."

I'm panting and trying hard not to scream out his name. My insides are pulsing and aching for him to give me what he has. I need to feel him jerking inside of me, but he keeps making deep thrusts. Over and over he moves deeply inside of me until his breathing goes ragged, and then he goes stiff and fills me with his heat.

I moan again, as quietly as I can manage, as my body goes into another deep orgasm, milking his cock for all it's worth. He bites my neck as he climaxes, most likely to stop himself from yelling too.

Our bodies slowly stop the squeezing and pulsing, then his bite eases and he kisses the place I know he's left his mark on. "Sorry, I kind of made a purple place on your neck again."

He eases his body off mine and pulls me up with him. He peppers my neck with small kisses, then he turns me to face him and pulls me in for a sweet hug. I put my arms around him and hold him too. "You know, Blaine, I really did miss you."

"I'm sorry, Delaney. I'm really sorry for staying away. I can't explain everything, but I just can't be that man—the man I know you expect me to be. I see the bad in this world. I just don't see the point in doing anything differently." He lets me go to put himself all back up.

"I think you were trying to make too many changes at one time, Blaine. I think that's the problem. You took on too much at one time. I have an idea to help you," I say as I straighten out my little outfit and make my way to the bathroom that's attached to his large office.

I snooped around before he got here and checked the place out. It's kind of a hobby of mine, snooping. The first thing I notice as I look in the mirror is a quarter-sized, purple mark on my neck and I run my finger over it.

Then he comes in behind me and trails his finger over it as he looks at it in the mirror. "I'll fix your hair to cover it. You taste too damn delicious." He leaves a kiss on the top of my head and turns to open a cabinet. "And I want to be honest with you, baby. I don't want to be forced to make changes either. I've made a ton of money being the man I am. I don't see any reason in the world to change how I do things."

"So you won't be having that meeting and bringing in people you ran out of business?" I ask with apprehension.

He shakes his head and comes back with a comb and a small rubber band. He starts combing out my hair as he says, "No, and I know you're not happy about that."

Not happy is a vast understatement!

29

BLAINE

I can see by her expression that she's pissed. "I don't want to fight."

"Well that's just too damn bad," she says as her hands go to her hips, the typical stance for her when she's about to go off. "You said you were going to do that, Blaine. You told me you already had the whole thing set up, the plans just had to be finalized. So what happened?"

"I changed my mind. I don't see the point anymore. I don't want you to be mad at me. It's …"

She interrupts me as she holds out her hand, her palm near my face, "Just business! I know. Blaine, here's the thing. You told me you were going to do something, and boom, just like that, you changed your mind without saying one word about it. That's worse than never coming up with the idea in the first place. Don't ever tell me you're going to do something and then just never do it. I hate that!"

"I just hurried into it. I don't usually do things like that. As a matter of fact, this is really the first time I've ever told people I was going to do anything and changed my mind about it. You see, I'm not that guy I was for that short amount of time. That was a fake person. You don't want to be involved with a fake person, do you?"

Her eyes move up and down as she looks me over. "Blaine, I don't want you to be anything you're not. But I have to let you know that I need to be able to respect you if we're to keep things like they are."

"That's another thing I want to change," I say and watch her perfect eyebrows raise.

"What? Do you want to end this? You want to stop seeing me?" she asks, and I see the hurt in her green eyes and that makes me ache inside.

I pull her to me and hug her, leaning my chin on the top of her head. "No. Not at all. I want more. I want what we have out in the open, and I want you to move in with me. I need you. I need to have you around me. And I can't go back to that hospital. I've had no idea how to ask you to do this. I also was afraid once you knew I'm not going to be making those big changes that you'd be the one who'd end things."

Her hand touches my chest, pushing me back gently as she looks up at me. "Blaine, I think this is too sudden. You're telling me you won't be the man I grew to care for. You're telling me you want to be that all-business-no-emotion man. I can tell you I won't be able to keep my mouth shut about how you do things."

"I can handle your mouth," I tell her, then take it with a sweet kiss. She's smiling when I end it and pull back to look at her. "And I'm not saying I don't want your input. I'm just saying I most likely won't act on any of it."

The frown that fills her face has my heart pounding with worry that she won't accept my offer. This is exactly what I was afraid would happen when I told her about me deciding my old ways are the best ways.

She has my heart right in the palm of her hand. I knew it would come to this. I knew if I let myself feel anything, I'd end up on the shit end of the stick. Now, here I stand, waiting for her to either give me what I want or take it all away from me.

The ball is in her court and I find her frown killing parts of me I didn't even realize had been brought to life. She's brought more out of me than I even knew. And, now, she may be about to kill all that she made.

"Blaine, I think moving in with you might actually be a good idea. I was thinking it was too sudden, but on second thought, it might be just what you need. You need to know everything isn't all bad. I know you truly enjoyed spending time with Terry, Colby, little Adam, and Tammy. You let the one negative, Meagan's father, take all the good away from your experience."

"It was more than just him," I say as I let her go and feel the hardness emerging inside of me again as I think about how unfair it is that those children have to suffer. There's not one of them who deserves what they're going through. Our God, if there is one, allows this kind of thing to happen. "I just know I was a lot happier when my mind was just on business. I do have room for you, though. I have lots of room for you."

She reaches out for me and pulls me back to her. I wrap my arms around her and love the way she makes me feel. Now, if she could just leave the kids at that damn hospital out of things and out of my mind!

"I think I can accept that, for now," she says, making me tense up again.

"For now?" I ask as I hold her back and give her a look that hopefully lets her know I'm not the kind of man who takes too well to being nagged. "You should know I hate to be nagged about anything."

"Nagged?" she asks, with yet another frown on her pretty little face. It seems I'm making her do that a lot today, and I don't like that at all.

"Sorry." I pull her back in close and hold her tight. "I'll just shut up now. Where would you like to go to dinner this evening?"

"It doesn't matter to me. I have to work until eight to cover for the nurse who's covering for me right now. It's going to be kind of late to go anywhere nice. I'd have to change and that would take a little while. Plus, I want to get to sleep early. I'm pulling a double tomorrow."

Just like that, I realize that, if she and I are going to get to spend much time together, I'll need to go to the hospital at least some.

And just like that, I think this will never work out.

30

DELANEY

Blaine has gone back and forth between being as tense as I've ever seen him to very relaxed and giving. It seems he's dealing a bit with an inner struggle he's not telling me everything about.

"I tell you what," I say, as I sense he needs me more than he's willing to tell me right now. "I'll call the nurse who's covering for me and work a deal out with her for the rest of today. I won't be going back up there until tomorrow. I know you have something to do at four, but after you get done, I am all yours. Take me anywhere you want or just take me to your estate. I don't care. The rest of the day and night is all about you, Blaine. Only you and me."

His body relaxes again and he smiles at me. "I knew there was a reason why I found you to my liking. You can get with your landlord while I take the meeting at four. It should only take me an hour to take care of that, then I'll be through for the day."

"Get with my landlord? About?"

"Moving out. Letting the place go," he says.

Then it hits me like a brick that he really wants a commitment from me. "That's a great big step."

Tension fills his body again, and this time, I can feel mine tense up too. "It is. I thought you understood. I want us to take this next logical step."

"Yeah, I get it. But don't you get that we don't really know if this is going to work out and that I don't want to have to start completely over? I'll just keep my apartment. That way, if things don't work out, I won't be devastated."

"It wouldn't devastate you for this to end?" he asks as he lets me go and turns away from me. "It would mess me up pretty badly if I never got to see you again."

"Wow! I didn't say that," I say as I throw my arms up in the air in exasperation. "I feel like I'm on a damn roller coaster with you today, Blaine. This is crazy. I mean seriously crazy. I think you need to see someone. A therapist or something. You have something going on inside of you that's up and down and all over the place."

He walks past me, leaving the bathroom and going toward his desk in a hurry. "I'm not crazy. Crazy people don't do the things I've accomplished. I feel odd right now. Uneven. Out of kilter. All because of my pops. Death is hitting me hard right now. I don't know what the fuck you expect from me. I'm grieving in my own way and fighting myself about things. You have no idea what's going on inside my head. My heart. My soul!"

My God, I've completely forgotten about him and all he's going through. I hurry to him as he sits in his high-backed, black, leather chair behind his large, oak desk.

"Baby, I am so sorry. I tell you what. I'm going to just stop all that now. I can give up my apartment. I get it now. You need to feel secure with me. I get it. I can do that for you. I'm so sorry I wasn't thinking about all you've gone through."

"No, keep the apartment if that's what you want to do. I shouldn't be bossing you around anyway. Do what you want to. Don't let me do that to you. I'm sorry. I'm a mess and I'm not really in the right frame of mind to make any lasting decisions. I think I've proven that already."

"Let's take this one day at a time. I'll bring the essentials to your place today. I'll make sure I have everything I need to make the place a home for me too. And, one day at a time, we can take this wherever it's going to go. And to start things off on the right foot, I'd like to let you know I've decided that it's safe to say that I love you, Blaine Vanderbilt. I know it for certain because you are so deep in my heart that it actually hurts when I've hurt your feelings, even inadvertently."

"I don't see how you could," he says as he looks at me through his thick lashes, his head is down.

"I can see you. I can feel you. I want to be with you and be here for you. So, how do you feel about me?" I ask as I take his chin and lift him to look at me.

I find his eyes a little glassy as he looks into mine. "I love you, Delaney. I've told you as much. Remember when I told you that I was falling in love with you?"

"I do, then nothing else was said. I certainly didn't want you to say anything you didn't really mean, especially something like that. Now, let me get my coat back on to cover up my slutty, little elf outfit and I'll go to my place to pack up my things. How about I meet you at your estate after your meeting?" I ask, as he looks a lot better.

"I would like that very much." He opens his desk drawer and fishes around, then comes back with a key in his hand. "This will get you in the front door." He writes down something on a piece of paper and puts it in my hand. "This is the code to the gate and the one under that is the code to the alarm system. The staff is there to let you in, but I want you to have this anyway. I'll let them know you're coming."

With the key in my hand, it starts to feel real. I'm going to move in with Blaine Vanderbilt. My family's enemy, who isn't going to be doing anything he told me he was. And, still, I'm moving in with him.

I have to ask myself, am I selling out my soul to the man who obviously isn't about to change a thing about himself?

Then I look at his light-brown eyes as they twinkle and have to smile. My heart is with this man. Perhaps with my influence and time, he will make some better decisions with his business. Maybe he just needs a positive influence.

He pulls one more thing out of the desk drawer and I see it's a small picture frame. Placing it on his clean desk, he turns it so I can see. "That's mom."

Strawberry-blonde hair and a smattering of freckles are outshined by a set of green eyes that sparkle like magic. "She has the same color eyes I do. But hers are much brighter."

"Yours are equally as bright, in my opinion. You remind me of her. I think that's why I took to you so easily. I think that's part of the reason I gave you the chance I've never given anyone else." I know his words are meant to comfort me, but they scare me a little.

I don't want to be the man's mother. But maybe he needs me to fill the void she left when she passed away when he was only five. I hope I have what it will take to make things work for us.

I don't think things are going to be easy. *But things that come easily are rarely worth much!*

31

BLAINE

The afternoon sun is peeking through the dark-brown curtains in Kate's office and managing to hit me right in the left eye. As I ease over to avoid it, I catch Kate giving me that look again—the one that says she's not a happy camper.

Picking up one of the dolls that resembles a Barbie doll, she shakes it a bit and the head falls right off. "See? Junk. And its brand new out of the packaging, which most likely cost more to produce than this piece of crap did. I bought thirty dollars' worth of toys from the Bargain Bin here in Houston, and out of the fifteen toys I purchased, two are still viable. The rest were easily broken within minutes."

"Children who get these toys are going to be very upset little individuals, Blaine," Kent adds. "Now, I found us a manufacturer that will deliver all we want to all of the stores within this upcoming week. They have reasonable prices, and we can mark our prices merely pennies below our competitors. You will still be the lowest price on the market."

I sit and look at the pile of debris on top of Kate's desk that was once a pile of toys for a brief amount of time. The alarm on my cell phone goes off, telling me it's time to end this meeting and get home to Delaney.

Her sweet face lights up my phone screen, as I set her picture to show with the alarm. Looking at her as I turn the alarm off, I get a solid voice coming from inside of my head. *Do the right thing.*

The right thing, it said once, and pretty loudly and commandingly. I look at the pile of junk again, then at the hopeful looks on my younger brother's and sister's faces, and it just comes out. "Do it."

"Really?" Kate says as she jumps up from her chair and runs around, grabbing me and pulling me up to hug her. "Oh, Blaine! You'll see—you'll still make money and the kids won't be heartbroken. I'll get on the phone to let the managers know we want those old toys off the shelves. I've found a recycling program we can give them too so they won't be completely wasted."

"Plus, we can write all that off as a loss and save money on this year's taxes," Kent adds.

"I hadn't even thought of that," I tell him as I shake my head and wonder why I've never thought of that before. "We could do that with returns to our stores too. We can send the things to be recycled, say once a month or something like that, and write all that merchandise off."

Kate's smile is enormous as she says, "Then my original return policy can be accepted."

With a nod, I agree, and she hugs me again. "Blaine, this is going to work! I'm so excited!"

Kent pats me on the back. "Let's go get some drinks and celebrate this big change."

"I can't. I have something going on I need to attend to." I pull my jacket off the back of the chair I was sitting in and turn to leave.

"What's the thing you need to attend to?" Kate asks as she grabs my arm, stopping me.

Looking back at them, I say, "Delaney is moving in with me today."

"What?" Kent says with a slack-jawed expression.

"Seriously?" Kate asks with a similar expression on her face.

"Why didn't you say anything about this before? This is exciting news, Blaine!"

"I just asked her a little while ago. She was in my office after that last meeting. I asked her then, and she agreed to do it. I think things will be better for us, with her living with me. I can't go back to that hospital again." I try to turn to leave, but my sister has yet to let my arm go.

"Whoa," she says. "Why can't you go back to that hospital?"

"It's too upsetting. Too depressing," I say and pull out of her grip.

"Think how the kids feel," Kent says. "Think about them, not yourself, Blaine."

"Yeah, they're sick and hurting, and you were a ray of sunshine in their dismal days. And you just stopped going all of a sudden," Kate says. "I thought you'd at least be going back around the week of Christmas, but it sounds like you won't be."

"I won't. I can't take all that suffering for no damn reason. It sets off bombs in my head that I'd rather leave dormant. It's better this way. And the kids don't care. How could they? They don't even know me," I say, then put my jacket on.

"I saw you with some of those kids, Blaine," Kent says. "You did manage to make them your friends. You need to get over yourself and go back. Really, it's just mean not to."

"Mean?" I ask, as I've never thought of not going back as being mean to anyone.

"Yes," Kate agrees. "It is mean. You made them think you cared about them, but then you just stopped going to see them. They have so damn little."

A pain starts in my heart, and I have no idea why that is. Could they be right? Could I actually be hurting any of them? Do I really care if I am?

"I need to go. Delaney will be waiting," I say and turn to leave.

"Think about what we've said," Kate calls out after me.

"And give Delaney our love," Kent adds.

I wave behind my head and nod as I leave her office. I have no idea why, but my brain is in a whirl as I try to wrap my head around things. I never meant to hurt anyone. *Not ever.*

Maybe I am selfish. Maybe I am being weak by letting my problems with humanity and the lack thereof in this world interfere in any good I can do for people. Maybe it's time to stop being this way.

With my brother's and sister's help, I've managed to figure out how to transform my stores into something at least a little bit better than my original ideas. Maybe with Delaney's help, I can manage to come up with a way to look past what my feelings are and think about the kids' feelings instead.

As I walk into the reception area, I see Blanch getting ready to leave too. "You have any special plans for this Friday night?"

She looks at me with a smile. "No. But I hear you do."

"Huh?" I ask, as I have no idea what she could've heard.

"Delaney told me about you two moving in together. She's a very nice young woman, Blaine. Your mother would've loved her." She takes my arm and joins me as we walk out of our offices toward the elevator.

"She talked to you?" I ask, surprised since she didn't mention anything about that at all.

With a nod, she says, "She did. Blaine, I know you and how you are, so please don't think I mean anything ugly by saying this. You need to put her first. You need to watch that streak of selfishness you have. Listen to the things she has to say. She seems like a compassionate and smart woman."

"Feisty too," I say with a laugh. "You don't have to worry about Delaney. She knows how to hold her own. She's not a woman I can walk all over, by any means. She is, quite frankly, perfect for me. She won't hesitate to call me out when I'm being selfish. Instead of making me mad, it makes me think she's adorable. I have no idea why that is, but it is that way."

Blanch smiles again and pulls me in for a hug. "Blaine, I think you've met the one for you. I'm so happy."

Maybe I have met the one!

32

DELANEY

Placing my clothes in Blaine's closet has given me just about the oddest feeling I've ever had. I've never lived with anyone before. I've lived alone since I left home five years ago.

As an only child with parents who both worked at their tire shop most of my life, I stayed alone a lot too. I have no idea how well I'll take to having limited time alone.

"You look at home already," Blaine says as he strides into his bedroom.

Stepping out of the massive walk-in closet, I find myself quickly taken into his strong arms, a kiss placed on top of my head, and a hand grabbing my ass, making me giggle. "I feel out of place."

He holds me back and gives me a scowl. "Well, stop feeling like that. I want you to think of this place as yours. Make yourself completely at home."

"You do realize that means I'll have to do a lot of snooping around. It's how I get to know my accommodations."

"I'll take you on the grand tour this evening. I just talked to the staff and I've given them the weekend off so you can really get comfortable here. I want you to take over the management of the estate. Make any changes you want to. I've told them all there may be some changes come Monday." He pulls me back close to him and rocks us back and forth. "I'm so happy you're here. You have no idea how happy you've made me."

He does look happier than I've ever seen him!

"I'm pretty happy too, Blaine. I'm excited to get to call this gorgeous place my home. It's so big that I think I'm going to need a map." I laugh, but he nods.

"I'll make you one. You'll get used to things quickly. I have no doubt about that. If you can manage to get around that huge hospital, you'll learn the layout of this house easily enough." Taking me by the hand, he leads me out of the bedroom and down the hallway that will take us to the main living area. "I want to give you something."

"Blaine, please don't start spoiling me already." I follow along behind him as he tugs me across the large living area to the side door that leads out to the mud room, and then into the garage filled with cars.

"I got you something," he says as he opens the door.

I see a deep-green Mercedes sitting in the parking spot closest to the door and I know what he's done. "You did not do this, Blaine!"

"I did, too." He picks me up and twirls me around. Then carries me over to some old car that's been refurbished. "Here you go. It's a Studebaker."

I bat at his arm and laugh. "You're not fooling me! Take me back to the real car."

He laughs, carries me back to the Mercedes, and opens the driver's door, then plops me down on the buttery-soft, cream-colored, leather seat. I look up and see there's a sunroof and so many extras I think I might need to take a course on how to work them all. "So, do you like it?"

My eyes fill up with tears. "Blaine, I love it. I absolutely love it. But I can't take this. It wouldn't be right."

"You will take it, and I will hear nothing else about that. I'm sure you can find someone to give your old car to. You won't be needing it anymore." He walks around and gets into the passenger side. "Now take me for a spin in your new car, Nurse Richards."

"Okay, but you have to let me pay the insurance on this," I say as I try to figure out how to start the car.

"Too late," he says. "I've already paid for the entire year of it. I managed to take a picture of your driver's license one night when you slept over. And your social security card, just so I could put you on my auto insurance. You are one highly-covered individual now."

"Wow! I don't know exactly how I feel about you going through my purse," I say as I think about the invasion of my privacy. But then I run my hands over the steering wheel and all that goes away. "This car is so beautiful. I know I'm going to be afraid to drive it. It's too expensive and gorgeous."

"And completely covered by insurance, and I know you have to be a safe driver. I've never ridden anywhere with you, but I know you have to be one. You are one, right? I mean your driving record showed no accidents or tickets of any kind."

I look at him and feel a little more of that invasion thing, but his smile eases that too. "Blaine, this was very nice of you. I'm sure I'll get used to it. And the answer is, yes. I'm a great driver."

"I tell you what," he says as he opens his door back up. "Let's go change and go out to dinner. You can drive us."

I get out of the car, too, and follow him back inside, giving a longing look to the new car. "I'll be back," I say to it as if it's human or something. *I just love it so much already!*

Wrapping myself around Blaine's arm, I hold onto him as we walk back to the bedroom. "This is unreal."

"No, this is real. This is reality. I am your reality, Delaney Richards. And you are mine," he says, then stops in the hallway, and I find myself pinned between him and the wall.

His thumb grazes my cheek as he looks into my eyes. "Blaine, this seems like a dream."

"That's exactly how I feel too. I've never felt this way. It's as if I'm standing at the bottom of a giant mountain that I'm about to climb. At the top are all the riches in the world. At the top is you." His lips touch mine softly.

As we kiss, I think about what this all means. I think about what my parents are going to say. I haven't mentioned one word about Blaine to them. I have no idea how they'll handle this.

His sweet kiss ends and his hands move through my hair. "This is going to work, Delaney. This is going to be better than either of us has ever expected."

I hope this gorgeous man is right, because if I have to give him up, I don't know how I'll handle that!

33

BLAINE

My knuckles are white is I grip the 'oh shit' bar on the passenger side of the car. *Delaney is not a great driver!*

"This is kind of a sharp turn here," I point out.

She zips around it without hardly slowing at all. "I know, but look how great this car hugs the curve. This is like riding on rails. I love it, Blaine!"

Her enthusiasm is nice. I just wish her driving was too. "I'm pretty sure the speed limit is seventy on this part of the highway."

"It is, but thanks to that radar detector, I can fly down this road, making such great time. It's incredible," she says as she pulls into the other lane without looking to make sure no one was behind her.

"There's not a radar detector in this car, Delaney. I didn't think you'd need one of those. So you better slow down to the posted speed limit. You don't want to get a ticket on your first day with the new car." I clutch the seat with my other hand as she looks back to her right and changes lanes yet again, for reasons I don't understand.

"Then what's this?" she asks as she points to the small, black box by the rearview mirror.

"That's the box that opens the garage door." She slows down and laughs.

"Oh. Well, I'll get myself one. I think I'll be going fast a lot in this beast of a machine," she says, horrifying me.

"You should really think about taking a defensive driving class too. I'll take one with you. It'll help lower our insurance rate." I look at her to see if she's interested in that at all, because she needs some kind of a class. "Who taught you how to drive?"

"My Uncle Steve. He's the reason my parents got into the tire business in the first place. He's a racecar driver and their company supplied his tires."

"Oh, now I get it. That's why," I say about her driving.

"Yeah, that's why they made a tire business," she says, then zips off the next exit, making me cringe as she comes to a hasty stop behind a large truck.

The lights will surely slow her down now as we make our way through the city streets to get to the restaurant she picked. She looks over at me with a smile filling her entire face. "I really love the car, baby. And I really love you."

Running my hand over hers on the steering wheel, I come up with a plan. "Can I drive your snazzy new car home, baby?"

Her eyebrows raise up high, and I get a little afraid, then she says, "Of course! It's a dream to drive. Didn't you drive it home from the dealership, though?"

"No, I ordered it and they delivered it. I'm itching to see how it drives. This is my first Mercedes purchase." The light changes and she has to drive slowly behind the big, slow-moving truck. I can see her frustration as she looks on both sides to find herself fenced in by other cars.

I'm thankful, though!

"I suppose that's how the rich do a lot of things. Just buy before you try," she says, then looks at me as she's stopped at another light. "Blaine, what about my parents? How in the world should I tell them about us? I don't know how they'll take the news. You're kind of the devil in their eyes."

"I was that in your eyes, too, and I fixed that, didn't I?" I ask as she finds a tiny opening and takes off to get into it. "Damn!" I grab the dashboard and think I must be about three shades paler than I was when I got in this car with her.

"I know. I caught that break just in time!" she says as she guns it right up until we hit another red light.

I'm overjoyed when I see the restaurant on the right, just ahead. I point and shout, "Look! There it is!"

"You sound pretty excited about that, Blaine," she says as she laughs and gives me a crazy look.

"Hell, yes, I am!" I say to mask the real reason I'm so damn excited to be at our destination.

"Blaine, you look a little tense. Does my driving scare you?" she asks. Her eyes tell me she's afraid my answer will be a negative one.

"Hell, no! I think you're an excellent driver. My problem is, I like driving. I'm just a little dominating when it comes to some things, like driving, sex, work, you know ...things like that."

It's not a complete lie!

She pulls into the parking lot, and I find myself thanking God we've arrived unscathed. Then I realize, I just thanked God. *I never do that.*

"I get it. I do. So, from now on, when we go somewhere together, I'll let you drive. I don't want to emasculate you. I was reading about dealing with dominant males so I could better understand you. The article said it was important to let them be who they are meant to be. You are all man. That's for sure." She gets out of the car, and I find myself thanking God again that I may never have to ride with her driving again.

That's twice in a matter of a minute!

I take her hand as we meet in front of the car. "Thank you for understanding. It's hard to have a relationship nowadays, with so many women not understanding what it means to be with a dominant male like myself." I laugh as I put my arm around her. "Glad to see you're on board."

"Yeah, well, you will have to chill on some of the things. I can give you the small victories." Her hand moves down my back and she pats my ass.

"Does that mean no more ass smacking?" I ask her, as she seems to really like when I do that.

"No, that doesn't mean anything like that. It means I like the dominate way you handle me in the bedroom. I don't want any of that to change, ever!"

Good, then we are on the same page and that makes me very happy!

34

DELANEY

December 15th:

With a couple of weeks behind us and many small conversations about how Blaine might be able to get past his problems with handling sad situations, I have come up with an idea that has him coming back to visit the children, who ask about him often.

They all made him Christmas cards, and I brought them home to him the other day. Every single one of them thanked him for his visits and said they'd love to see him again if he ever could find time.

As he read the cards, I saw the mist in his eyes, and when he finished, he asked me how in the hell I dealt with it all. When I explained how I had cried when I first started this career, which is a tough one, he gained a better understanding.

Since he had jumped in head first before, I've slowed him down a little. We'll be putting small, artificial trees that are pre-lit into the rooms of the kids whom he made friends with. Then we'll decorate them so he can spend some time with each one of them.

It should be light and easy, and we'll stay the hell away from Meagan's room, since her father demanded it. Meagan is getting worse, anyway. I would hate for Blaine to see her. He's coming along pretty well. Seeing her and how her father is might send him back a few paces. *That's the last thing I want.*

Mr. Green pulls to a stop in front of the hospital entrance, and I hop out and go to find a couple of orderlies to come grab the supplies. Out of the kids who were here for Thanksgiving, four are still here. So those are the ones he'll visit today. I don't think he can handle meeting the new ones. Four is more than enough for now.

Blaine is a man who exudes confidence in almost every situation. It had me thinking he was without any kind of insecurities or had nothing he was unsure of. I was wrong.

I think he was sent to cross my path for a reason. And maybe he's helping me figure some things out about myself too, like how to have patience and more understanding of people. We all have our little things that give us fear or uncertainty. Not one of us doesn't have something we need help to overcome or understand.

Coming back with a couple of men to help carry the things inside, I take Blaine's hand and take him back into the hospital for the first time since Thanksgiving. I can see he's nervous, and when we get to the elevator and Meagan's mother steps off it, I'm the one who gets nervous.

Her eyes are red from crying. She blinks when she sees us. "You two are together now?" she asks as she looks at our clasped hands.

"We are," I say and step aside, pulling Blaine with me so she can pass by us.

She looks at me and Blaine, then over her shoulder as if checking to see if anyone is behind her. "Can I talk to you two for a minute?"

I don't see this as good in any way. "Mrs. Sanders, we have some things to take care of, and your husband was more than clear. He wants Mr. Vanderbilt nowhere near your daughter."

"Yes, I know that. I also know he had you removed from her nursing staff as well, Nurse Richards."

Blaine looks at me. "He did?"

I nod. "Yes. I didn't want to bring it up to you. I know how he makes you feel."

"Meagan asks for you both," she says, making me feel a little surprised. "Every single day, she asks for you two. She says she needs to tell Mr. Vanderbilt something very important."

"I don't know how we can do that," I tell her. "Neither of us are allowed in her room, and she's not able to leave it."

Her eyes cut off to the side as she looks behind us. "He's coming. I have to go. I'll come talk to you as soon as I can. We have to figure out something." She walks away quickly, and we step onto the elevator the orderlies have been holding for us.

"I really hate that asshole," Blaine mutters as the doors close and we see Mr. Sanders meet up with his wife.

"Don't think about him. Let that all slip right on out of your mind. Colby, Terry, Tammy, and little Adam are the only people I want you to think about today." I give his hand a squeeze as the elevator stops and we get out and make our way to the nurses' station.

"Look who I've brought," I say with a giggle as the other nurses look at us.

I told them all about moving in with Blaine, and I was told everyone was well aware of the attraction we had for one another and most knew it would end up getting serious.

Paul steps out of a patient's room and his eyes land on us. He makes his way to us and extends his hand to Blaine. "Looks like you've made our Nurse Richard's dreams come true, Mr. Vanderbilt. She's never looked happier or had a better attitude. Congratulations."

"Thank you," Blaine says as he shakes his hand. "She's made my dreams come true too."

The nurses all give us an *awww*. "Yes, we're adorable," I say, then wave everyone off. "We have trees to put together, ornaments to hang, and rooms to brighten with Christmas cheer. Let us get to work."

The cluster around us disperses, and we take the first tree and bag of Christmas decorations to Colby's room. When I push the door open, I see the teen sitting on his bed, Indian style, his headphones on and his electric guitar in his arms, like I usually find him.

"He loves his present, Blaine. And he's got a song he wrote. He'd like you to hear it. Make sure you ..." I say, then his fingers are on my lips.

"You don't have to tell me to let him know I like the song. I'm not a jackass."

With a nod, I walk up to Colby, and he finally opens his eyes and takes off the headphones. His face brightens as he sees Blaine. "Mr. Vanderbilt! Dude!"

"Mr. Vanderbilt?" Blaine asks as the two high-five. "I thought I told you to call me Blaine?"

"Blaine, yeah," Colby says and nods my way as Blaine still holds my hand, "So, you two, huh? I saw it coming."

Blaine and I laugh a little. I blush as Blaine gets another high-five from the kid. "I hear you have a song you wrote. So, can I wear those while you play it?" Blaine asks him.

Colby is quick to take the headphones off and hand them to Blaine. "Yeah, man! I've been tweaking it, and I think I've got a great song here. Listen and please give me some critical feedback. I need an honest opinion. My family and these nurses tell me what I want to hear, I think."

"Brutal honesty is the only way I know how to dish it out," Blaine tells him as he sits next to him on the bed and puts on the headphones. "Let it rip anytime you're ready."

I get busy setting up the little tree as the two have their fun and I love the way Blaine gets along with the kids. He's going to make a great dad ... or I wonder if he wants to be called pops.

Then I laugh at myself for getting so far ahead in this thing he and I have barely started. I have no idea if we will even get so far as to make it to the altar, much less have kids.

I have no idea if he even wants kids for that matter, or if he does, how many he wants. I have no idea about a lot of things where that man is concerned.

By the time they're finished with their little jam session, I'm done with the decorations, and Colby turns his attention to what I've been doing. "Wow! A tree and Christmas decorations. Thanks, Nurse Richards." He looks at Blaine and nudges him with his shoulder. "So when's the big day?"

Blaine looks at me with a smile, then winks. "I'm not sure yet. I have to make sure Nurse Richards really likes me before I go popping that question. If you knew how scared I was just to ask her to move in with me, you'd laugh."

"I wouldn't worry too much if I was you. She glows when you're around. Not so much when you're not," he tells Blaine, and I find myself blushing again.

"Okay, boys. We have three more trees to get to. It seems there're trees for all today and we have to get to that business," I say and go take Blaine's hand, taking him away from what looks like his new best buddy.

"You glow, huh? I've noticed that. Only I thought you looked like that all the time," Blaine whispers as we leave the room.

"I didn't realize I was doing that," I say as we go back to the nurses' station to pick up the things to bring some holiday spirit to another kid. "I'll try to stop."

"I don't think you can, and I'm going to do everything I can to keep that perfect glow going on inside of you, Nurse Richards." His arm runs around me as he takes the box with the small tree out of my hand and we head toward Terry's room. "I wonder how much you'll glow when you're pregnant. I bet it will get even brighter."

His thought has me wondering how we both thought about that nearly at the same time. I wonder if things really will get that far with us. I wonder if we will get married and have a family.

I suppose stranger things have happened.

Just before we get to Terry's room, I hear a voice come from behind us. "What the hell is he doing here?"

Looking over my shoulder, I recognize the voice and see Mr. Sanders standing in the hallway just outside his daughter's door. "Do not engage him, Blaine." I pull him along with me to get inside of Terry's room.

"I thought I told you to leave my daughter alone, Vanderbilt!"

Blaine stops, and I go into a panic as I hear Mr. Sanders' footsteps quickly approaching. I have no clue as to what Blaine will do to the man.

Why does this man have to be such an asshole?

35

A CHRISTMAS WISH BOOK FIVE

A Holiday Romance

By Michelle Love

Dreams. Passion. Aspirations.

Blaine finds an understanding in himself for Meagan's father.
Delaney finds it hard to understand how Blaine can take how the man is threatening him so calmly.
A brief visit with Meagan's mother has the couple's interests divided.
Blaine is interested, but Delaney is afraid.
Will Meagan really be able to change how Blaine sees the world? Or will Blaine even get the chance to talk to the little girl he thinks will change his life?

36

BLAINE

December 15th:

Despite Delaney's best effort to pull me into Terry's room, Meagan's father is in full-on asshole mode and grabs my shoulder before we get all the way inside of the room. "You need to leave!" he shouts at me.

Letting Delaney's hand go, I turn back and look the man in the eyes. I see something in the light-blue recesses of his red-rimmed eyes. *I see a man who is terrified.*

Placing my hand on his shoulder, I say, "Look, Mr. Sanders, I know you're afraid for your daughter. I know you're looking like crazy for someone to take all your anger out on. I'm not the guy who's going to take it, though. My advice is for you to go talk to that preacher who comes around here every day. He's the best man to help you with what you're feeling right now."

"Get your hand off me," he growls. So I move my hand as his face goes red with rage. "You don't know a thing about me, you rich son of a bitch. Don't act like you do. My world is being torn in two. I want you out of here. You came in here and have spoiled these children. I can see right through you. You have no soul, Mr. Vanderbilt."

"That is enough!" Delaney hisses at the man as she grabs my

hand. "I've had enough of you, Mr. Sanders!" She pulls me the rest of the way inside Terry's room and closes the door in the angry man's face. "He has gone too far with this!"

I see Terry sitting up in his bed, looking worried. "What was that man's problem?"

It's only been a few weeks since I've seen this kid and I find his dark hair, which had been thick and curly, is gone. The way it makes me feel is awful. Then I think about what my brother and sister told me, and I stop thinking about myself and think about Terry.

Who gives a shit how his hair loss is making me feel? It's him I should be thinking about!

"That man is a very scared person right now with his daughter being so sick, that's what's wrong with him," I say. "People's grief and anxiety come out in different ways. He's just going through some bad things right now, and I'm obviously the one he's chosen to take it out on. It's okay. Now, tell me how you've been doing. I see you've decided to get into that Vin Diesel look. You're rocking it."

He runs his hand over his bald head and smiles at me. "You like?"

"Very hip," I tell him, then go sit in the chair next to his bed. "Wanna play some football while Nurse Richards puts up some Christmas decorations to brighten up your room?"

"Yeah, I have some time to whoop your butt in a game." He tosses me a game controller. "Now, what's had you so busy you couldn't stop by for a game in three weeks?"

"Business," I lie. "So, update me on your progress, Terry. Tell me what I've missed."

"It's all the same," he says as he starts the game.

"No, it's not all the same," Delaney says as she stops placing ornaments on the tree and looks at me with a shimmery light in her green eyes. "There's very good news. His tumor is shrinking a little each day. If he keeps making this kind of progress, he'll be on his way home within a few weeks."

I shake my head as I look at the fifteen-year-old young man and catch a little smile. "Home? Man, I don't even remember what it feels like to be there."

"It'll be good to get back there," I say. "There's no place like home. You know, I heard Santa was going to come by to see you, Terry. He and I are good friends, you know."

"Is that right," he says, then laughs. "Well, I'll just have to start thinking about what I want him to bring me for Christmas, won't I?"

"I would, if I was you," I tell him, then score a touchdown. "Yes!"

"You made that look a little too easy, Blaine. I bet you can't make even one more of them," he says, and I can see his mind working on how to stop me from winning this game.

The intercom in the room comes on with a squeak then I hear a man's voice say, "Nurse Richards, I need you and Mr. Vanderbilt in my office."

Delaney rolls her eyes as she comes to the intercom and hits the button. "Yes, Mr. Davenport. We'll be there right away, sir."

"Who is that?" I ask, as I've never heard of him before.

"He's the head of security here," she says, then takes the game controller out of my hands. "You'll have to pause your game, Terry. Sorry."

"Man!" he whines. "I was this close to making a touchdown, myself."

I laugh as I get up and follow her out of the room. "I'll be back. And you weren't close to anything."

Getting into the elevator, I notice Delaney hitting the basement button. "His office is all the way down there?"

"Yes, they keep him in the basement. That's where all the security monitoring equipment is. I know that damn Mr. Sanders is behind this. Get ready to get angry, Blaine," she says as the elevator stops and we step out to find a tall man with short, dark hair, wearing a blue uniform that resembles a police officer's.

His badge has his name on it, making it easy to see this is the man who called us down here. "Mr. Davenport," I say as I extend my hand. "I'm Blaine Vanderbilt."

He takes my hand and gives it a firm shake. "Nice to meet you. Follow me, please."

Delaney and I follow the man to a door on the side of the long hallway. The cement floor makes the sound of our footsteps echo loudly. It's chilly down here, so I wrap my arm around Delaney as she runs her hands up and down her arms.

When we step into his office, we find it warm and on the cozy side. He takes a seat behind his desk, and we sit in the chairs on the other side. "A Mr. Sanders has asked me to talk to you two. He's worried about the children you're visiting and giving things to."

"It's none of his business," Delaney snaps.

I put my hand on her knee in an attempt to keep her calm. Her cheeks are already growing pink, and I think the little Pitbull she can be at times is trying to get out.

For some reason, I find myself calm. *Eerily calm.*

37

DELANEY

Fury is right at the surface and I have to fight to remember this is just Davenport's job. It's not him I'm angry with, it's Meagan's father. Blaine's hand moves to my knee and he gives it a little squeeze. I suppose he's trying to calm me down.

But I don't know if I can be calm about this!

"Look, we aren't even going to his child's room. I see no reason why you needed to bring us down here to tell us anything!"

"It's okay, baby," Blaine says as he looks at me with a calm expression. "Let the man do his job."

"Thank you," Davenport says, then continues, "Mr. Sanders is going to have a meeting with the other parents this evening. He's not happy at all with the way Mr. Vanderbilt is doing this for some kids and not all of them. I know this is just an excuse he's come up with. He wants to get the other parents to sign a petition to ban Vanderbilt from making any visits to the children here."

"This is ridiculous!" I shout, and Blaine's hand leaves my knee, then he runs his arm around my shoulders.

"Shh. It's okay," he says. "If the parents don't want me to visit their kids, then that's up to them. Frankly, I doubt the man will get everyone to agree with him. I know Tammy's mother won't."

"It's the damn point!" I shout again. "I'll go talk to the asshole, myself!"

"No, you won't," both Blaine and Davenport say.

"Why the hell not?"

Davenport leans forward and looks directly at me. "Because things could escalate. So, just stay away from the man. I brought you in here to let you know about the meeting, and that, if there is a petition brought to me, then I will have to follow protocol and Mr. Vanderbilt will be banned from coming here anymore."

"I don't know why that man has to be so difficult," I say, then get up to leave. "We've heard what you had to say. We have things to do. Kids to see and trees to put up. It would be appreciated if you would stick up for Mr. Vanderbilt just a bit. He is doing nice things and that damn man is doing nothing but being a jackass!"

I leave the room and find Blaine coming out behind me. "Hey, you need to cool down."

With a quick spin, I face him and find him looking like he doesn't have a care in the world. "Why? So he can get away with this?"

"Because this is purely his problem. It has nothing to do with you. And not even me, really. He feels out of control because he is out of control where his daughter is concerned. The only thing he might be able to control is me being here."

"Why pick on you?" I ask. "I'm not going to allow that."

"Baby, this isn't a thing for you to fix. I don't think there's anything to worry about. When the other parents go to his little meeting—and let's just see how many even show up for it—then you'll see that things will end."

He moves me inside the elevator and pushes the button to take us back up. "Blaine, I really hate this. You came here at my cajoling and this happens to you. I feel terrible. Don't you see why I feel the need to fix it?"

"I do," he says as he pulls me into his arms. "But I'm a big boy. I can handle it."

"You shouldn't have to face this kind of adversity when you're doing a nice thing." A protectiveness over him fills me as I hug him tightly.

He may look like a tower of strength, and right now he's even exhibiting that same strength, but it infuriates me that anyone would do this to him.

The elevator slows to a stop and he lets me out of the hug, leaving one arm draped around my shoulders. Making our way back to Terry's room, I see Mrs. Sanders standing at the nurses' station. She heads our way, and I find my insides getting tight. "Damn it," I whisper. *I am more than tired of dealing with this family today!*

"Please come with me," she says, once she's close enough for us to hear.

"No way," I tell her. "Your husband has made himself crystal clear about anything to do with his family."

"He's gone. He won't be back for three hours. I need you to come with me, please," she begs as she wrings her thins hands. With tired eyes, she looks at Blaine. "Meagan said to tell you that Crystal is with her. I don't know what that means, but she told me to tell you that."

Blaine's face goes pale. "My mother's name was Crystal."

"We can't go in there, Blaine. The camera in the hallway will catch us going in. I'm sorry, but we just can't. Tell Meagan we would if we could, but we're not allowed in her room. You have to explain that to her. This is not anyone's fault but your husband's." I take Blaine's hand and try to pull him away from the woman who's making him feel terribly.

He doesn't move though, as she says, "My husband is mad at you, Mr. Vanderbilt, because Meagan keeps talking about you. She keeps saying she's going to go away with Crystal, but she can't until she tells you something. He thinks if you talk to her, she'll die."

"Is her condition that dire?" he asks me.

I nod. "It is. But there's always hope." Turning to face Mrs. Sanders, I continue, "And this notion about her talking to Blaine then passing away is ludicrous. I've seen patients who have said they saw people who'd passed away in their rooms, and guess what, not all of them died. I don't know how to explain any of it, but I know Blaine nor I can go into that room."

"If we are disguised, we could," he says. "Say, if we visit as Santa and maybe an elf, or something along those lines. Then we could go in and the camera wouldn't be able to tell it's us. I could even have other Santas and elves running around the hospital, spreading Christmas cheer."

"Blaine, that would take some preparation," I tell him, not at all liking his idea. He needs to stay away from the kid, or he could end up facing some stiff charges.

"It would," Mrs. Sanders says. "And that is a great idea. I could make sure my husband has something to do to keep him away from here. I have a very different opinion than he does. If it is time for our daughter to go home, then I will accept that. But I still have hope that she can beat this. I also think you need to hear what she has to tell you."

"Why don't you tell her to tell you and you'll make sure he gets the message?" I ask in an attempt to stop this insanity. Sanders could have Blaine put in jail for going into that room. I will do everything I can to stop Blaine from going in there.

"I have, but she said she has to hold his hand and show him something. She also said Crystal will tell her what to say. She doesn't know what it is yet. I think the Santa costume thing will work." She looks down the hallway toward her daughter's room. "I should get back to her. Please let me know when you'll be able to get this plan underway, and I'll make sure my husband is nowhere near here during that time."

"I will," Blaine says, then I get him to move his feet and start pulling him away with me. "Maybe in a couple of days. I have to get things together."

"Come on, Blaine," I say as I tug at him to hurry. "We have things to do."

"Yes, we do. We have a lot of things to do. This will take some planning, and I think five sets of Santa's and elves will do. Some of my employees can help out with that."

"You can't possibly be serious about doing that," I say, then push open Terry's door.

"Oh, I am very serious. I have a chance to talk to my mother. I know that sounds crazy and I shouldn't believe it, but something is telling me it's true."

Something is telling me it's not!

38

BLAINE

When that woman said my mother's name, chills ran through me. I wanted to run down the hall and into that little girl's room more than I've ever wanted anything in my life.

We saw the parents of the kids I visited with today and all of them said they would attend the meeting Sanders is having this evening. They said they'd sing my praises.

As I sit in the back of the Suburban with Delaney, I find myself feeling very empathetic for the man who has it in his head that if his daughter talks to me, she'll die. *No wonder he's acting so crazy.*

Taking Delaney's hand, I lift it up and place a kiss on top of it. "If that was our little girl having to deal with everything Meagan's having to, I might act the same damn way her father is."

"You wouldn't go after an innocent person, Blaine. You're not like him," she tells me, then leans into my side and places her hand on my chest. "And what's this talk about our kids?"

"I think you'll be a great mother. What do you think about me?" I ask as I run my hand through her hair.

Her eyes shine as she looks up at me. "I think you'll be great at whatever you do. I also think you have it in your head that little girl will tell you something to make you believe in something, and I want you to know, that's a longshot."

"It's a shot I have to take, Delaney. You have no idea how much I felt when that woman said my mother's name. It was like lightning went right through me. What if she can help me believe in something?" I ask as I hold her even tighter.

The way she's looking at me has me thinking she doesn't believe in this kind of thing. With a nod of her head, she says, "I guess if she can help you, that'd be great. God knows you need some help in that department. But what if what she says only throws you further into the fray?"

"The fray?" I ask, as I have no idea what she's talking about.

"The place where you dangle between worlds. Not quite a believer, but not quite not. I think you're closer to the believing side right now. If she says things you don't understand or things that make you think it's all made up or just plain wrong, then I see it hurting you."

"She's only a little girl. I don't expect much, baby. I just need to do this. I really do need it." Mr. Green pulls into the driveway of the estate, taking us back home for the evening, and I start thinking about the phone calls I need to make to get things going.

As we pull all the way up to the house, I see my brother's car, and he and my sister are sitting inside of it. "Who's this?" Delaney asks as we stop.

"Kent and Kate." I get out of the car and help her out too. My sister and brother get out too and meet us at the front door.

"Hey, Blaine," Kate says, then smiles at the woman under my arm. "Delaney, how are you this evening?"

"I'm just fine. Blaine didn't tell me you guys were coming out here. What a nice surprise," she says as she moves away from me and hugs my sister.

I lead everyone into the house, where we're met by the housekeeper. "Evening, Vanderbilts. Do we have guests for dinner?"

Delaney takes Kate's hand. "Please tell me you two will join us for dinner this evening."

"Sure, if Blaine's okay with that," she says as she looks my way.

"Of course," I say. "Add two more to the dinner plan. We'll be in the main living area. When it's ready, would you let us know?"

"I will," she says, then hurries away to let the cook know plans have changed.

Going straight to the bar at the back of the living room, I get out a short glass and fill it with ice. "Feel free to make yourselves whatever you want."

Delaney picks up a wine glass and grabs a bottle of red wine out of the wine chiller. "Care to join me in this bottle, Kate?"

My sister nods, and Delaney fills two glasses and tucks the bottle under her arm. Picking up the glasses, half full of the red liquid, she makes her way to sit across from Kate. "Thank you, Delaney. So how did the visit to the hospital go today?"

"Great, except for one monkey wrench one of the patient's fathers is throwing at Blaine. That man is a real menace." I watch Delaney take a long drink of the wine, as if she's really needing something to ease her tension.

"What's he doing?" Kate asks.

I take a seat next to Delaney while my brother mixes himself up some kind of a fancy cocktail. I merely filled my glass with Scotch, not looking for anything more than little settle-me-down drink.

Electricity is coursing through my veins with excitement. I lean forward as Kent sits down at the opposite end of the sofa from Kate and tell them, "There's a little girl in the hospital who is very sick— near-death sick. Her mother came to us and told me the little girl has a message for me from someone named Crystal."

Kate nearly spits out the wine she's just drunk, and Kent's eyes go wider than I've ever seen them go before as he says, "No way!"

Delaney clears her throat. "Yes, that's what the little girl's mother said. But let me tell you, as a person who has been around quite a few people who have been close to death, things aren't always what they seem to be."

"What do you mean by that?" Kate asks as she attempts to take another sip of her wine.

The cook's assistant, Maggie, comes in with a tray of appetizers and places them on the table. "Chef Roxy said to let you know dinner will be ready in an hour. Salads will be served in forty-five minutes in the small dining room, if that's all right with you, Miss Richards."

"It will be fine with me," Delaney answers, already taking well to the running of the place. "And I'd love it if I could have some iced tea in a pitcher on the table too. I've been craving some sweet tea all day."

"I'll make sure it's there," Maggie says, then leaves us with the tray of cheese and apple slices.

Kent picks up a piece of cheese, then asks, "So what do you mean by that, Delaney?"

She settles in, kicking off her heels and pulling her feet under her as she leans against my side. "You see, the neurons in the human brain begin to fire in odd ways as the body begins to die. Things start shutting down and it affects the brain. Dreams can occur while they're in a semi-awake state. Lucid dreaming is one way of describing how it works."

"This little girl," Kate asks. "Is she on a lot of pain medication? You know, is she maybe hallucinating?"

"Could be," Delaney says. "She is on pain medication. She's also in the final stage of her illness."

"Is there any hope for her at all?" Kent asks as he looks sad.

"Of course," Delaney says, then smiles at us all. "I have seen things happen many times. I've seen people beginning to make funeral arrangements for their family members only to have to cancel them when the person came back around. The human body is amazing. Some believe it's divine intervention that brings them back to our world."

"God?" I ask as I feel another cold chill move through my body.

Delaney's eyes settle on mine. "Yes, God, Blaine."

And it really hits me. Meagan may show me what I have been searching for my whole life. *The truth!*

39

DELANEY

I can see it, there in his light-brown eyes—the flicker of hope. The idea that what that little girl might say will have the ability to cement a faith in him that he's lacked.

Blaine and I have had a few discussions about his beliefs. He's shaky, at best. With the pain of having a mother who left them one afternoon with the promise of arriving back home the next day with a new addition to their family only to never come back, Blaine holds a lot inside of himself. He has little faith in the world or in there being anything real that is watching over us.

"I have to let you know that you could be in for a real disappointment, Blaine, if you go through with your plan," I tell him.

"You have a plan?" Kent asks as he looks intrigued. "If it's anything to do with the woman I never got to meet, can I be a part of it, too, Blaine?"

"Oh! Me too!" Kate says as her cheeks grow pink with excitement.

"You should all calm down," I tell them, as I know things never go the way people think they might when dealing with this type of thing. "I've seen the mother of a child ask her young son about her father who had passed. The boy kept saying he smelled cigar smoke that no one else did."

"Phantom smells, huh?" Kent asks as sits back, taking a sip of his fruity-looking drink. He pulls a piece of pineapple out and eats it as he looks at me with an expression that lets me know he thinks I'm about to tell a spooky story.

The story I'm telling is not spooky. *It's disappointing!*

"I suppose you could call the smell a phantom one, if you wanted to be dramatic," I say with a laugh. "But really, it was the oxygen that was being forced into the kid through his nose to help him stay alive. His mother, though, led him as she told him her dead father used to smoke cigars. With her interest, I think the child began to focus on something that was not really there."

"Okay, Delaney," Blaine says as he looks at me with a no-nonsense look on his handsome face. "But Meagan knows nothing about me or my mother. So why would she make this up?"

With a shrug, I say, "Why does anyone come up with anything?"

"You seem cynical," Kate says. "I guess you've seen so much, it's made you that way."

"I'm not cynical. I believe in God with all my heart. I just know that it's not likely this little girl will say anything to make someone who's not been a real believer to make such a huge change in their mind." I look back at Blaine. "Tell me, if you actually saw an apparition of you mother, would it make you believe in God and heaven?"

Blaine stares blankly at me, then he looks at his sister then his brother. "I don't know if that would make me believe anything other than this world is really crappy. To think of mom trapped here is even more awful than thinking of her as just no longer existing. Maybe Delaney is right. Maybe I shouldn't go see the girl."

Kate shakes her head. "I don't think you're going to be shown a ghost, Blaine."

"She said she had something to tell me," Blaine says, then looks at me. "I do think if some words were told to me that only mom would know to say, then I might gain some faith."

Kent nods in agreement. "Yes, if she said something only he would know about, that should make him feel like there's another side. That she's not trapped here or non-existent any longer."

"And how about you two?" I ask. "What kind of beliefs do you have?"

"Pops took us to church every Sunday, up until Kent was about fifteen. I suppose he felt like he'd done his duty and introduced us to the Lord," Kate says.

Blaine looks away. "I went with them until I was twelve, then I refused to go anymore. Pops was disappointed in me, but he told me he wouldn't shove something I didn't want down my throat."

I feel compelled to let his brother and sister know the risks of Blaine going to see the girl. "The thing you don't know is that the little girl's father has banned Blaine from his daughter's room. He's having a meeting tonight to try to get him banned from the entire hospital."

"I don't think that's going to happen, though," Blaine says. "I have a few supporters there."

"Most likely it won't happen. But even if he doesn't get banned from the hospital, he and I are both banned from Meagan's room. If we go into it without permission, then we could be arrested," I tell them and watch their faces fall.

"Crap!" Kate says, then sips her drink.

"That does put a damper on things, doesn't it?" Kent asks.

"A very big damper on it," I say.

"But I have a plan," Blaine lets them know. "And you both can help. I need four Santa and elf teams to be in the hospital at the same time Delaney and I are in the same costumes. Then the camera won't catch us going into the girl's room. It will catch one of the five sets of people who are moving around the hospital that day, but no one would be able to point out exactly who we are."

"I like it!" Kent says, making my heart plummet.

I had really hoped they'd see the risk and decide it wasn't worth doing. *Am I the only one who's worried about this turning out very badly?*

40

BLAINE

I can see by the look on Delaney's face that she expected my siblings to be on board with her, and they're anything but that. *We are cut from the same cloth!*

"The salads are ready to be served," Maggie says as she enters the room.

We all get up, and I catch Delaney taking the bottle of wine with her. She seems a bit down with the news that my plan will go off, despite her objections to it. "You know, even if we do get arrested, I have the money to get us bailed out quickly and will hire the best lawyer to defend us both," I let her know, then pull her close to me and kiss the top of her head. "You'd only see the inside of a jail cell for a short amount of time. Most likely, not even overnight."

"Sure, that makes me feel better," she says with a frown as we lead the way to the dining room.

Taking our seats at the table for four, I take Delaney's hand. "Tell you what, let me say grace over the food."

Her eyebrows arch in surprise. "Do you know how to do that?"

Kent laughs as he takes her other hand. "Sure, he does. He's not a heathen, Delaney."

Kate takes my other hand and Kent's, and the four of us form a circle. "Bow your heads and close your eyes," I say and make sure they all done as I've said to. "Lord, we want to thank you for this food. We also want to thank you for everything you've done for us and will do for us. I hope you see fit to let my mother come through the little girl and give me a sign that you are real. Amen."

When I open my eyes, I see Delaney looking at me with that frown still on her face. "Blaine, that is not how faith works. Faith is believing in something you can't see or hear. If it was supposed to be shown to you no one would call it faith."

"You can't understand, Delaney," I say as I pass the salad dressing to her after drowning my salad in it. "If you've never doubted, like I have, then you don't understand how I feel at all."

"I guess so," she says as she puts a tablespoon-sized dollop of the dressing on her salad, then passes it to Kent. "You know, there are things you do have faith in. You have faith all those toys are going to fly off your shelves at your stores."

"That's only because I've seen it happen," I tell her. "By the way, Kent, how's that all going? I can't believe I've been so involved with getting Delaney all settled in that I haven't checked our sales even once since the new toys started filling our shelves."

"I can't believe that either," he says. "And sales have doubled since last year. With the advertisement about the toys being of improved quality, we've done better than any of your past year's Christmas sales."

"Seems you guys were right about things," I say and find myself pleasantly surprised.

I had a bad feeling the sales wouldn't increase and we'd make less money than previous years. Seems I was wrong. I wonder what else I might be wrong about.

"Tell me about her, Blaine," Kent says as he stabs a piece of lettuce with his fork. "Kate can't recall much about our mother."

"She was pretty and nice. She smelled like honey most of the time. I'm not sure why that was, but she did. Honey and lemons. I think that might have been from cleaning the house, though. Pops ended up smelling like lemons, too, after she left us," I say and find Delaney's hand on my leg.

"She didn't leave you. You shouldn't think about her like that. She had finished her job here and was sent on," she tells me.

"Her job was not finished," I say with a huff. "And I suppose you're right. I shouldn't say she left us. I should say she was taken away from us."

"Well, now I'm sorry I said anything at all about it. I don't want you to think that way either," she says, and that frown is still on her pretty face.

I kiss her cheek. "I'll try to speak in a positive manner. How about that?"

She nods. "Did she do anything special that you remember?" she asks. "My mother used to cut up my meat for me. She did it until I was about fifteen. Dad's the one who made her stop."

"Mom did tons of stuff for me. She always made macaroni and cheese for dinner because it was the only food I would eat every time it was on my plate. I was a picky eater," I tell her, then look at Kent, who never got anything from her. "I made sure we got macaroni after that. I would remind pops when we went grocery shopping that we needed it."

"I wish I would've been able to know her," Kent says with a sigh. "It's hard never knowing your mother. I wonder how people who don't even know who their mother and father are make it in this world."

"Life seems unfair at times," Delaney says. "I see it all the time. But there are plenty of times when life is more than fair. No one has it all bad. And no one has it all good. Look at you guys. You lost your mother, but you had a great father. And Blaine's managed to make a hell of a lot out of himself, and with his help, you two are doing the same thing. I'm sure your mother looks down and feels nothing but pride in her family."

Kate wipes a tear away, then takes a drink of her wine. I know Kate missed mom far more than we boys did. She was the lone female in the house. There was no one for her to talk to about female things. Or boys.

We were hard on her where boys were concerned. If she brought one up, pops, me, and Kent would tell her to stay away from all boys. They were out for one thing and one thing only. And now I look at my sister, who is twenty-eight and has never had a real relationship and I think we were too protective. Mom would've made sure she had a normal life as a teenage girl.

"You know, thinking about Mom has me thinking about you, Kate," I say, making her look at me.

"About me? Why?"

"Well, it's brought to mind that you have yet to have a real boyfriend. I have noticed a man at the office who watches you a lot. He's not a bad guy. You might think about checking him out sometime. His name is Randy."

"Randy Holdings," she says with a smile. "He's talked to me a few times. I didn't realize he liked me."

"I did," Kent says. "I didn't tell you anything because I'm so used to keeping men away from you. But I've seen his attention to you as well. He is a nice guy."

Kate gives us both a look that tells me she's a bit on the shy side when it comes to men. "You guys have kind of impaired any skills I might've formed to understand how to act with men."

"I can help you out there," Delaney says with a smile. "You have me around now. And men are easy. Show the tiniest amount of interest in him and you'll have him eating out of the palm of your hand. You are stunningly beautiful, Kate."

My heart grows with love for the woman on my right. Her kind spirit makes her even more beautiful to me, and I wonder if she was put in my path for a reason. Maybe Delaney is meant to be our matriarch, falling into the place mom's death left vacant.

That role needs to be filled!

41

DELANEY

D ecember 23^{rd:}
The bus full of Santa-and-elf teams Blaine has put together, using his brother, sister, and other members of his staff, is ready for action. Each Santa has a bag full of goodies to hand out to every last kid in the entire Children's Hospital.

Mr. Sanders was unable to get enough signatures on his petition to get Blaine banned from the hospital, and Blaine has come with me every day to see his four favorite kids. He had posters made up to let the other kids know Santa would be visiting them today to give them all something special to make their holidays a bit better.

I'm uncomfortable in the shapeless elf costume with the long, pointy, green shoes that feel odd on my feet. Once I have to put the elf mask on, which Blaine said was a necessary evil so we don't stick out like a sore thumb, I'll really be uncomfortable.

I have to admit, after the makeup that Blaine had done on all the Santa's, they all look alike. Their fat suits match right down to the last button and so do their white beards and little wire-framed glasses. I can't tell one from the other.

The bus, which has been wrapped to resemble a train, has the words *Polar Express* written down the sides. It pulls to a stop in front of the hospital entrance. "Here we go," Blaine says. "Stay in character now. You all have the areas you will be visiting, so let's get this show on the road. Ho! Ho! Ho!"

The bus erupts into ho, ho, ho's as the other Santa's seem to be cheering. Blaine hands me my mask with the silly pointed hat attached to the top of it. He makes sure my hair isn't visible at all, and we get out after all the others have. "Here we go, baby. I can't explain how excited I am."

I can't explain how nervous I am!

Ten of us in all, we move into the lobby, and my heart stops as Davenport comes toward us with a frown on his face. "Okay, I'm gonna need to see a little ID here fellas."

Silence falls on us all as the others have been briefed not to reveal their true identities. The other Santas and elves look back and forth at each other with odd looks on their faces.

"Just kidding!" Davenport shouts as he laughs. "I know Santa doesn't need an ID. Go wish the kids a Merry Christmas, guys." He waves and goes to the elevator to go down to his surveillance room to monitor things.

"Scared me there for a second," Blain whispers to me.

I laugh nervously. "I'm still scared."

"Calm down, little elf," he says, then adds, "Ho, ho, ho."

The sounds of the happy Santas fill the lobby, then disperse as we all take separate paths to separate areas of the hospital. My heart is pounding as we go to the set of elevators that will take us to what Blaine has called his destiny.

The man can be so dramatic sometimes!

The elevator stops on our floor, and as we step off, I nearly pass out, as the hallway is filled with the parents and families of the patients. A lot of them have cameras and most have their phones out, recording us.

"Oh, Blaine, this is terrible," I whisper, so no one else can hear me.

"It'll be fine," he says, then makes a big wave. "Merry Christmas!"

"Look, it's really Santa," a little girl says as she comes running up to us. She tugs on Blaine's red, velvet pants leg. "Hi, Santa. Remember me? I'm Polly and my sister is here. She's very sick and I have only one thing to ask you for this year."

"Of course I remember you, Polly," Blaine says with a deep voice that I can't recognize as his at all, and I find myself pretty relieved by that. "And what would you like to ask Santa for this year?"

"I want my sister to get better and get to finally come home," she says with a smile on her face.

Just as I worry that Blaine won't be able to come up with anything to say to her and work hard on trying to make my voice sound different, he says, "Well, that's a great thing to ask for. Aren't you a wonderful sister, Polly? I think I have a present in my sack for a sweet little girl like yourself." He pulls a prettily-wrapped package out of his bag and hands it to her. "Here you go, and remember to be good. Christmas is right around the corner."

"I know, Santa," she says as she holds the package in her arms as if it's precious to her. "Thank you so much!"

I have to smile underneath my mask, as he pulled that off better than I thought he'd be able to. And he didn't even make a fake promise that might scar the little girl if her wish doesn't come true.

Dragging the other red bag that's also full of presents behind me, I follow Blaine as he goes down the hallway to the first room on the right. Tammy's room.

Here's where we'll see if we're pulling things off. If any of his four favorites can tell it's us, then we shouldn't try to go into Meagan's room. I'm interested to see if her mother, Patsy, is able to tell it's us as well.

Tammy has her long, blonde wig on as we come inside her room. Her mother is videoing us as Blaine says, "Ho, ho, ho. Merry Christmas, Tammy!"

I made sure to give every child's name to all the Santas so they could amaze the kids further. I think it was genius on my part!

"Santa, you are real?" she shouts, then gets off her bed and runs to hug him. "I was afraid you'd just be a man in a suit."

"Nonsense, little Tammy," Blaine says with a resounding, deep, thumping voice. "Now, let me see what I have for you. Excuse me, my little elf helper. I do believe you have her present in your bag."

I open the bag, find the gift with her name on it, and hand it to him. Then I make an attempt at talking very high and elf-like, "Here you go, Santa."

Tammy giggles and looks at me. "Your voice sounds like you've been sucking on a helium balloon."

I giggle with the same high tone to my voice. "Thank you, Tammy!"

If we didn't have to go into Meagan's room, I'd actually love this. *But we do, so I'm still more nervous than I've ever been in my life!*

42

BLAINE

With the majority of the kids behind us, we come to Meagan's door. Her mother's the only one at it as she smiles at us, then pushes the door open. "Won't you come in, Santa? I have a little girl here who is so excited to see you."

I smile and nod. "Is Meagan ready to see Santa?" We head into the dimly-lit room. Mrs. Sanders closes the door behind us and stays on the other side to make sure we aren't interrupted by anyone.

"Santa?" Meagan asks with a weak voice. "Is that really you?"

We get close to her, and I run my hand over her head. A red bow has been taped to her hairless scalp, and I see a mere shell of the little girl I visited not that long ago.

"Yes, it's Santa, Meagan. I brought you a gift from the North Pole," I tell her. "Can you get Meagan's gift, elf?"

Delaney shuffles through the bag, taking her time like I asked her to, in order to give the little girl time to see if anything comes through. Meagan's eyes have dark circles under them and she looks so tired. "Santa, can you tell me something?"

"Anything, Meagan," I say and watch her reaching out for my hand.

"Can you take off your glove and hold my hand?" she asks me.

With a nod, I pull the glove off and hold my hand out to her. "Santa, can you tell me if you know a man named Blaine?"

Delaney stops digging through the bag and looks at us. I can tell she's freaking out that Meagan has recognized me somehow. Her mind must be sputtering with what to do now.

"I do know a man named Blaine," I tell her as she peers up at me.

"Good. Crystal's telling me that I can tell you what she has to say. She told me you will let him know. You will let him know, right, Santa?" she asks, then looks just over my right shoulder.

I get a cold chill and feel my back going colder than I ever recall feeling before. "I will deliver whatever message you have for him. Who is Crystal?"

"She's this very pretty angel who's staying with me most of the time. She has little freckles across her nose. Her eyes are shiny and green. She's nice and she promises me there's nothing to be afraid of if I have to make the transition. If my body doesn't get better."

I feel a trickle of adrenaline move through me as cold air stirs near my right ear. "Is she here with you now?"

"Listen closely, and you might hear her. She's trying to talk to you. You should close your eyes and listen as hard as you can," she tells me, and I do as she's said to and concentrate harder than I've ever done before.

I can't hear a thing, but my ear is growing numb with the freezing air that's hitting it. The sound of a picture being taken makes me open my eyes, and I see Delaney has out her cell phone and is taking pictures of me.

She isn't saying a word, then she puts the phone down. With that mask on, I have no idea what her expression is and no idea why she took pictures of me.

"I can't hear anything, Meagan," I tell the little girl, who's looking at me with wide eyes.

"I see. I guess she has to tell me, then, and I'll tell you. It's been a long time since she was able to talk to anyone. Except me, that is. I'm the first person she's been put in charge of making feel safe with the transition. That's because I am special," she says with a grin.

"You are very special," I agree.

"What would you like me to tell him, Crystal?" she asks as her eyes follow what must be the woman she's seeing, moving her gaze to the other side of her bed. Then she looks at me. "She wants me to tell you that she's proud of how you, Kate, and Trent have turned out." Her eyes go back to the other side of the bed. "Oh, okay." She looks back at me. "Kent. Not Trent."

I sigh and feel a weight moving off my shoulders that I didn't even realize was there before. "How is my father?"

She looks back to where I guess my mother's spirit is and nods. "He is fine and she sees him often, Blaine." Meagan smiles at me. "You fooled me. You're not really Santa. That's okay. I'm sure the real Santa won't forget about me, Mr. Vanderbilt. And Crystal told me not to tell my daddy about this. So I won't. I always do what Crystal says, on account of her being an angel."

"Good to know. Do you know that angel was once my mother?" I ask and look at the other side of the bed, longing to see what this little girl sees.

"I do. She's not worried about you because she never worries," Meagan says. "But she wants you to know there is another side. This world is not all there is. And you never need to be afraid of anything. Living, or dying. We are being watched over, but things happen anyway. Nothing is meant as a punishment. We all come here to experience different things."

I find myself wanting to ask so many questions, I have no idea which ones to make the most important. "Can she answer any questions for me?"

Meagan looks away then back at me. "Ask one and she'll see if she knows the answer. She says she doesn't know everything."

"Why does suffering exist?" I ask, as that's been one that's always hit me.

Meagan doesn't skip a beat. "She says you may as well have asked why love exists. Why are there bees? Why are there rivers and lakes? She says, simply because it does exist, like everything else. There's no reason to question it, the same as you wouldn't question why macaroni and cheese tastes so good to you."

Mac and cheese. It is my mother!

"Can you tell her that I love and miss her?" I ask.

"You just did, Blaine," she says with a laugh. "She's right here. Just because you can't hear her doesn't mean she can't hear you." Meagan looks back at Delaney. "And Nurse Richards, Crystal says to tell you thank you. Thank you for caring for Blaine and her other children. She said they really need you and to please never give up on any of them."

"You know it's me, too?" Delaney asks in her regular voice.

"Not me, I didn't," Meagan tells her. "Crystal knew that." Meagan looks at me with a frown. "Is that true, Blaine?"

"Is what true, Meagan?"

"That my father's treatment of me was one of the things that made your heart nearly go hard again?" she asks, then looks at the empty spot on the other side of her bed.

"I guess it is true," I admit.

She looks back at me. "Daddy is just afraid. He's not really a mean man. And I understand him. So please don't worry about me or how I'm being treated. Don't let anything that you might see as mean or unnecessary cruelty affect what you know to be true. Someone is always watching over us all, whether it seems like it or not."

"Thank you," I tell her and look at the spot my mother is most likely occupying. "And, thanks, Mom. I can't wait to see you again."

Meagan laughs a sweet laugh. "I know, Crystal. That is funny." She looks at me, then says, "Time is a human thing. She said to remember that. When you see her again, it will be as if you never were without her. And she also said you should marry Nurse Richards."

"Did she now?" I ask and chuckle. "Well, maybe I will ask her someday in the near future."

"She said you better," Meagan says, then laughs and wiggles as if she's being tickled. "Okay, okay! You're silly, Crystal!"

"I suppose we should get out of here. People might start

wondering about us being in here so long," Delaney says, then hands me the present we bought for Meagan.

I hand Meagan the present we bought for her. Something her father would approve of. We stay to watch her open it and find her clutching the book to her chest. "Thank you! Oh! I've always wanted a book to keep me company. Thank you so much!"

"It has pictures on every page and the words aren't too long or hard. And maybe your mommy and daddy could help you read it," I tell her as I run my hand one last time over her head.

She opens it and smiles at the very first page, then turns it for me to see. "Just like my angel," she says about the picture of an angel hovering over a small boy as he crosses a bridge over raging waters, seemingly alone.

"Just like your angel," I agree and smile at the little girl who has so many reasons not to believe in anything, but with the help of her angel, my mother, she's more than happy with her life just as it is.

Life is amazing!

43

DELANEY

Pulling the elf costume off, I finally get out of the uncomfortable thing, then fall onto the bed. Blaine is quick to stand over me, looking down at me with a smile and only his Santa shirt on, but left open. He's holding some champagne on ice. "Tired, baby?"

"Not really. Just so ready to be out of these clothes."

He pulls me up and unzips the back of the white corset that was holding my breasts in so no one would notice that I was a girl today. I breath out in relief, and he pulls me up to him, holding me. "You look amazing, my little elf. Ready to play Santa and the naughty elf?"

Reaching for the bottle of cold, crisp alcohol he's holding, I find him batting at my hand. "Oh really?" I ask with a laugh.

"I need you to earn this drink. Kiss me like you want me," he says with a deep voice that tells me he's feeling naughty himself. He takes his Santa hat off and places it on my head. "And you better make me feel it, baby."

"I do want you, so that's not going to be hard at all." I wrap my body around his and devour his neck. The noises he makes while he grows at an alarming rate against my core lets me know he's liking the kiss and I may soon get a glass of the bubbly to quench my thirst.

44

BLAINE

With my Santa hat still on her head, somehow, I point at Delaney's phone on the nightstand as I hold her satiated body in my arms. "Wanna show me what you took pictures of when I was talking to Meagan?"

"Oh!" she says, then sits up and grabs her phone. "I didn't want to take this out in front of anyone else. But look at this."

She hands her phone to me, and I find the pictures of me in the Santa suit in the dim light. A cloud of smoke is near my ear and in the center of the smoke is a pinpoint of light. Picture after picture shows the same thing, only the smoke moves and the light always stays at the center.

"Wow!" I say as I can't stop looking at the pictures. "This is amazing!"

"And you never heard a word, Blaine?" she asks as she looks at the pictures too. "It's like the spirit was right there."

"I felt the cold, but I didn't hear anything. Did you ever hear anything?"

She shivers and runs her hands over her arms as if she's cold then shakes her head. "No, I never heard anything either. But I saw that and knew I should take some pictures for you to see it too."

"I wanted to hear her voice so damn bad," I tell her as I run my finger over the screen.

"I'm sure you did," she says, then cuddles me. "I wish you could've heard her."

"Me too. And I strained to see her the way Meagan did. I tried so hard. I just couldn't. I wonder why some people can see and hear things like that and some can't."

She kisses my neck, then whispers, "Now, haven't you learned not to ask questions like that? I'm sure the answer is ... *because, that's why.* Now I know from where my parents got their answer to every question I ever asked."

I laugh as I think about how many times in my life I've heard nearly every adult say, *because I said so.*

"So, in your opinion, you and I couldn't see or hear my mother, but Meagan could because the powers that be said so?" I ask her, then run my hand over her naked back and lift her up to straddle me as her kisses on my neck are growing a bit more passionate.

"That's right. Why even waste time thinking about it?" she mumbles as her mouth moves with hot kisses over my neck. "You should lie back and let me show you things you never knew before."

"Well, okay," I say, shimmy my body down on the bed, and watch her move her body around until she's securely attached and moaning with how good it feels.

"Will I ever not feel this way when you're inside of me?" she asks as she moves her body up and down.

"I hope not," I say as I watch her body move in waves, her long hair falling across one shoulder and her eyes closed.

"I hope not, too, because this feels amazing. You feel amazing and you make me feel," she stops and moans as I flex my cock.

"Amazing! I know," I finish her thought for her. "Open your eyes for a brief moment, baby." She does and I take her chin in my hand and look into her eyes. "Can I ask you to marry me now? Since mom said I should?"

"I think if you did, I'd say yes. Since I know your mom said you should." She leans down and takes my face between her palms and looks at me for the longest time as she barely moves her body to keep my dick stimulated. "I love you more than I've ever loved anyone. I think I'd do anything for you, Blaine. So, if you decide to ask me to marry you, you can bet your ass I'd accept that offer. But you better take that commitment seriously. I won't ever let you go."

Taking her wrists, I pull her hands away and hold them to my heart. "Do you feel that?"

She nods. "It's your heartbeat. I'm a nurse. I know these things." She smiles at me, making it beat a little harder.

"Well, then, Miss Smarty-pants. Tell me who this heart beats for, since you're a nurse and all." I kiss her nose, then lick her cheek.

"Yuck, and it better beat for me," she says, then leans over and licks my cheek. "Because mine beats only for you."

As I push her up so I can watch her as she moves and takes me back to the world only she's ever taken me to, I think about how I can't see life going badly with her as my partner. Not when my mother thinks it's a good idea too!

A CHRISTMAS TO REMEMBER BOOK SIX

A Holiday Romance

By Michelle Love

∾

Hopes. Dreams. Aspirations.

With what seems like a visit from Santa, himself, Blaine finds himself hopeful his Christmas wish might save little Meagan Sanders.

Delaney's not sure anything, short of a miracle, can save the poor, little girl. The couple spends a romantic Christmas Eve night at home and make some commitments for their future.
But will their first argument as fiancés happen the very night they get engaged?

45

BLAINE

December, 24th:

Hauling a box full of Santa and elf costumes up the stairs to the costume-rental shop, I lead my brother, who has another box of them to turn in, with me. With Christmas Eve upon us, I have big plans for tonight with Delaney. She's making some quick rounds today at the hospital before I pick her up as soon as I get done with my errands.

"Don't forget about tomorrow, Kent," I call back to him. "I'd like to have lunch around noon. I know you have that company Christmas party that I'm forgoing so I can have an extra special Christmas Eve with Delaney."

"Did you get her a ring?" he asks as he moves up beside me.

I put my box down to open the door for us to go inside, then grin at my younger brother. "You'll just have to wait and see."

He laughs as he goes inside, then holds the door for me so I can get my box and go inside too. "I see. No telling anyone about what it is you're doing to make her Christmas so special. I get it. You're afraid you'll jinx it."

"That's right. You never know how things will turn out in this crazy world." I see the lady behind the counter give my brother the once over.

"Good morning, gentlemen. I hope this Christmas Eve is finding you both well," she says in greeting.

"It is," Kent says and leans on the counter. The lady is wearing a slightly-sexy elf costume. Delaney's was much sexier. "And I see this day is treating you pretty well too."

She giggles, and I see it's time for me to make my exit so my brother can make a date. "I'll leave this return up to you, Kent. I have some things I need to get to."

"Yeah, I got this," he says with a suave tone to his voice. Lord help the girl. He's got her in his sights.

As I get to the door, I see a man dressed as Santa coming toward it, so I pull it open for him. "Here you go, Santa."

"Thank you," he says and gives me a nod. Then he stops and looks at me with an odd expression on his white-bearded face. "So, tell me what you'd like this Christmas, young man."

With a laugh, I say the first thing that comes to my mind, "Santa, there's a very sick little girl in The Children's Hospital. Meagan Sanders is her name. I'd like to see her make a recovery if that's not too much to ask."

With a wink, he says, "It may not be. One never knows about these things." Then he comes inside and I smell sugar cookies as he walks by me. "You have yourself a Merry Christmas, Blaine."

"You too, Santa," I say then walk out the door. I stop suddenly when I realize he's said my name. "Hey! How did you ..." When I turn back, I don't see anyone there at all.

I go back inside, take a look around, and go back to the counter where my brother is all but kissing the attendant. He gives me a look that tells me to get lost as he says, "Can I help you?"

"Did either of you see a man in a Santa suit?" I ask as I look around for the man who seems to have disappeared.

"Very funny, Blaine," Kent says. "No. Did you?" He rolls his eyes as he looks back at the woman.

"Forget it," I say, as I see neither one of them would've seen anything with the way they're only looking at each other. So I head back out and go to the car.

Mr. Green greets me at the back door of the Suburban. "It's getting chilly out here. You better put that coat on the next time you get out of the car, Mr. Vanderbilt."

"It is getting cold," I say, then wonder if he saw the man. "Did you happen to see me talking to that man in the Santa suit?"

"Seriously?" he asks as he looks confused.

"Yes. I was standing at that door, talking to a man in a Santa suit. If you looked that way, you'd have seen us talking, I should think."

"I saw you come outside, then turn around and go back inside, then you came out again. And no one has gone up or down that sidewalk except you and your brother. Are you feeling okay?" he asks with a concerned expression. "Because you're kind of going pale."

"I feel fine. I guess I'm tired is all. We can go now. I have to stop at the jewelers to see if what I ordered is ready," I say and lean my head back on the seat.

That seemed so real. I don't know what to think about it. I guess I need to forget about it. My imagination must be working overtime with last night's activities.

Closing my eyes to see if I can get some rest, because maybe that's my problem, I find something drifting in the air. A smell I can't quite place. I can't rest and open my eyes. Rolling the window down to talk to my driver, I ask, "Did you spray a new air freshener in here?"

"No sir," he says, then I see him looking at me through the rearview mirror. "Maybe we should make a stop to see Miss Richards at the hospital first. Maybe she could get a doctor to make sure you're okay, sir."

"I'm fine," I say. "I just smell a sweet smell. Kind of like honey, with maybe a hint of lemons.

"Honey and lemons?" he asks, then takes a huge sniff of the air. He shakes his head. "No, sir. I don't smell anything but the leather seats."

"Thanks," I say, then roll the window up. I take another sniff. "Yep, lemons and honey." Then it hits me. "Mom!"

I look around the car and try hard to see anything at all—any smoke or a light of some kind—but I see nothing. The car stops and I put my coat on. Just as Mr. Green opens my door, I feel cold hit my ear. But that's probably just the chilly air. "Thanks, Mr. Green. You stay in the car when I come out. I can let myself in and out of the car. It's getting colder by the minute out here."

"Yes, sir, it is," he says as he shivers a little. "Thank you, sir."

With a nod, I leave him and go inside the jewelry store I ordered from a few days ago to see if they've managed to get what I asked for. The smell goes away, and I'm left thinking this is all in my head.

"Good morning," the man at the counter says as I come inside. "My, it's looking like real Christmas weather out there, isn't it?"

"It is. I think this is the coldest I recall a Christmas Eve ever being." I shake the man's hand and notice him looking over my shoulder. "I'm Blaine Vanderbilt. I have an order and I'm hoping you have it in and ready to go."

He looks back at me with a smile on his face. "Should I be discreet?"

"I guess so," I say, as I have no idea why he'd say such an odd thing.

Reaching under the counter, he unlocks something and comes back up with a little black box. He then places the box directly in front of me and opens the lid. "Does this meet with your expectations, sir?"

I take the ring out and look at it, finding it flawless, then give him a nod. "It does. Do I owe you anything else?"

"No, you paid online. Let me put this in a bag for you. Or should I gift wrap it?" he asks as he looks over my shoulder again. "You know, so she can open it."

"I actually have a funny way I'm going to give it to her, so I don't need it wrapped. Just the bag will be fine, thanks." I look back over my shoulder to see what he could be looking at and guess he must be looking out the door at passersby.

He's an odd little man, anyway!

"Here you are, sir," he says as he hands me the bag. "You two have a Merry Christmas."

"We will," I say, then start to walk out the door. Suddenly I think his words were kind of odd. Why did he say, 'you two?'

Making my way back to the car, I get in and instantly smell the honey-heavy scent with the touch of lemon in the background. "Mom? Are you in here? Can you give me some kind of a sign if you are?"

The window rolls down and I jump at the sudden sound, finding Mr. Green looking back at me. "Were you saying something, sir?"

"I was talking to myself. You can take me home now. I have to wrap this thing up before I go get Delaney."

"Yes, sir," he says, then turns around and rolls the window up.

I lean back and smile. "So, I guess you're going to hang around me for a while. That's cool."

I just wish I could see her!

46

DELANEY

Sugar cookies are everywhere—the nurses' station, the children's rooms, and the break room. I've found out something about myself—I have no willpower. *None!*

"This one looks like Santa," Tammy tells me as she holds up a bright-red, sparkling cookie. "You want him?"

"I shouldn't," I tell her as I look longingly at the cookie that would make number four for me in the last hour.

She wiggles it a little. "But it's really good. Momma made them for me."

"Oh, a different recipe. Then I should try it," I say as I take the cookie out of her little hand. With one bite, I know I will finish the whole thing, as it melts in my mouth. "Mmmm."

"Told you so. Momma's taking some to the Christmas party at her new job. She told me she wants to make a good impression for when she can start actually going to work there. She thinks Mr. Vanderbilt is the best person in this whole entire world," Tammy says, then nibbles on a cookie that looks like a bell—an expertly-decorated bell that she didn't even take the time to admire.

"These cookies are gorgeous as well as delicious," I say as I point at the cookie in her hand. "Do you see how much work went into that one you have there?"

She stops and takes a long look at it, then pops it into her mouth. Well, at least I got her to take a moment to appreciate it, anyway. It's better than nothing.

The sound of the speaker system cutting on has me looking up to see if it will have anything to do with me as I swallow the last bite of the cookie. "We need all available medical staff to room 573, now."

"That's Meagan's room," I whisper to myself. "I'll be back to finish you up, Tammy."

Hurrying out of the room, I go down the hallway and find her parents standing outside of her door. Both look frantic as I get to them. Her mother grabs me. "She stopped breathing!"

I look at her father, asking silently for his permission to go inside of his daughter's room, and he nods. His face is pale and he looks worried and afraid.

I'm the first to respond and the only person in the room, other than the little girl who is lying lifelessly on the bed. I find the slightest hint of a pulse and start CPR on her small, frail body.

I'm usually very calm in these situations, but for some reason, my heart is pounding. I knew it could come to this, I tell myself as I make chest compressions, then breath into her lungs and check to be sure my breath is filling them.

Another nurse makes it in, and she takes over the chest compressions while I keep up the recitation. The fifth time I put my mouth to hers, I feel air coming back out of hers. "She's breathing!"

The doctor on call comes into the room, tossing out orders as he does. "We need her on a ventilator. Did you get her back for us, Richards?"

"Yes, sir," I say and step back to let his team assist him. Stepping back even further as I hear something, I keep moving until I'm at the far corner of the room.

A light sound is tickling my ears. I can almost make out the words that are light and airy, as if moving on a breeze. But there is no wind in this room.

I look up to see where the air conditioning vent is and see it's clear across the room and nowhere near where I am, so I can't be hearing anything through that. The sound begins to move, and I walk in the direction I hear it going and find they're about to hook Meagan up to the ventilator.

Suddenly, the little girl sits upright and her eyes seem to search the faces around her, then she finds me. "Tell her I need her. She left. Tell her I need her, please!" Her body falls back and her eyes close.

I find everyone looking at me with odd expressions, then they get back to work on her. I turn and leave the room. I know she must mean Crystal, but how the hell can I find her?

Her parents are hugging each other as I walk out of the room. "I got her breathing again. You can go back in if you'd like."

Turning to leave them, I find a hand on my shoulder. "Thank you, Nurse Richards," I hear her father say.

I turn back and look at him and see lines around his face that weren't there when they first came here. "You're welcome."

"I'm sorry." He moves his hand and turns away from me, and I understand he doesn't want to talk about anything. He just wants that to be known.

"Thank you," I say and walk away.

The only thing running through my mind is what that little girl said to me and what I can do. I go to the chapel on the first floor. It's empty, so I go to the altar and kneel. "Please send Crystal back to Meagan Sanders, Lord. Amen."

I have no idea if that will work, but I don't know what else to do. Then my cell phone vibrates in my pocket, and I pull it out to find it's Blaine. As I answer the call, I have no time to say a word as he says excitedly, "My mom is with me!"

"I'm not even going to ask you why you think that, even though that would be the most rational thing to say right now. I'm just going to tell you to speak out loud and tell your mother that Meagan needs her right now. She just quit breathing a few minutes ago, and I had to resuscitate her. She sat up in the bed and asked me to get her."

"I'll do that. Is Meagan going to be okay?" he asks with a fearful voice.

"I have no idea, Blaine. This isn't in any of our hands."

Nothing is in our hands, it seems!

47

BLAINE

"Okay, I feel kind of stupid doing this," I say out loud and hope my staff doesn't hear me. "Mom, Meagan needs you. You have to hurry to her. Please help her, Mom."

I wait and listen, as if I might hear the slamming of a door as she leaves, which is insane, but I listen for some kind of sound anyway. After five minutes of hearing nothing, I stop. I didn't ever hear anything before, so I don't know why I thought I would this time.

Roxy comes into the room, where we've set up a Christmas tree, with a platter of beautiful Christmas cookies she places on the table, then stands back to admire them. "They turned out nice, don't you think, Mr. Vanderbilt?"

"I do think they look very nice. And how do they taste?" I ask as I go to pick one of them up. I pick up a reindeer and bite its head off. "Yummy!"

She laughs as she leaves the room. "I'll be bringing in a few platters of little, yummy things for you and Miss Richards to enjoy while you spend this evening together, then I'll get out of your way so you two can be alone."

With a smile, I finish wrapping the last box that's holding

Delaney's ring in it. She will never think there's a ring in this huge box!

Even though I know things are going tough at the hospital right now, I can't stop thinking about how good it's going to be to have Delaney be a real part of me forever.

If she accepts, I want to be married before the new year begins. I want everything to start out new and fresh. All of it. Then I think about her parents. I seem to have totally forgotten about them.

Going to the bedroom, I find the paper I had her fill out so I could contact them about the meeting that I ended up blowing off. But now I think I might just go with that idea again.

Dialing up the number on the paper, I find a woman answering the phone. "Richards' residence."

"Mrs. Richards, my name is Blaine Vanderbilt, and I ..."

She interrupts me, "Wait? Who did you say you are?"

"Blaine Vanderbilt. Your daughter and I ..."

"The Blaine Vanderbilt? The man who owns the Bargain Bin store chain? That man?" she asks, sounding more than a bit confused.

Then I hear a roaring sound in my ear. "Blaine Vanderbilt?" a man shouts. "Let me talk to that son of a bitch!"

"Ma'am, please let me explain," I say, but hear the phone being shuffled around.

A booming voice makes me hold the phone away from my ear. "What the hell do you want, you son of a bitch?"

"I don't know if what I was going to ask you would be a smart thing right now. You see, sir, your daughter and I are ..."

"My daughter? Delaney? How do you know her? What have you done with her?" he asks.

"I haven't done anything with her. I don't know what you're implying. Hasn't she told you about us?" I ask and wait, listening to the sound of dead air.

Finally, he says, "Us?"

Shit! *She has not told them a thing about me!*

"Yes, sir. You see, I met your daughter around Thanksgiving. She and I dated, then moved in together."

"Holy shit!" he says. "I have to get off here. I have to call my daughter."

And just like that, he hangs up. I'm not sure what to do, so I call right back and find I get a busy signal. Then I call Delaney to give her the heads up, but she forwards my call, and I know she's on the line with her father.

Shit! *I think I've just ruined her Christmas!*

48

DELANEY

Taking the vibrating phone out of my pocket, I see it's my parents calling and want to kick myself for not calling them sooner today. "Hi, I'm sorry. I had to get to work early this morning. I was going to call you two, I promise."

"Delaney Richards, your mother and I have just received a very disturbing phone call," dad says.

"Oh no! About what, Dad?"

"About you living with our mortal enemy! That's what! Now tell me that bastard was lying to me."

"He called you?" I ask as I try to figure out how to tell them everything. But it sounds like Blaine might have already done that, the fool!

"Yes, and he said you two were living together. Now, I know that can't be true. So, you tell me the truth, young lady," he says in his dad tone that he uses only when needed.

"Okay, I knew you guys would be upset if you knew that I was fraternizing with the enemy. But he's changing, Dad. He's very nice to me. He always has been. He's changing his business ways too."

"I am so ashamed right now," he says, sounding a bit devastated.

"Dad, don't be. It's all right," I tell him. "There's nothing to feel ashamed about."

"I'm ashamed I have a daughter who would sell her family out like you're doing. Stop seeing that man, this instant! Do you hear me?"

"Um, Dad, I'm not going to do that. Now tell me what he said to you. He must've had a reason to be calling you."

"I don't know what the hell he called for. To upset us, I guess," he says, and I know Blaine better than to think that's why he decided to call my parents without talking to me, at all, first.

"Let me call him, then I'll call you back. Maybe he was going to invite you to Christmas at our place."

"Our place? Delaney, you cannot be serious about this man. He's evil! The devil and him have an agreement. I'm sure of that. No one gets rich off of selling complete shit! No one!"

"Dad, he's not a bad man. I promise you that. Not anymore. I'll call you back." I end the call without another word, as there are no words to make my father understand what I'm doing with Blaine Vanderbilt.

What was Blaine thinking?

49

BLAINE

When my phone rings again, I know who it is, and I know I'm in trouble. "Delaney, I'm sorry."

"Why would you call them, Blaine?" Her voice is weak, defeated sounding.

I feel awful. "Baby, I thought you had to have told them something about us. I'm sorry. I was going to invite them to join us tomorrow. I was going to send a private jet for them in the morning. That's a nice thing to do, right?"

"It would be," she says. "If they'd have known about us. Dad sounds like he might have a stroke, he's so mad. He told me he was ashamed of me, Blaine. He's never told me that before."

"Damn, baby! Ashamed is a pretty strong word about you being with me. I'm not a monster."

"In his eyes, you are. He actually thinks you made a deal with the devil. He really thinks that, Blaine. So, in his mind, I'm in bed with the devil. I don't know what I should do about this."

"Well, what does that mean?" I ask, as it sounds like she's kind of thinking she needs to do something different. *Like leave me!*

"It means I need to fix things with my parents. I need to make things right again."

"I'll buy them brand new cars," I say, then shake my head, as that's too small. "A new house too! Anywhere they want one. I'll get them anything they want and even give them a great settlement for their company—one that will last them for the rest of their lives! How about that?"

"Dad's not one to accept bribes. But something along the settlement lines is a good idea. We can brainstorm when I get home. Speaking of home, I get off in an hour. Are you going to be here to pick me up?"

"I am. I got your present this morning. I hope you like it," I say and feel a little better now that it doesn't seem like she's going to leave me because of her parents.

"I have to pick yours up. It's being gift wrapped. We'll have to stop off at the studio to pick it up on our way home," she says, intriguing me.

"Want to give me any hints, baby?" I ask with curiosity.

"Here's one," she says, and I can hear the smile in her sweet voice. "You can find out tonight when we open the presents we're giving each other, brat!"

"I knew you would be that kind of woman," I tease her. "The kind who makes you wait for it. See you in an hour."

"I can't wait. I'm so tired. I'm going to need a nap when I get back home."

"Okay, I'll take a naked nap with you. And just to further entice you, the chef has made all kinds of delicious-looking cookies and snacks, so get ready to pig out later."

She groans, which I didn't expect would be her response to such good news. "See you in an hour."

Just as her call ends, I find my phone ringing and see it's from her parents. I steady myself to get yelled out and answer with a timid voice, "Hello."

"This is Delaney's mother."

I sigh, relieved it's not her father. "Yes, ma'am?"

"My husband ran to the store, so I took the time alone to call you. I hope you don't mind," she says with a very nice attitude, so this should go better than the last phone call went.

"Look, my husband is very upset with this news. So upset, he headed out to get himself something hard to drink. I don't like what this is doing to him. Now, I'm calling you to beg. You took our business. And I'm afraid you taking our daughter is too much for the poor man. Please think about ending things with her. I'm afraid for my husband's health if you don't."

"Okay, look, here's the thing. I love your daughter. I love her more than I knew was possible. What you're asking me to do isn't something I can do. But listen to me. I'm going to make you and your husband a settlement for the business you lost because of me. A great settlement that will take care of you both very well for the rest of your lives."

"What about all the other businesses you shut down? What about those people?" she asks, and I find myself shocked she wasn't happy about what I just offered.

"Well, I'll deal with each case on an individual basis."

"But you will rectify things to the best of your ability with the others as well?" she asks me, making me feel like she's a pretty great negotiator.

"I will. Since you and your husband are people I want to make happy because I love your daughter, I'd like to start with you guys. If you two would come to our estate for Christmas, I'd be glad to discuss things with you both. If you could keep your husband from killing me, that is."

She laughs, then stops abruptly. "Wait. Did you say our estate? Whose house are you inviting us to? Your parents?"

"No, this place belongs to me, and since Delaney is such a huge part of me, I always incorporate her when I talk about this place. I think of it as ours. She's taken over running it since she moved in, and it's never felt more like a home than it does with her here."

"That's sweet," she says, and I hear it in her voice that I might be able to win her over, at the very least.

"I can send a car to get you two in the morning and take you to the little airport in Lockhart, where a private jet will bring you to

Houston. I'll have my driver pick you guys up and bring you out here. I had lunch planned around noon, but I can push it back. It's not a problem at all. My brother and sister will be here too."

"Where're your parents? Won't they be there too?"

"They've both passed on. So, what do you say? Talk it over with your husband and let me or Delaney know."

"Passed on? Already? How terrible!" She sounds very sincere as she adds, "I'll let my husband know that. It might help soften him up some. Bye, now."

As I put the phone down, I have to wonder if I'll be in trouble with Delaney for what I've just done. But I can't let that stop me from extending the olive branch to her parents. I want us to be one, big, happy family, after all.

Roxy comes into the den, wiping her hands on a towel. "Mr. Vanderbilt, I'm off with the rest of the staff. We wanted to let you know that we've volunteered to help prepare and serve the food at the homeless shelter where you made the food donations. We thought that having your entire staff, both personal and company-wide, helping the homeless have a nice Christmas might help your reputation a bit this year. That's our present to you and Miss Richards."

"She will be very happy to hear that. We both want you all to enjoy this next week off, so you all can have a break from work. That's Delaney's gift to you all. She felt terribly that she had very little money to buy you guys gifts."

"About that, Mr. Vanderbilt. We don't need an entire week off. We'll take the typical Christmas day off and one more day, but we can come back. This place is huge and hard to care for alone," she says as she gestures to the huge place.

"Nonsense," I tell her. "We'll have family to help on Christmas day, and she and I can fend for ourselves after that so you all can enjoy some much-deserved time off."

"Promise to call me if you need anything. I can get a skeleton staff together on short notice." She looks at me with her no-nonsense look.

With a nod, I say, "If we get into a jam, I will call you. Now, go enjoy the Christmas bonuses that should've arrived in your bank accounts. You might find you want the week free with what you'll have to spend."

Her eyes go wide. "Sir, you've already given us our bonuses two weeks ago. Don't you remember doing that?"

"This is a special bonus. For years of hard work. So go home and see what Santa brought you, Roxy."

With a smile, she turns, and as soon as she gets out of the den, I can hear her shoes moving much faster with my news.

I never knew it felt this damn good to give!

50

DELANEY

With the present I got for Blaine wrapped up in a way that will never let him know what's really inside of it, I walk back out to the car with the box. The lady who runs the shop did a fantastic job on it, and I'm looking forward to seeing if Blaine is impressed by it.

Getting a gift for a man who has everything is damn hard!

I place it in the back seat of my Mercedes he's driving me around in as he cranes his neck to get a look at it. "That's pretty big and boxy."

"It is," I say and slide into the passenger side. "What's the size of mine?"

"A secret," he says, then smiles at me. "A great, big secret."

"Great and big?" I ask as I think about what he might have bought me. He's already given me a car, but he has tons of them so it could be another one. Or a house in some remote area. He could've done that too. With a man of his wealth, one never knows what she might get when gift-giving time comes around.

"How's Meagan?" he asks, and my smile disappears.

"Not good. The pastor has been with her and her family all day. They've called in the rest of the family too."

"Is that how they do things when there's nothing else they can do?" he asks, and I see him swallow what looks like a lump in his throat.

"Yes," I say, then take his hand. "But these things happen. At least you got the gift she gave you. Your faith."

He nods, then glances at me. "I saw Santa today."

"Oh, Blaine!" I say with a laugh. "Now that's a little too much faith."

"No, really! Stop laughing at me!" He looks a little irritated, so I stop laughing.

"Sorry. So, tell me about your sighting. Was it in the sky, driving his eight, tiny reindeer? Or somewhere more personal than that?"

"It was more personal than that. He talked to me. He asked me what I wanted for Christmas." He glances sideways at me.

"And what did you tell him you wanted, Blaine," I ask, trying very hard not to smile and attempting to take him seriously.

"I told him I wanted Meagan to get better. I'm not saying I'll lose what I've found if she doesn't, but man, how great would it be if she did get better?" His smile tells me he's taking this way too seriously and is doomed to go very low if the poor girl doesn't make it.

"Blaine, you need to understand things better. That little girl's body is shutting down. It would take a miracle to save her now. Please don't get your hopes up. I'd hate to see you dive down into the depths of despair because Santa couldn't save her."

"I won't," he says with an annoyed tone. "I'm not an idiot. I know Santa isn't real."

And now I feel like an ass!

"Hey, why don't we talk about how we're going to get my parents to chill out over us?" I say, to steer away from the subject of Meagan.

"I talked to your mother," he says, making me freak out.

"What? Did you call her? Blaine, damn it!"

"Chill, baby! She called me. And I told her about the money I'd give them in an amount we could mutually agree on. I invited them for Christmas, and she said she'd talk to your dad."

"She called you?" I ask as I try to stop shaking with the anger that has risen up in me like molten lava in a volcano.

"Yes. Right after I got off the phone with you. She called, and I was not about to not answer the call, even if it was your father calling to cuss me out some more," he says, and now I feel badly that Dad cussed him out.

Running my hand over his shoulder, I apologize, "Baby, I'm sorry. I got mad too fast."

"As usual," he says, and I punch him in the arm.

"Oww," I whine, as that was a mistake. *His bicep is like a rock!*

"Ha," he laughs. "Maybe don't punch me."

"Yeah, yeah." I rub my hand as we pull into the driveway of the estate. "So how did Mom act?"

"Nice. I think she'll smooth things over, and hopefully, they'll decide to join us tomorrow. But for tonight, it's just me and you, baby. I hope you're ready for one hell of a romantic Christmas Eve."

"What all do you have planned, my personal Santa?" I rake my nails along his arm and purr.

"You sound a little naughty there, my personal sexy elf. And my plans will be revealed one at a time. First, let's get this thing parked and into the house. A nice, hot bath is in order, I would think, to relax you for the fun and festivities of the night," He stops the car, and I can see a glow in his light-brown eyes.

"I think you're going to make this the most memorable Christmas Eve ever."

Getting out of the car, he comes around and gets my door open before I even get my seatbelt off. As he helps me out, he pulls me right up into his arms. "I'm going to treat you like my queen tonight. I want you to know how much I really love and care about you."

Wrapping my arms around his broad shoulders, I lean my head against his wide chest. "Blaine, you make me feel loved and cared for every day. I can't imagine a day where I would doubt your feelings for me. I hope you can feel that coming from me as well. I love you more than you will ever understand. If I never got another thing in my entire life, I'd never complain, because I have you and that's a gift in itself."

The house is warm as he takes me inside. "I've made a fire in the den, where we'll be spending the evening. It's nice and cozy in there, and I can't wait to give you the gift I got you. But first things first. To the tub with you, my sweet."

Relaxing in his arms has never been easier!

51

BLAINE

W hen I was a boy, things were vastly different at Christmas time than they are now. Pops would wrap our presents in the paper from the Sunday comics of the local newspaper. We would eat a canned ham for our Christmas dinner, along with mac and cheese and green beans. Nothing fancy at all.

Our presents would be things that we could use. New bags of underwear and socks for all three of us. A new set of pens and pencils for school. And every year we would get a brand-new coat. Our stockings were filled with fresh fruit—never any candy. I don't know what pops aversion to giving us candy was, but we got it very rarely from him.

There was never any mention from any of us as to why Santa never came to our house. I had friends whose families made huge deals out of Santa bringing their gifts in the dead of night while they all slept. It just never was that way at our house.

I suppose pops was too busy working and taking care of us that he didn't think about doing things like waiting for us to go to sleep on Christmas Eve before he brought out the presents and put them under the tree.

Holding Delaney as we lay out on a blanket on the floor in front of the fireplace, with Christmas lights blinking happily on the tall Christmas tree off to one side, has me thinking about the future.

"You know, I think tonight is the night I want to make up the ideas of how our family will spend this night. What kind of traditions did your family have for this night, baby?"

She's lying between my legs as I lean my back against the sofa. We've donned our matching Christmas PJ's, which are red with candy canes all over them. Her hands move up and down my thighs as she says, "On Christmas Eve nights, we'd go to my Gammy's house. She and Pawpaw would make us dinner. Usually pot roast. They were my father's mom and dad. His other two brothers would come most of the time, too, with their families."

"That sounds nice," I say as I pull her hair over to one side and press my lips to the side of her neck. "What do you think we should do?"

"Something like this. Spend the night here with our kids. If you wanted to invite your brother and sister and what will one day be their families, then you could," she says, then turns in my arms and sits in my lap sideways so she can look at me.

Grazing my knuckles across her pink cheek, I say, "I think I'd like this night to be just about us and our family. The actual day of Christmas can be for the rest of the family too. All of them—your parents too. But on Christmas Eve, I'd like it just to be us and those we create together."

"And just how many of those creations do you think you'd like to make to form our family, Blaine?"

"Nine or ten," I say and watch a smile spread over her gorgeous face.

"Lower please," she says, then giggles. "How about two?"

I shake my head. "Four or five. I want a big family, baby."

"We'll see," she says, then kisses me. "I'm not ruling it out yet."

"I'm not worried. I can talk you into having my babies. So, about those kids we'll have one day—should we let them believe in Santa or bypass that whole thing?"

"You know, with everyone being at our grandparents' home and having to travel to get there, we never got to do the Santa thing. I think we should do it for our kids. Don't you? Did your family do the Santa thing?"

Shaking my head, I say, "No. I think we should do it for our kids too. I think it would be fun to watch them be surprised on Christmas mornings."

"Me too." She kisses me again. "I think we've just made our first decision as parents, Blaine."

"Weird, huh? Since we don't even have one kid yet," I say, then laugh. "Maybe it's time to open the presents we bought for each other. I'm kind of dying to know what you got me."

"Me too. But that huge box has me totally without a clue as to what you have in there. I can't think of a thing that big, except maybe a dishwasher, which I do not need," she says as she looks at the huge box next to the tree.

"You haven't commented on the wrapping job I did."

She looks at me with a grin. "I was told if I didn't have anything nice to say, then I was not to say anything at all. But since you asked, it looks like a monkey wrapped that box."

"Yeah, just wait until you pull that wrapping paper off," I tell her, then kiss her and find her soft lips yielding to mine as her hands move over my back with soft caresses.

Before I know it, we're getting carried away, and I'm lifting her up to straddle me. Then I remember what I'm about to give her and stop the kiss that became passionate much too quickly. "Let's slow things down a bit. You give me your present first."

With a sigh, she climbs off me and goes to get the present she got me. Coming back with it, she sits down, Indian-style, and I imitate her. Then she hands me the present. "This comes more from the heart than the pocketbook."

"Good. I like those kinds of presents the best. And might I say, the wrapping paper is lovely, baby." I pull the large, red, shiny bow off the box, then untie the red ribbon that's holding the box shut. When I take the lid off, I look up, see her biting her lip, and looking a little on the anxious side. "Don't worry. I know I'll love it."

"It's just that you have everything, and I had no idea what to get you. If you think it's lame, just tell me so I never repeat this," she says, then leans forward to peek into the box. "Good. I was afraid the lady used the wrong frame, but it's the right one—the gold one."

Lifting the frame out of the box, I see it's a picture of me, my sister, and my brother when we were kids. "This is the sweetest thing I've ever been given, baby." My parents loom above us with smiles on their faces, as if watching over us from heaven. "I don't know how you managed to get all these pictures into one, but this is cool."

"The lady who did it just needed a picture of each of you, and she kind of collaged them together to form this one. Kate sent me the pictures through our phones. That lady is pretty artistic, isn't she?" She moves to sit next to me and looks at the picture with me.

"Thank you, baby. This is the most thoughtful thing I've ever had, and I will cherish it forever. I wonder where I should hang it."

"You know the entry room, Blaine?" she asks as she takes the picture out of my hands, gets up, then places it on the sofa. "I think that's where our family pictures should go. You know, so people who come to visit us can get a glimpse of who we are and where we come from as they come into our home."

"I can see it now, pictures of our wedding day, the day our kids are born, things like that. I like it!"

This woman is going to make the best wife ever!

52

DELANEY

I can see it in his yes—he does like the picture and that makes me very happy. I was a little worried he'd think it was cheesy.

He's sat me on the Queen Ann chair that's near the Christmas tree and is going to get the huge box my present is in. I really have no clue what it could be. When he picks it up as if it weighs nothing, I find that hard to believe.

"What did you get me, Blaine? A box of air?" I ask with a laugh.

"You'll just have to open it and find out." He sets the box down right in front of me. "Here you go, ma'am. Have fun."

"So, should I just rip into it or what? Is the thing inside breakable? Or alive? Should I be very careful?" I ask, as I have no idea how to go about getting to the contents of the large box.

"Just start pulling the wrapping paper off and go from there, Delaney." He stands there, watching me with a big, old smile on his handsome face.

I shred one large piece of reindeer-covered paper at a time until I get to the box. Opening the top of it, I find another present inside. Pulling that one out, I give him a quizzical look and find that smile still plastered on his face. "Okay, Blaine, what are you doing here?"

"Just keep unwrapping, baby. You'll get there soon."

This box is wrapped a little better. It has nice snowflake-covered wrapping paper and a large, white bow on top. And when I get to the box top, I open that and find yet another wrapped box. "Blaine?"

"Just keep going," he says, with what's going into a goofy smile.

I unwrap the plain, red paper-covered box with a black bow on top and find a ton of black tissue paper inside of it. "Finally, the real gift."

At the very bottom is another box. This one is small and expertly wrapped in black, velvety cloth and tied up with a pretty, silky, red ribbon. As I pull the ribbon to untie it, I catch Blaine biting his lip out of the corner of my eye.

Inside, I find a little, black box and notice Blaine going down on one knee in front of me. As I open the lid, he says, "Delaney Leeann Richards, I'd like to ask you an important question tonight. The ring inside of that box is a token to remind you that you are loved. You are loved more than you will ever know, and I am the one who is giving you that love. In return for the love I give you, I'm asking you to give yourself to me. I want to make you mine forever. I want to make you the part of me that's been missing. Delaney, will you marry me?"

The word is stuck in my throat under a knot that's grown there. The ring is exquisite. There's a large diamond in what looks like a platinum setting. Small diamonds encircle the large one in the middle. It looks like it cost a fortune, and I'm overwhelmed by it and the fact this gorgeous man is actually asking me to marry him.

I feel the tears falling down my face and then his hands are on my cheeks, wiping them away. "Well?"

I nod and choke out, "Yes. Yes, Blaine, I'll marry you." Sobs come out of my mouth for reasons I can't comprehend. I've never been so happy that I've cried before. It's an odd feeling.

Blaine takes the box out of my shaking hand and takes the ring out of it. Steadying my left hand, he slides the ring onto my finger, and I feel the weight of it—a weight that will remind me that I am not an 'I' anymore. I am part of a 'we.'

I'm pulled up and hugged and my heart is pounding. This is real!

I'm going to marry a billionaire!

I am going to marry the man I never, in a million years, ever thought I'd even meet. He was our enemy, and now I will be his wife!

Shock is moving through me, slowing my tears and my heart rate. "I love you," I tell him, then kiss his neck.

"And I love you, baby." He takes my arms and holds me back to look at me. "And you and I will soon be a family. I have one more thing to ask you."

Wiping my eyes with the back of my hand, I ask, "What would that be?"

"I want to forgo the condom and start trying to have a baby. I want to start tonight."

"Wow! I mean, wow! Um, uh, that's a lot to think about."

With a sexy smile, he says, "You just committed your entire life to me. I think a baby is small potatoes to that, don't you?"

"No," I say as I shake my head. "Blaine, that really is a big step. I don't know about that just yet."

Taking my pajama shirt by the lapels, he pulls me close to him and starts to unbutton it. His knuckles graze my naked breasts as he pushes the shirt open, then off my shoulders. It lands on the floor with a soft sound, then he hooks his thumbs into the elastic waist of the pajama bottoms and pushes them down too, leaving me naked in front of him.

Taking my hand, he leads me back to the blanket on the floor in front of the fireplace and tosses a pillow off the sofa onto it. He moves me to lie down on the blanket and props my head up on the pillow. Then he stands back up and unbuttons his shirt, revealing a bit of his muscular torso a little at a time. The way the fire and Christmas lights bounce off his perfect body has me mesmerized. When his PJ bottoms hit the floor, my eyes are drawn to his erection.

At this point, he'd usually be putting on a condom, somewhat discreetly. But he's not doing that, and as a matter of fact, I did not hear the tell-tale sounds of one in the pocket of his pajamas.

My eyes must be telling him what I'm thinking as he says, "I threw them all out."

"You were pretty sure of yourself," I tell him as I give no hint of what I feel about that.

"I want to see a version of us running around this house. I want to see your tummy swollen with that little version of us. Aren't you curious at all about who we'll create together?"

His hand moves up and down his cock, making it grow a bit more, and my mouth starts watering. I lick my lips and wiggle my finger for him to come to me and let me taste him.

He stands perfectly still as his hand keeps moving up and down his long, thick dick. His head shakes slowly, and I can't believe he's doing this to me.

I don't know what choice I have!

53

BLAINE

Her green eyes dance as she looks up at me. "So you want to become a daddy, do you?"

I nod and keep moving my hand along my cock to entice her. "So, what do you say?"

She wiggles her finger at me again. "I say come here, Daddy. Let's make a baby."

Heat fills me with her words, and I am on her before she knows it. Pressing her shoulders to the floor, I hold her down as I pull one of her juicy tits into my mouth. She moans as I suck hard and lick the nipple over and over until her body is shaking with her first climax.

"God, I didn't even know I could have an orgasm like that," she says, then I flip her onto her stomach and straddle her back, barely sitting my ass on hers as I rub her back, making her moan again. "That feels so good."

"I'm going to pamper you so much you're going to be spoiled by it." Leaning over, I kiss all over her back and move down so my lips can graze over her luscious ass.

Spreading her legs, I kiss her from behind, running my tongue back and forth between her two openings. Her body starts shaking again after mere minutes of this attention and her groan tells me I've sparked orgasm number two.

I've been reading about ways to help ensure a sperm meets an egg, so I get up and grab another big pillow off the sofa and lay it on the blanket next to her. Turning her over, I lift her up and place her ass on top of the pillow to elevate it. "We're really doing this, aren't we?" she asks.

I nod, and a tear runs over one of her cheeks. She holds her arms open, and I move into them at the same time I move into her. I kiss the tear away. "I want you to have my baby, Delaney. I want you and me to become a family."

As I enter her, feeling her flesh to flesh for the first time, I have to moan with how amazing it feels. I never want to sheathe myself from this feeling again.

My cock grows even larger with the sensations of her silky, warm inner lining as it moves back and forth, creating a need in me I've never had before.

Faster I go, making her body quiver with each hard thrust. Her nails gouge into my arms as she holds them tightly. I ease up to see her face as I slam into her. "Tell me you want this."

She looks deep into my eyes, her head moving with each thrust I make. "I do. I want to have your baby, Blaine. I do!" She grits her teeth with another orgasm. It squeezes me, but I'm not about to give it up yet.

"Ahhh!" she screams and wraps her legs around me, pulling her body up to mine and hanging onto me. "Blaine!"

Leaning back down, I kiss her neck, then bite it, making her body shake and continue to pulse. I can feel her nails digging into my back as she writhes underneath me.

Her body is on fire and her breathing is hard and ragged. I go on and on until her body goes loose again and the orgasm is all the way over. Then I pepper soft kisses all the way down her neck as I slow my strokes.

Small kisses I give her until our mouths meet. She takes my face in her hands and holds me while her tongue does some magic in my mouth. Her foot runs up and down the back of my leg and her body squeezes me tighter each time her knee comes up.

I grab her leg and pull it up so I can go deeper into her and feel like I'm bottoming out so I thrust as hard as I can to reach that point over and over until her body is quivering again and she moans, "Please, Blaine. Please, give it to me."

Her body is begging me too and I can't hold back any longer. The liquid heat moves out of me and into her and I can't even think as it shoots out with a vengeance.

Our breathing is so loud it fills the room with the love we're making. Her moan is low and long as she gets what she wanted. Her hands move in slow circles over my back.

I hold her in the same position, her leg pulled back and our bodies pulsing around the others until nothing is left. Then I let her leg move back down, but I stay where I am, inside of her.

She wiggles on the pillow. "Can this thing be moved?"

"Let's wait a few minutes to let things soak in."

She giggles a little, then runs her hands through my hair. "Blaine, I want you to know that I really love you. I can't even think about my life before you came into it. It's so crazy. It's like that was just time—not anything special. Then you came along and every day has a special place in my memory bank. It's so weird and amazing at the same time."

"I suppose that's what happens when you meet the one for you. I feel like life was merely lived a day at a time before you came along and filled my mind, heart, and soul." I kiss her with a soft, sweet kiss. "I promise to try my best to make you happy every single day."

"There will be bad days, too Blaine. Don't think every day will be so happy," she says.

I pull back and look at her, then give her a wink. "Baby, even a bad day with you beats a day without you. I'll take the bad with the good. I get it now. Things happen, both good and bad. There are times in everyone's life where the bad outweighs the good and vice versa. I'll take them all with you by my side."

"I don't know what I did to deserve you." Her voice is shaky, and I can hear the tears that are about to spring forth again.

So I kiss her cheek. "Shh. No more tears for the rest of the night." I move off her and lie on my side, wiggling the pillow out from under her. "Tonight is all about you and me starting our lives together, for real. So let's decide some things. The first thing I want to decide, so we can tell everyone tomorrow when they come, is what day we will get married on."

"I'd like to get married on a date that has importance to you. Say, your mother's or father's birthday, perhaps." Her eyes sparkle as she looks up at me and runs her fingertip over the bow of my top lip.

Taking her finger, I kiss it, then say, "I'd like to get married on New Year's Eve in Las Vegas."

"That's a week from today," she says as she shakes her head. "That's too soon. There's no time to make any plans. How about in the spring?"

"No," I say and pull her to me, then turn over with her on top of me. "I want you to carry my name when the new year begins. I want that belly big by the spring, and I don't want our first kid thinking we weren't married when we started making him."

"Or her," she says with a giggle. "I thought I'd have a church wedding."

"They have chapels in Vegas."

"You know where else they have a chapel, Blaine?"

"Everywhere," I say. then tug her close so I can kiss her. "So what do you say to Vegas for New Year's Eve? I'll bring the whole family if you want, or it can be just you and me, alone."

"I say no to that. But I have an idea. It can still be on New Year's Eve, but it will be at the hospital, so the kids can be there. They were there when this whole thing began. I'd like them to be there when we say our vows too."

Her idea sounds good. But there most likely won't be one very special little girl there, and that empty place would dampen my spirit.

I wonder how Delaney will take being told no to where she wants to have our wedding. Badly, I bet!

THE GIFT BOOK SEVEN

A Holiday Romance

By Michelle Love

Miracles. Forgiveness. Happy Endings
*In the conclusion of 'The Billionaire's Gift,' Blaine and Delaney find out if
her parents will accept their marriage plans.
A Christmas snow fall may be a hazard to getting to spend Christmas with
their families.
With all of those things to worry about, the couple may not get the wedding
they wanted, as things go out of their control.
Will all of the problems have Delaney doubting if marrying Blaine is the
right thing to do?*

54

DELANEY

December 25^{th:}

Oranges and pinks seemingly stain Blaine's skin from the reflection of the embers of what's left of the fire that was raging in the fireplace when we first settled into the evening in the den. The lights on the tree went out with the timer they were set on, telling me it's past midnight.

"Merry Christmas, baby," Blaine whispers in my ear as he holds me loosely in his arms. The blanket on the floor isn't enough to keep us warm any longer, as the fire nearly dies out. "Ready to head up to bed?"

"I am."

Effortlessly, he picks me up, wrapped in the blanket, and carries my satiated body to the bedroom we share. We're now an engaged couple with no way to agree on where to get married.

I want to be married at the chapel in the hospital, and he's against it. He won't say exactly why he would rather fly out to Vegas instead of having something a little more traditional, but I have a strong hunch little Meagan has everything to do with it.

Not wanting to argue right after our engagement, I've closed my mouth about the wedding destination for now, anyway. I have a feeling I'll have everyone's vote on my idea when our families get here. *If mine is coming.*

Kicking the door closed behind us, Blaine pads over to the bed and places me on it gently. "Here you go, baby. Climb in under those covers, and I'll join you in just a minute."

He heads toward the bathroom while I get under the blankets and snuggle down, already feeling sleep coming for me. Pulling my hand out from under the blanket, I take one last look at the gorgeous ring he gave me to make sure this is all real.

Blaine not only wants to get married ASAP, but start our family as well. He's a man on a mission. I think it's safe to assume that he will pursue me tenaciously until a little stick lets him know I'm carrying his child.

The light of the full moon that's peeking through the sheer curtains reflects off the ring. It glimmers and glows with the light, and my heart skips a beat as I think about the future.

Mrs. Blaine Vanderbilt is the name I will soon carry. Nurse Richards will be no more, and Nurse Vanderbilt will be the one who watches over the sick children at the hospital.

Blaine comes out of the bathroom and catches me gazing at the ring. "You really do like it, don't you?"

"It is a thing of great beauty, Blaine. You made an excellent choice. I know I'd never have chosen this for myself. It looks too expensive. And please never tell me what you paid for it. I'm already afraid to wear it. You know, because I might lose it."

He climbs into the bed, laying out on his back next to me, and pats his chest, his gesture for me to lay my head on it. This is the way he likes to fall asleep every night since we moved in together.

His arm goes around me, holding me and making me feel safe, secure, and loved. Slipping my hand under the blanket, I settle in and know my dreams will be the sweetest ever. He's made me happier than I was before somehow. I was pretty damn happy before he proposed, so that was some feat.

"Before I let you fall asleep, I want to ask you a question, and I want you to give me your honest answer," he says as he runs his hand through my hair. "Do you really not want to be married in Vegas?"

"I really don't. I didn't have a lot of dreams about the day I got married, but I don't think the sound of slot machines and tons of strange people being around is how I want to start our marriage. I want it small, with family and friends around. A quaint, little affair." I turn to look at him and find him smiling at me.

"I don't think they have slot machines in the wedding chapels there. But I get what you're saying, and I don't want you to go to sleep thinking we are on opposite sides. I will put my problems to the side and give you what you want. That day should be what you want it to be, rather than me being selfish about that."

"Really? You would really put whatever is bothering you about the hospital out of your mind and actually enjoy having the wedding there? Because I want you to enjoy it too," I say as I search his eyes for the truth.

His hand moves in a soft caress across my back as he looks into my eyes. "As a husband and father, I will have to make sacrifices. Being selfish is a luxury I no longer have. Let me do this for you and for us. Let me put into practice how I will need to be if I'm going to be a great husband and father, which I'm striving for."

"Then I will let you do that. I think you'll enjoy it more than you think you will," I say and lay my head back on his chest, feeling even better than I did before. I have a plan now, and that fills me with a content feeling.

"As long as I'm marrying you on that day, that's all I need. It's all I should need, right?" he asks, as if I could argue with his point.

"Of course. Now let's get some sleep. I'm half expecting an early phone call from mom telling me they've decided to join us for Christmas. You do realize that means they'll be staying here for a few days?"

"Few days?" he asks, then chuckles. "Baby, they can stay until after the wedding, which will be next week. We can take them shopping for clothes to wear, and I'll get the settlement all squared away. They will leave our house with a bank account the likes they probably haven't even dreamt of."

"My parents are going to be rich?" I ask as I look at him with renewed energy, as I just never realized what would happen for them if they accepted his settlement. *I never thought about them being rich!*

"Yes, they will be rich. I also will be throwing in a house for them. I have one on a Lake Tahoe and one on the beach in Miami. Which one do you think is more their speed?" he asks me with a grin as he runs his fingertips along my shoulder, sending chills through me.

"Lake Tahoe, definitely. How big is the house? It can't be too big. Mom's getting too old to clean a big house."

"It comes with a staff. You should know that by now, Delaney. And it's big. A log-cabin-style mansion," he says, and my blood really gets pumping.

I sit up and laugh. "My God, Blaine! They're going to think they've died and gone to heaven!"

"Pops wouldn't let me give him hardly anything. A Cadillac last Christmas was the first thing he actually accepted. I bought that place for him and took him up there, and he flatly refused to live there. Even when I told him he could have Kate or Kent or both of them live there too, he refused it."

"That's kind of sad. You just wanted him to be happy. I'm sorry." Leaving a kiss on his cheek, I lay back down on his chest and run my finger through the sunken line between his abs. "I wonder why he wouldn't let you do that for him."

"Stubborn pride and the fact he saw my money as bad money— money taken from people who really needed it and needed the things they purchased to be worth the money they paid for it. And he hated the fact that I ran small, privately-owned businesses out of business," he says with a sad tone to his deep voice.

"But you're changing all that. Too bad it took his death for you to see it needed changing."

"Yes, too bad about that." He kisses the top of my head. "Let's go to sleep. baby. We have a big day tomorrow. We have to heat up all that Christmas dinner Roxy made for us."

"At least I don't have to really cook," I say and close my eyes. "Goodnight, Blaine. I love you."

"I love you, Delaney. Good night."

55

BLAINE

The snapping of branches tells me someone is coming. From out of the darkness emerges a single light. It hovers six feet over the snow-covered ground. The sound of the footsteps stops, but no person stands where I thought I'd see one.

The full moon's light overhead filters through the dense forest. How I got here, I don't know. An owl hoots from far away and the light in front of me grows larger and glows brighter until there is nothing but light in front of me.

The flapping of wings fills my ears as the light is so bright I have to shield my eyes. Then it goes dark—completely dark—until the moon's light has vanished.

My eyes adjust to the darkness as a booming voice calls out, "You've asked for something."

"Who are you?" I ask as I begin to see two large, round, yellow eyes a few feet in front of me.

"Who," he says.

"Yes, who are you?" I ask again.

"I am Who." He moves a step closer, and somehow, I can see him. It's as if he has an inner glow and he is a six-foot-tall owl. "And you asked for something, didn't you?"

"I'm not sure what's going on. Where am I?" I ask as I look behind me for any sign of light and only see large trees shrouded in darkness. "And why am I talking to a giant owl?"

"You are talking to an average-sized owl where I come from. And you are here, in the primordial forest. In this place, magic can happen. And what you have asked for requires magic."

"You must be talking about what I asked Santa for when I met up with him yesterday. You have to be talking about Meagan Sanders. I asked for her to get better. Are you here to grant that wish, Who?" I ask the tall bird with fluffy, white feathers and glowing, yellow eyes.

"It is only you who has the power to grant that wish. Are you prepared to pay the price for her to get better?" He moves one wing out, showing the ultra-white underside of his easily five-foot long wing, as if he's pointing in that direction. "If you will come with me, I can show you what it will take to make your wish come true. Then you can decide if you're willing to pay that price."

He starts hopping away and I follow him. "I thought prayers worked differently than this."

His head spins around and he looks at me. "Oh, you didn't ask for that in a prayer. You wished for it. That's the difference. Yes, prayers require no trade. Why didn't you think to ask for her health to be returned in that form? That would've been much smarter, don't you think?"

"I suppose it would've. Can't I change that now, though? Can't I simply say a prayer now?" I ask and find the owl stopping and turning his body around too.

The tip of his wing touches my shoulder. The soft ends of the white feathers touch my cheek, and they are the softest things I've ever felt. "I'm sorry. Her life is in peril right at this moment. That's why I came to get you. You made the wish instead of a prayer. You can always say one now if you want. No one can ever stop you from doing that, of course."

I bow my head, close my eyes, and say, "Lord, I am asking for your help. Little Meagan Sanders is near death. She's just a little girl. I'm asking for you to please let her get better. End her suffering. Please,

Lord. Amen." I open my eyes and look at the owl. "Do you think that worked?"

"How should I know? I'm in the wish department, not on the prayer side of things." He shrugs his feathered shoulders. "Do you want to continue on with your wish or end things here and see what happens?"

"Will I have another chance to go through with this if the prayer doesn't work out?" I ask as I weigh the odds.

"No, this is it." He stares into my eyes with his yellow eyes glowing as if a fire is inside of them.

"I'm not sure what to do. Will I have a choice about what the payment for her life is?"

He shakes his head, and I find myself wondering what price I am willing to pay. "You know she is not yours to worry over. You don't have to do a thing. You've made your prayer. Who would expect any more from you?"

"I'm just afraid of what will be asked in exchange for her life. You see, I've begun my life now. I have a woman I'm about to marry and we want children. We're already working on our first. There are some things now that I will not trade. If I'm asked to trade any of their lives, I won't do it."

"I have no idea what you'll be asked to trade. I do know it's always something which is dear to you. I should let you know, most who are given this rare opportunity do not go through with it. They find the trade-off too hard to make."

I think about what he's said and wonder what I would give up for little Meagan to live. Then it hits me. "She is in God's hands, isn't she?"

The owl merely shrugs. "How am I to know that? I am in the wish department, remember? That God stuff is something I'm not a part of. I am the creature who hears a wish, and some I give the opportunity to see their wishes come true. Wishes come to me, while prayers go to another place. So, do you wish to continue?"

An odd sensation runs through me. With sudden clarity, I know what my answer has to be. "No. No, Who, I do not wish to continue.

She is in the best hands she could be in. Who am I to get in the way of what God has in store for her? Who am I to judge him? Who am I to think I know better than our creator?"

A flash of light startles me and I fall back on the snow-covered ground. "Ouch!"

56

DELANEY

"Blaine! Wake up and look outside. It's snowing!" I shout, then feel terrible as he falls out of the bed, landing on his ass.

"What the hell?" he says as he looks at me with a disoriented expression.

I rush to help him up and stifle a laugh. "I'm sorry I shouted and woke you up that way. But I was so surprised when I saw the flakes of snow falling past the window. I got up and pulled the curtains back, and when I saw the ground already covered in snow and more falling, well, I got excited. Houston hardly ever gets snow."

"Yeah, I know," he says and looks around the room as I help him up. "It's just that I was having a very odd dream, and in it, I fell on the snow-covered ground, and that's when I woke up. It's so weird."

"You must've incorporated my words in your sleeping mind," I offer as he looks completely out of it.

"Whatever it was, it felt real." He takes my hand and pulls me down on my knees as he goes down on his too, next to the bed. "Delaney, will you pray with me for Meagan? She was near death in my dream and I'd like it if you and I prayed for her right now."

Tears immediately spring to my eyes, and I nod. "But Blaine, you shouldn't ask for what you want. You should ask for what's best for her in his eyes. And you should ask for the strength to handle whatever that may be."

"Okay, I think I have the ground rules down. And thank you for doing this with me and not making me feel like a fool about wanting to do this with you."

Running my hand over his cheek, I say, "I am going to be the other part of you. Never feel like I'll make fun of anything you do or want me to be a part of. Especially where God and prayer are concerned."

"And that's what makes you perfect wife material, Delaney." He kisses my cheek, then gestures for me to bow my head. Taking my hand, he lays our clasped hands on the bed between us.

As he starts praying out loud, I echo his words silently in my own head. I can see he is passionate about having someone hear his pleas for the little girl.

"Lord, I am just a human. I have no control, nor want any. I only want you to hear me when I say I care for that little girl who may be close to death right now. I know she is sick for certain, and I'd like to voice my concern over her. Lord, I am asking you to help her. I am asking you to do what's best for Meagan Sanders. I am also asking for your help for me to handle whatever that will be. And while I have your ear, I'd like to also ask for you to do what's best for Terry, Colby, Tammy, and little Adam, too, as well as all the rest of the sick children in the entire world. I know that's a lot to ask for, but I have the faith that on this day, the day you gave us your son and our savior, that you have the ability to make miracles happen. I'd love it if Meagan Sanders could be the recipient of one today. No matter what that miracle is, Lord, I will accept it. In Jesus name, we pray to you, Amen."

My heart sores as I can feel it in the room, Blaine has completely given this over to God, and for the first time, I can hear it in his voice. *He does believe!*

Turning to him, I take him in my arms and hug him, then I feel wetness on my shoulder and know he's crying. "Shh. It's going to be okay."

"I know it will. I do." He sniffles and pulls back to look at me.

Seeing tears go down the handsome man's face does more to me than I expected it would. It sends pure love in a rush all over my body. "I can see it in your eyes. You get it now, don't you?"

"I think so. I think I understand that this world is not ours to control. We should do the best we can for one another while we're here. But all the begging and pleading a person can do won't stop even one thing from happening. All we can do is pray for the best to happen and for the strength to accept it if it means that person has to leave their body. And one day, we will all meet again, in another place."

"That's what I believe too, Blaine." Kissing his cheek, I get up, pull him up with me, and take him to look out the window. "And we have snow on Christmas. Now, that's a real gift from God, don't you think?"

His fingers touch my chin, and I look up at him. "You are my gift, Delaney. He sent me to that hospital to find you. The moment I laid my eyes on you, I knew something was happening. Your hatred of me was a thing I had to make it past, but when I did, I knocked those walls all the way down. I will thank him for you every day until he gives me my last breath."

His emotions get the best of me, and I start crying and have to hug him, hiding my face in his chest. "Blaine, you're so sweet."

"I think you are, and I'll strive to be the man you deserve. You are an angel. You are my angel and you're one to those kids you take care of too. I'll never try to take you away from that. So you should be prepared for me to make myself just as much a part of that part of your life too."

"You already are. Having you visit doesn't have to stop with the holidays. You can still bring cheer to the kids who find themselves in that place that's so scary to most of them and boring to nearly all of them."

Lifting me up, he carries me back to bed. "We have a few more hours to sleep, and I've just decided to add something to our morning. A quick visit to the kids is in order, I think."

Crawling back under the blankets, I watch the snow fall, as I've left the curtains open. "It's just gorgeous out there. The full moon and the white snowflakes that seem to be dancing around in the gentle breeze. It's hard to close my eyes with a scene like this going on."

Putting his arm around me, he pulls me close so I can lay my head on his shoulder. Our heads touch as we both gaze out the window. "It is nice to see," he says, then sighs. "I don't believe this was on the weatherman's radar last night. I wonder where this came from."

"The North Pole, I suspect," I say with a laugh.

As I lie here with him on our first Christmas, I have to thank God for him too. He is my gift as well. *The best one I've ever had!*

57

BLAINE

The morning is perfect. A nice blanket of snow completely covers the ground as we pull out of the garage in the four-wheel-drive truck. Snow is still falling, though nowhere near as thickly as it was during the early morning hours.

"This is incredible," Delaney says as she looks out the window, taking in the sights of snow-covered trees with icicles hanging from their thick branches. "What a Christmas day this is going to be. It's off to such a great start."

"It is," I say, then take her hand and give the top a little peck. "And thanks for the Christmas lovemaking this morning. It was right up there with one of the best times ever. But, with you, every time is better than the last."

She giggles, and I watch a light pink fill her cheeks. "It was pretty great, and you're right. Each time is a little better than the last. Look at that squirrel, Blaine. He's playing in the snow. How cute!"

Slowing down so she can watch the little creature as it frolics around in a substance I doubt he's ever seen before, I watch her instead of the animal. Her face is all lit up as she's obviously loving this.

Her cell rings, startling us both and the squirrel, who must've heard it too, as he bolts back up the tree. With his antics over, I start moving forward again. We haven't even gotten out of the driveway yet. We'll never get anywhere at this pace.

"Merry Christmas, Mom," she says, then crosses her fingers. "Did you guys make a decision?"

She presses the speaker button so I can hear, too, and I find my stomach clenched as I have no idea if I'll like what she's going to say. So far, this day has been fantastic. *I'd hate for it to get messed up already!*

"I talked to your father and we'd like to come today. If that's still okay."

"It is," Delaney says, then lets out a sigh. "I have so much to tell you. Your lives are on the edge of complete change, Mom. I can't think of a better present you will ever get after today. Blaine will get on the phone and make the arrangements to get you two here. Thank you, Mom. I love you."

She holds out her hand and looks at her ring, and I can tell she's fighting herself not to tell her mother over the phone about our engagement. Reaching over, I take her hand and give her a nod, then whisper, "You can tell them when they get here."

"Okay. I assume you'll let us know when to expect the driver?" her mother asks.

"We will. I'll call you here in just a little while to let you know. Blaine's driving right now, but when we park at the hospital, he'll make the calls he needs to make. Bye now."

Her smile makes it more than evident she is one happy chick. "They're coming around, aren't they?"

"And after you give them the news about the house and the settlement amount, I think we will have no problems out of them at all. Add in the fact that we're getting married and will soon give them a grandchild to spoil, and we're pretty much golden."

Things are falling into place the way I'd hoped they would. Delaney has agreed to become my wife. She's on board with the baby idea. And now her parents are coming to our home and will soon be on board with our decisions too. *I hope!*

"You should let your brother and sister know we have to push back lunch. I say let's push it back to two or so," she tells me.

Handing her my phone, I say, "Give them each a text. I doubt either of them is awake yet. Those office parties can get pretty out of hand. The later lunch may be more of a present to them than you think it is."

With a laugh, she takes my phone, taps out the message, and sends it to them. "I wonder if they'll bring dates today. I'd love to see Kate get a man. She's so pretty and sweet. She'd make some man very happy."

"You know any single doctors?" I ask as I pull onto the highway that's been cleared of any snow and salted down to prevent any of the falling flakes from sticking.

"I know plenty of them. I don't recommend getting into a relationship with one unless you don't mind spending a ton of time alone, though. They are some busy people. Most have practices they see to all day. They make early morning rounds at the hospital, some as early as five in the morning. Most come back to check on their patients on their lunch hour, grabbing a bite to eat in the cafeteria before going back to their offices. And even after their offices close, they come back and usually stay until nine or so, checking on their patients again,"

"That does sound like something that would make a relationship tough. Yeah, don't tell any of them about my little sister. I'd like her to have a man who has time for her. And speaking of time, I'd like you to make sure you're not put on any more double shifts. As a matter of fact, I'd like it if you told your boss that you can work the morning shift only. That way you and I can spend our evenings together."

The way she looks at me has me a little worried as I wait to see why in the world she'd argue about this. "And if my boss tells me she can't do that?"

"Then tell her you don't even need the job. That should make her see things your way," I say and take the exit to get to the hospital. I'm pleased to see these streets have been cleared of snow as well.

"I suppose I could play that hand," she says as she seems to be thinking about it all. "But what if that backfires on me and she tells me she can't do that and if I need to quit, then let her know?"

"I doubt it will turn out that way. There is a shortage of nurses as it is. Why let you go just because you want a certain shift? You're not asking for a lot. And let her know about our plans to have a baby. Because once a baby comes, then I think you'll need to go to part-time or maybe stop working all together." I glance at her as I pull into the hospital's parking garage.

She's wearing a frown and that can't be good. "I think you need to understand this is important work to me. I might go to part-time while our child is young, but when they start school, I'll go back to full-time. And here's another thing you need to consider. You, too, can work part time or do some of your work from home and you can also care for our child. It's not all up to me. We can share the workload of taking care of our children."

And just like that, she's told me how our parenting is going to be, and I have to admit, I love her take-charge attitude. Who knew I'd like a woman who made some of the rules? *Not me!*

58

DELANEY

A s we walk into the main lobby of the hospital, I see the lady behind the desk looking at me with laser-focused eyes, and she hurries to come to me, waving her hand at me as she calls out, "Nurse Richards, I have something to tell you."

Blaine's hand squeezes mine and he whispers, "Please don't let it be bad news."

I nod in agreement. "Yes, Mrs. Packie? What is it?"

She looks into my eyes, and I can see she's excited as she says, "The little Sanders girl."

Blaine interrupts her. "Please stop right there. I don't want to hear this."

"But it's amazing," she says.

Blaine, who was turning away, stops and looks at the woman. "It is?"

"Yes," she says, then a smile lights up her face. "That little girl was pulled off the machines last night at her parents bidding."

"They pulled her off on Christmas Eve?" Blain asks. "That man stops at nothing to do the most inappropriate things."

"I don't know if he was so wrong this time. Maybe it was a little Christmas magic that helped her. All I know is that she woke up feeling good. When her blood was drawn and sent to the lab, the results were out of this world. Everything was absolutely normal. Not a trace of any abnormalities."

"You're serious?" Blaine asks, then I find him pulling me along behind him as he hurries to the elevator. "We have to go see her!"

"Blaine, I'm not sure her father ..."

He cuts me off. "He will let us see her. You watch!"

The elevator opens up, which I'm thankful for because Blaine was eyeing the door to the stairs. A three-flight run of them would not be anything I'd like to do.

The doors close and Blaine pulls me in for a hug. I can feel his heart pounding hard in his chest. "Maybe our prayers worked, Delaney!"

"Maybe. Like I said, I've seen things happen no one could explain. But you need to know that sometimes it looks like things are in remission and suddenly the disease can come back with a renewed vengeance. I just want you to be aware that could happen." I watch his face and the smile is still there.

"I know this doesn't mean the little girl will never face another bad thing in life. But at least this bad thing may be out of her way. That's all anyone can ask for." The doors open and he's dragging me along behind him, as there is just no way I can keep up. His long legs make such quick strides.

Every person we pass along the way to Meagan's room is all smiles. "It's another miracle!" Nurse Pradhan tells us as we pass her. "A real Christmas miracle!"

Before we get to Meagan's room, the door to Tammy's room flies open, and her mother, Patsy, is wide-eyed. "You two! Oh my God! You're not going to believe this."

Blaine smiles at her. "I know. We heard Meagan is making a recovery."

She shakes her head and grabs my hands. "We just got back the results of Tammy's blood draw this morning."

Blaine's hand starts shaking in mine as he whispers, "No way."

Patsy starts jumping up and down. "She's normal! Her blood

count is perfect! She's in remission is what her doctor just told me. My baby is going to be okay!"

I hug her as Blaine stands there with his mouth open. "I wonder if anyone else got these kinds of results from this morning's blood draw."

"Congratulations, Patsy!" I call out as Blaine takes my hand and hurriedly goes down the hallway. Little Adam's room is on the left, only three doors down from Tammy's, and he stops at it, making a quick knock. "Adam?"

The door is pulled open and Adam's father, a young man of only twenty-two, opens it. He and Adam's mother were only seventeen when they had the little five-year-old boy who has a malignant mass under his right arm. "It's gone!"

"What?" Blaine says and hurries to the little boy who is sitting up on the bed, holding his arm up.

"Look, Mr. Vanderbilt," he shouts as he runs his hand over the smooth surface where a massive lump was only yesterday. "It's gone. It just went away. I feel so much better too."

Blaine moves his hand over the place the cancer had been. "This is amazing."

"We're waiting on the lab results and for the doctor to come talk to us, but we know it will be great news," his father tells us.

Blaine gives the little boy a hug. "I'm so happy for you, Adam. I'll be back to see what the doctor tells you. I need to check on a couple of other kids." Taking my hand, he pulls me along as he hauls ass. "Oh, Merry Christmas!"

I manage to pull the door shut behind us as he hurries toward Colby's room. When he pushes the door open, we both stare at the clean room, void of any of Colby's things. "What the hell?" I ask as we walk back out and go to the nurses' station. "Beth, where's Colby?"

"I don't know," she says. "I just came on to my shift. I was running a little late. I let the kids open their presents this morning. Rhonda gave me a little time to do that with my family. I'll check on that for you."

"Let's go see Terry," Blaine says, then grabs my hand again, and this time I manage to keep up with him as adrenaline is flowing through me.

I stop him just before he pushes the door open. "Okay, now, don't get too excited. The chances he's also got great news are slight. And we don't want to let him know about the other kids who are doing so well."

Blaine nods and pushes the door open. Terry's mother is in the room, packing up his things. "What's happened?"

She looks at us with a smile. "Go to the chapel and find that out for yourselves."

Leaving the room, Blaine says, "I want to see if Mr. Sanders will let us see Meagan before we go downstairs."

I nod and we go toward her room. At least we know there's good news, even if the man is still being a jackass. Knocking on her door, I call out, "It's Nurse Richards and Mr. Vanderbilt. We'd like to ask you ..."

The door is opened, and I'm caught up in a hug, then I see Blaine is too. Her mother and father are in tears as they hug us. Then they let us go and point toward the chair at the side of the bed.

There sits Meagan. It's the first time I've seen her out of bed. She has on a red dress and a red bow is taped to her bald head. Her blue eyes are shining like diamonds as she looks at us. "Merry Christmas, you two. Are you having a good one?"

Blaine lets my hand go and walks over to her, picking her up. He can't even talk as he hugs her. So I talk for him, "We are having the best Christmas on record. And I think you are too."

"I am." She pushes against Blaine's chest and sees the tears running down his cheeks. Wiping them away with her little hands, she says, "I'm better now. So you don't need to cry."

He nods and tries to smile, then bites his lower lip—to keep it from trembling, I'm sure. I step up beside him and smile at her. "He's very happy. Those are happy tears. I've never seen him cry those. You're pretty special to make that happen, Meagan."

"Yes, I know that. And don't worry. I'll make the most of the gift

I've been given. I won't take one single day for granted. I promise." She hugs Blaine again. "Thank you for your help."

He closes his eyes, and I can tell it's taking everything in him not to fall apart. "We should go see what's happening in the chapel, Blaine."

With a nod, he sets her back down and looks at me. I know he can't talk yet, and I think Meagan does too. "I'll be leaving the hospital as soon as I gain five pounds. So I'll see you around. Maybe we can have lunch together one day."

"We will see you every day, Meagan. And I will make it my personal mission to get that weight back on you. So be prepared to eat well, my little princess," I tell her, then take Blaine's hand and leave the room, making sure to give her parents a nod as we go.

Blaine falls against the wall after we walk out and pulls me in for a hug. His body is shaking, and I know this is the most emotion the man has ever felt. I let him hug me until his body stops shaking and he clears his throat. "Okay, I've taken charge of myself again and am ready to hear other news. To the chapel, baby."

As we head to the elevator, his arm tight around my shoulders, I can feel the difference in the atmosphere. A positive charge is in the air, surrounding us all up here on this floor right now.

When we get on the elevator, Blaine looks at me with shimmering eyes. "Is this real, baby? Am I dreaming this?"

"It's real, Blaine. This is the most miraculous thing I've ever heard of. But I have to admit, I'm afraid of what kind of news we're going to have about Colby. So please hold on for whatever that is."

He nods as the doors open and we walk out, heading to the small chapel where I hope to be married on New Year's Eve. Now, more than ever, I see this place as a place of hope.

The doors are wide open and Christmas music is playing softly. At the very front of the room, two young men are on their knees in front of the preacher who is praying over them.

Blaine and I sit in the back, waiting for Terry and Colby. We hold hands and give each other looks of complete joy to find Colby there, next to his friend. I still don't know what's going on with them, but I know they're both alive, and that's got me feeling better than I did before.

The preacher ends his prayer and the boys stand up and shake the man's hand, then turn back and see us. We get up as they hurry to us. Both have the broadest smiles on their faces.

"It's a miracle, Blaine!" Colby says.

Terry nods. "It is! And we both wanted to come see the preacher and give ourselves to the Lord. We're going to get baptized in a little while."

"You can stay for that, can't you?" Colby asks. "Because after that, I get to go home. Home!"

"Me too," Terry says with so much enthusiasm that it's heart wrenching. "Home!"

Blaine has a huge smile plastered on his face. "This is so amazing. I just can't believe it. All of my favorite patients are better."

"All of them?" Colby asks.

I nod. "Yes, every one of the kids who Blaine's visited and made friends with have been given great news this morning. Isn't that something?" I pat Blaine on the back. "Seems his prayers were answered."

"You prayed for us?" Terry asks with a wrinkled brow. "Last night?"

"No, it was very early this morning. And Nurse Richards prayed with me." He holds up my left hand. "I asked her to marry me last night and she accepted. We're getting married right here on New Year's Eve. I hope you two will join us."

"For sure!" Terry says and gives Blaine a high-five.

Colby gives him one next. "Wouldn't miss that for anything! I'll be here."

"I could use a couple of best men," Blaine says. "You two want the job?"

"Yes!" they say, together.

"This is insane," I say. "Did you guys see the snow?"

"We did," Colby says. "As a matter of fact, when I saw it, I went to wake up Terry so he could see it too. We were together when the lady came to draw his blood, and she got mine then too. And, later, the doctor came and told us the great news at the same time. It was awesome!"

"I can't even imagine," I say. "I've never even heard of anything like this. Not ever!"

"I just wish every child here could've gotten the same news," Blaine says. "But I'll take what I can get. I'm happier than I've ever been, seeing you guys like this. Healthy and happy."

"How about a little Christmas breakfast before our ceremony," Terry asks.

"You got it," Blaine says, then we head toward the cafeteria.

"I'm going to go talk to my boss. You three go eat, and I'll catch up with you soon," I tell Blaine who gives me a nod and then a kiss on the cheek.

"Go show off that ring and make sure to let everyone know about the wedding," he says as I walk away from him.

I wave back at him, then turn around and go see what I can get accomplished with my boss. Hopefully, with all of the other miracles, I'll get the change in my schedule I'd like to have.

"What has happened around here?" Paul asks me as we meet in the hallway. "Have you heard all the wonderful news?" His eyes go right to my left hand and he takes it, looking at the monster on my finger. "Delaney Richards, are you going to get married?"

"I am. On New Year's Eve. Right in our little chapel. You should come," I say, then take my hand back. "And what about these miracles? Have you ever seen anything like this?"

Walking beside me, he says, "You know, I read about a thing like this once. It wasn't on Christmas and it wasn't all in one day. It was a week, and thirteen children's test results suddenly changed. All of them got better during that week. It was a rare case."

"So, we are the new rare case, I assume." I skip a couple of steps, as I feel light and overjoyed. "And we get to claim a part in history!"

"I'm sure there will be people wanting to interview Blaine. He's the common factor in all of the children. Even Meagan Sanders, in a way. He was banned from her room, but she was one of his original group he made frequent visits to. And now he has your hand in marriage too. Well, he gets what he wants, doesn't he?"

"I suppose he does," I agree.

"Did you ever read that article that was written about him a couple of years ago?" he asks me. I shake my head. "It was written by a man who he ran out of business with his super stores. The man claimed to have seen Blaine coming out of a building that was a known place for Satan worshipers. He made claims about Blaine selling his soul to the devil to earn his wealth."

My father has thought that for a while too. But I didn't know there was an article. And I have no idea if what the man who wrote it said is true.

Could Blaine have really done such a thing?

59

BLAINE

Leaving the chapel, I can hardly wait to find Delaney and tell her my news. Making my way to the nurses' station, where I think she'll be, I find myself feeling like I'm floating on air.

When I see her talking to her boss, I see her frowning and have no idea if I should interfere or not. So I wait and watch her as her arms go up. She goes a bit red in the face, then she slams her fist on the counter top, and I decide I should see what's up.

Moving in behind her, I wrap my arms around her waist. "What's up, buttercup?"

Her boss looks kind of testy, then snaps, "She's not getting her way. That's what's up. And if you think I'm about to give her special treatment over the other nurses, you're mistaken."

"Oh, I see." I had no idea it would be so hard to get a set shift for her. "There's more than one hospital she can work at. You sure you won't reconsider?" I ask the woman, who just seems kind of grouchy. She's not normally like this. It makes me think something is wrong.

"Are you telling me she'll quit if I don't concede to her demands?"

Delaney looks mad as hell. "They are not demands. I'm being more than fair. I said I'll do the remainder of this schedule for the month of December. That's pretty nice of me, considering I have a wedding to plan. I've got double and midday shifts that will take up my time for getting things done, but I'll do it and not make things hard on you or the other nurses. But the new schedule should have me on the first shift and only five days a week."

"Monday through Friday," I add. "No weekends. You do realize she doesn't have to work at all, right?"

"Yes, I heard she's going to be Mrs. Billionaire. So why even keep working, Delaney?" she asks, and I see it in her eyes. *It's the green-eyed monster also known as jealousy.*

"I love my work," she says. "But Blaine's right. This isn't the only hospital to work in."

"Have him buy you one, Delaney. Then you can make your own schedule. A couple of hours each morning and let the rest of the staff work the hard hours. When did you stop being a team player?"

"She's on my team now," I say and pull Delaney back with me. "If you won't make the next schedule the way she asked, then leave her the hell off of it."

Delaney is not saying a word. Her body is tense, and I feel terrible about asking her to do this. Everything was great up until this point, and I feel like it's my fault.

"I think we should get home now. Terry and Colby changed their baptism time to later in the evening. There's no reason to wait around. Your parents will be here in a couple of hours, and I'd like you to be mellowed out by that time. This little matter ..."

She cuts me off with a glare as she stops. "This is my career. Not some little matter!"

"I'm not saying it's not important. I know it's important to you," I tell her and pull her along so we can get out of the hospital and to the truck where no one can eavesdrop on our conversation, which is sounding more and more like an argument.

"Well, I may not be able to have things the way you want them to be."

I wait until we get outside, then I say, "You shouldn't allow your career to be defined by one place. Your career—your passion—can be done anywhere. This is not the only place to be a nurse. And that woman in there is just jealous of you and the money you're marrying into. She shouldn't even be a boss."

The walkway has been covered with snow again that hasn't melted off yet, and I find it slippery. "They should've thrown some salt on this already. Come on, let's go back inside and get some or someone's going to get hurt."

As I turn around to go back, I feel her hand slipping in mine and yank her up before her ass hits the ground. "Oh!" she shouts as I pull her back up.

"See? Damn! You were nearly hurt!"

As we go back into the hospital, I hear a voice, and my name is coming out of some woman's mouth. "Yes, that's right. I remember that article on Blaine Vanderbilt. The one claiming he was into Satanism."

Fury explodes inside of me. I can't believe people are bringing up that old article written by that crazy old man!

Delaney looks at me with a nervous expression on her pretty face. "Don't worry about that, Blaine."

That's easier said than done. I know all too well how things can get out of hand with rumors. And right now is not a time I'd like shit like that to be thrown around. *Not with Delaney's parents here in town for the week!*

How is it that you can do so many good things and it doesn't over-shadow the stupid or bad shit you've done?

The truth about what happened in the warehouse is that I was there to make a deal. Not with the devil per say, but the person I dealt with was, indeed, an evil man. And I knew that. But I bought the clothes from his connection anyway.

Young children were used in the factories that made those cheap clothes. Women were used too. All the employees worked under horrible conditions, and I made money on that torture.

And that did make me an evil man. I'm making a change today that will help me on my new path. The right path. What makes me mad, is that no matter what good I do, it's the bad I've done that will follow me.

A helpless feeling comes over me—a feeling I shouldn't have on this day that's so full of miracles. Delaney asks the lady at the reception desk, "Do you happen to have any salt back there for the sidewalks. Mr. Vanderbilt is worried about people slipping and getting hurt. We'll put it out if you have some."

She retrieves a bag of it and hands it to me. "Here you go, Mr. Vanderbilt. How nice of you."

I know she overheard that woman talking, too, and I find it hard to look into her eyes. "Thanks," I say as I take the bag from her.

"Mr. Vanderbilt?" she asks, making me turn back around. "Don't listen to what anyone says about that thing that happened a couple of years ago. Who cares about that? I've seen you do a lot of good recently. That's what matters in this life. There's not one of us who hasn't done things that are bad in one way or another. Don't let it get to you. You're a great man and getting greater all the time."

I look her in the eyes and find a smile on her face that lights her pretty, brown eyes up. "Thank you. That means a lot to me."

She nods, and we go to sprinkle salt over the slippery surface of the sidewalk people have to use to get into and out of the hospital. Delaney pats my back as I move along it. "Blaine, you really can't let things like that get into your head."

"I know," I tell her. "I talked to the preacher while ago, and he told me where I can get a marriage license. He also told me he was available the whole day of New Year's Eve to perform the ceremony."

"Good!" she says with a huge smile. "Thanks for taking care of that."

"I also will be coming back up here tonight with my family, if they want, and with you and yours, hopefully. I'm going to get baptized." I look back at her and see her eyes shiny with unshed tears.

"Really?" she asks as she reaches out for me.

"Yes." I put the bag of salt down and hug her. "Have you been baptized?"

"I have," she says. "When I was ten. But if you want me to, I'll do it again with you."

"You would?" I ask, as I didn't think about that. But it would be special. "I'd love that."

"It's a good idea, anyway. I was too young to really know what that meant then. Now that I have a real faith that resides in me, I'd like nothing more than to renew my devotion to our Lord and Savior with you, my soon-to-be husband."

Placing a light kiss on her rosy lips, I say, "And soon-to-be father of your children."

She blushes and pulls out of my arms. "We have so much to do. Hurry, let's get this finished and head home. I can't wait for my parents to get here."

Hurrying to clear the sidewalk, I finally get it all done and place the empty bag in the trash can as we head to the truck. Helping her up into the tall truck, I see my future in her green eyes and know that, no matter what, we'll make it through this life together.

Climbing into the truck too, I find my phone going off with a text and read what my sister has written. *Can I bring Randy with me today?*

"Seems my sister has found a date. She'd like to bring him today."

Delaney claps her hands. "Yes! Tell her yes, Blaine!"

So I type back in the response and text my brother next. *Kate's bringing a date. You should, too, or you'll feel left out.*

Starting the truck, I pull out of the parking space to go back out to the estate. When my phone dings with his reply, Delaney picks it up and reads it to me, "Already have one. You remember the sexy elf from the costume rental, right?"

"I knew it," I say as I pull onto the road that's beginning to get a little slippery. "Damn, they need to de-ice these again too. What a cold day we're having here in Houston!"

"It feels weird, doesn't it?" she asks as she puts my phone down. "It's like a wonderland. One that can't possibly be real. I keep thinking I'm about to wake up and find this entire thing is just a dream. Including you, Blaine."

"I hope it's not," I say as I pull onto the freeway and find it a little slick too. "Damn it! Would you call the sheriff's office or something and tell them the roads need to be de-iced again? This is ridiculous!"

"Okay," she says as she looks up the number on her phone. "Should you pull over?"

"No, I've got great tires and this is four-wheel-drive, but not everyone has this. And if you look behind us, you'll see a car has just slid off to the side of the road. Report that to them too."

The snow begins to get thicker, and I can see the makings of a real disaster. I hope this wonderful day doesn't end in tragedy. *This started out as the best Christmas ever, after all.*

"Hello, this is Nurse Delaney Richards, and I'd like to report a vehicle that's slid off the road on Interstate 10, near mile marker 112. There's ice on the roadway and the snow is beginning to fall harder. So it's time to de-ice them again."

"I'll send an officer to the area. Thank you," the dispatcher says, then the call is over.

"That's about all we can do, Blaine," she says as I take our exit off the highway and find this road is worse than that one was.

"We are in for a slow ride, baby. I hope this clears up by the time your parents get to the airport or they'll be sitting there for I don't know how long."

"Can't you get them out in a helicopter? Your place has ample room to land one."

"They won't fly in the snow. If there's a break in it, I might be able to get my neighbor down the road to go get them. Max Lane has a badass machine and he's got tons of experience flying. Maybe I should call him to be sure he can do it, though. It is Christmas, after all."

"Do you know how cool that would be to fly them to the estate in a helicopter? Blaine, you have to ask him to do it. Offer him some money to entice him," she says.

I laugh and say, "He won't take my money. He's got enough of his own. But he might not want to risk it. He's got a wife and kids. But I'll see what he says."

Making the call on my speaker system, I find him answering, "Well, Merry Christmas, neighbor. How's it going?"

"It's better than I ever expected. I got engaged last night."

"No way! You'll have to bring her by to meet the missus. Lexi can help her acclimate to being the wife of a rich man," he says. "What's she do?"

"I'm a nurse. My name's Delaney Richards." Delaney answers. "Hello, he has you on speaker, Max."

"Hello to you too, Delaney. It's nice to see my friend and neighbor has met the woman for him. It's about time. He's been all work and no play. I've invited him to every one of my gatherings, and he's always been way too busy."

"Well, I'll make him go to the next one. It's important to know your neighbors," she says.

"That it is. We have an extensive friend base and adding a new couple sounds great. You two planning on a family anytime soon?" he asks, and I knew he would because he and all of his friends began having kids from the get-go, once they married.

"We do. Your kids will have friends down the street before you know it," I tell him. "I'm calling because Delaney's parents are flying into the airport on a private jet and the car ride is pretty treacherous right now. I don't suppose you'd like to fly your helicopter over and pick them up for us? I know it's a little more than the typical favor neighbors do for one another—not exactly a cup of sugar or an egg or two."

"Sure thing," he says without any hesitation. "When they get there, call me, and I'll check the weather and the radar. The trip there is only ten minutes. It'll be a snap to get them to you guys. Have you told them the news yet?"

"Not yet, so don't let it slip, Max," Delaney says. "And thank you so much. I'm a nurse, like I said, so if you, your wife, or any of your kids get sick, you can call me and I'll come see if I can be of help."

"Cool," he says. "Will do. Give me a call when they touch down."

"Wow, a helicopter pilot as our next-door neighbor," Delaney gushes. "How cool is that? Mom and Dad are going to freak. I can't wait!"

And with one little phone call, I've made her day even better. *This is getting a little too easy!*

60

DELANEY

With the snow still falling, I'm getting increasingly more worried about my parents getting stuck at the airport. Kate and her date, Randy, as well as Kent and his date, Tiffany, managed to get here, thanks to their four-wheel drive vehicles. But the jet had to land at a small airport in LaGrange to wait for the snow to stop in Houston.

"It looks like we have a few trays of appetizers, Blaine. Roxy made a ton of food." I pull the tray of cut-up veggies and dip and place it on the counter top. "Maybe you could take this tray out to them and take a bottle of that white wine too. I feel terrible for making them wait even longer to eat, but I still have a bit of hope mom and dad will make it here within the next couple of hours."

His lips touch my cheek, and I feel an instant heat deep inside of my stomach. All his sexual attention last night, this morning, and even when we got home from visiting the kids at the hospital has my libido overloaded.

Fighting the urge to turn to him, wrap myself around him, and take that sweet kiss and turn it into more, I slide the platter to him and turn to take the other trays out of the fridge. Those have to be heated.

His chuckle as he takes the tray and leaves me alone in the kitchen lets me know he saw the reaction I had to his innocent kiss. And, damn the man, even his chuckle sounds sexy as hell to me right now. I think the man has put me in heat, like some kind of animal!

Turning the oven on to 425 degrees, like Roxy's directions, which are taped to the top of the aluminum pan full of tasty looking little savory treats, state, I turn back to see what the directions are on the other tray. My cell phone rings and I see it's my mother. "Mom, how's it coming?"

"The pilot said we're taking off again. How's it looking there?"

I peek out the window over the sink and see the snow has lightened up. "It's a lot better. I suppose the pilot must've seen an opening in the weather if he's going to make a break for Houston. I'll let Blaine know you're headed there now. He'll have his friend pick you guys up, if the weather permits. You may have to sit a while in the airport. I'm sorry about this. I wish the weather was cooperating. But it is beautiful out here with the snow."

"We wanted to tell you not to hold your dinner for us. We can eat leftovers. It's not a problem," she says, sounding chipper about it.

But I know my mother, and she's not one to be an inconvenience to anyone. "No, we're waiting for you guys. I've just started to heat up a couple of trays of appetizers and have set out a vegetable platter for our other guests."

"How many are there?" she asks, sounding worried. "I don't want a bunch of people waiting on us, Delaney."

"It's just his brother, sister, and their dates. And it's okay. They're eating. No one is going hungry. So I'll hold it until you guys get here. End of discussion," I tell her, then watch Blaine walk back into the kitchen. "Blaine's here. Let me tell him everything and call me when you land in Houston. Love you, bye."

"Tell me what?" he asks as he strolls toward me. His hips move in a rhythmic fashion, and I don't know why I can't take my eyes off his rippling body. His white, button-down shirt is tucked into dark-gray pants, his abs move underneath the slightly tight shirt, and my insides are getting jiggly.

On their own accord, my hands move up his arms, then I grab his lapels and pull him in for a kiss. I melt into him as our lips touch and his hands move up my back until they're tangling in my hair as he pulls my head back a bit, parting my lips. His tongue comes in and I relish the taste of him.

The sound of a woman clearing her throat stops our kiss, and we look to see who has interrupted us. "Steamy," his sister says as she goes to the fridge. "I'm just here for a bottle of water. Don't mind me."

A bit embarrassed by what she caught us doing, I move away from Blaine's arms and grab the aluminum tray as the oven beeps at me, telling me it's heated up and ready. "Sorry about that."

"Don't be," Blaine says, then moves in behind me, cuddling me from behind. "It's what people in love do, baby. Right, sis?"

She laughs. "How the hell should I know?"

"Blaine!" I hiss as I try to shrug him off. "Come on!"

With a deep chuckle, he lets me go. "You were going to tell me something."

"Oh, yeah! Damn, that whole thing completely slipped my mind."

"Nice to know I have such an effect on you," he says and comes at me again.

I step to the side of the island in the middle of the huge kitchen to put something between us. If I let him keep this up, we'll end up in the laundry room with me bent over the washing machine while he takes me from behind. My insides clench with the thought and I'm sorry I even let that little scene go through my head!

"Blaine, I was about to tell you the pilot of the private jet is bringing my parents to Houston. You need to get with that neighbor and see if he can make it." I take another few steps to go around the island as he follows me.

Kate leaves the kitchen, giving us a sideways glance as she does. "I think I'll be an aunt very soon by the way you two are acting."

Heat fills my face. "Blaine! You have to chill! Damn, baby!"

"One more kiss," he says as he catches me. "That's all I need, then I'll chill. But I can tell you right now, tonight I'm going to make you mine all over again. Every last inch of you."

My knees go weak as he takes me easily into his arms. My breasts smash against his hard chest. Then he's kissing me hard and wanting, and I'm thinking about that laundry room and how much time we have to get the deed done. But his phone rings, vibrating his right front pocket. It's very near my personal pleasure zone, and the sensation makes me moan.

Our mouths part and he looks at me with lust-filled eyes. "Should I answer that or let it finish you?"

I know I'm blushing again as my cheeks heat and I break into a sweat. "Blaine!" I give his chest a faint punch and step back as he releases me to answer his phone.

"It's Max," he says, then answers the call. "Hi, Max. I was just about to call you."

"Good, so they're on their way here?" he asks.

"Yep, they left LaGrange a few minutes ago. What's the weather looking like?"

"Great for at least the next hour. We have a nice clear spot, then more is possible, but not likely. I was hoping that pilot was watching things and moving on. I'll take off to get them. It's Mr. and Mrs. Richards, right?"

"It is, and I'll tell them to look for the tall hulk of a man," Blaine says, making me wonder what this man looks like. "They'll be coming in the gate where the private jets land. You know where that is."

"I do. I'll have them to you in no time," Max says.

"Oh, tell him I have a pumpkin pie for him to take home. He should come inside when he gets here. I'd love to meet him," I call out as I pull the pie out of the fridge. Roxy made six of them, and I doubt we could ever eat them all.

"I will certainly do that. I'm always up for free pie. See you guys soon."

Blaine puts his phone back in his pocket and moves toward me again. "Okay, now, where were we?"

Holding up my hand, I tell him, "No! You and I have to heat this meal up. So no more kissing until later. Much later! We have so much to do, baby."

"Well, hell!" he says and turns to start getting things out of the fridge. "Can you turn the other two ovens on to start heating them up? We have a lot of stuff here."

With a smile, I turn the ovens on and think how nice this is. Our first Christmas together, and he and I are working together in the kitchen. We're so domestic already. *It's adorable!*

61

BLAINE

Her red apron with white trim makes her look like a little homemaker. So cute and spry, she moves around the kitchen. *I can hardly keep my hands off her!*

But she's insisting we get this done, and I'm not about to piss her off today if I can help it. Her hair keeps getting into her face as she hustles to get things out of the oven. "Let me help you, baby. I can get these things. Why don't you set the table and call Kate in here to help us?"

"Good idea," she says, then gives me a peck on the cheek. "I'll be right back. They should be here soon, I think."

I watch her hurry out of the kitchen and think about what a great team we make. I'm a little nervous about her father, but hopefully that won't go too badly. Then the sound of chopper blades cutting through the air has my stomach going tight, and I know the time has come.

"Blaine!" I hear her call out. "They're here! Come on!"

She runs into the kitchen and grabs my hand. "Slow down, Delaney. We have to get coats on. It's cold as hell out there."

"Our coats are on the rack in the entry room, clear across the house, Blaine. Crap! We need to ..."

A knock on the back door, off the kitchen, stops her from saying another word. I walk over to the door with a knot in my stomach from the nerves I'm feeling and trying hard to hide. "No need. That's them now."

Delaney rushes to my side, taking my hand. "Okay, let them in. Damn, I'm nervous!"

I kiss the side of her head, for luck mostly, then open the door. Max stands at the door as her parents come up behind him. "I brought you two a couple of presents."

We step aside to allow him to come in. He's carrying an old, brown, beat-up suitcase and sets it to the side of the door. Delaney lets my hand go as she's grabbed up in a hug between her mom and dad. "We missed you," I hear her mother's muffled voice say.

"We sure did," her father says, then they let her out of their arms and her mother looks at me.

Her smile is wide as I extend my hand to her. "Nonsense," she says, then hugs me. She's a thin woman, almost frail-like in stature. Her hair has gone gray and she keeps it short. I can see her eyes were once as green as her daughter's are now. They have faded, most likely due to the stress of being so poor.

I can't help but feel badly for that. But I push it away, as I know I am going to rectify that for them. "I'm glad you could make it, Mrs. Richards."

She lets me out of her thin arms and smiles at me, then steps back to stand beside her stoic husband. "I'm glad you invited us. This has all been amazing. The private jet and then a helicopter ride too! We're on excitement overload!"

"I've ridden in a helicopter before," her father says. "I worked on offshore rigs when I was younger. Now those chopper pilots were notorious for scaring the shit out of their passengers. I have to say, Max here is a hell of a lot better than any I've ridden with before. You can tell he's experienced."

Max's hand lands on my back with a swift pat. "Blaine has yet to ride with me, despite being invited many times."

"I was a very busy man, but that's all about to change," I say, then extend my hand to her father. "It's nice to meet you, Mr. Richards."

He shakes my hand as Delaney comes to my side, running her arm around me. His eyes stay focused on her. "We'll see if you still think that after our visit here, Vanderbilt."

"Dad," Delaney warns him. "Be nice. Don't bring out the redhead in me."

Her mom laughs, and by the way her white-haired father cuts his eyes at his wife, I can tell he's been on the bad end of redheads before. I feel for the poor man if they've both ever gotten crossways with him at the same time!

Delaney kisses my cheek. "I'm going to show them to their room so they can freshen up." She heads off with her parents behind her. Her father stops to pick up the one suitcase they've brought with them, making a pang of guilt hit me square in the heart. Delaney looks over her shoulder. "Nice to meet you, Max. Don't go anywhere. I have that pie for you and your family."

"I'll be right here," he says, then looks at the counter with the half-empty trays of appetizers Kent brought back in here when they started setting the table. "And that looks like some good stuff right there. Do we have mini lobster rolls here?"

"We do. Try one," I say and pick up one too. "My chef used phyllo dough to wrap them. They are light, airy ..."

He finishes my description after he swallows the bite he took. "And scrumptious! It seems you and I need to have a little potluck one Sunday evening. My chef, Hilda, is a wiz too. She specializes in authentic Mexican cuisine, but she's great at anything."

"We will have to do that. Domestication has fallen all over me since I met Delaney. I never saw myself as this man I'm quickly becoming."

With a nod, he says, "I know what you mean. When I met Lexi, she was a diamond in the rough. And so was I. Together, we brought out more in each other than either of us knew was lingering just under our surfaces. Love is fantastic. You're in for a whirlwind of emotions, feelings, and sensations."

"So what you're saying is, this is just the tip of the iceberg?"

"It is. You think you know what love is now. Wait until you watch your wife bring your children into this world. Your love for her grows deeper and the love you have for your child isn't even a thing one can describe, it's so encompassing."

"Wow, you make it sound a lot better than most married men do."

"Most men don't take the time to make the intimate connection it takes to really get to the meat of a marriage. It takes work and patience. But like anything that turns out well, it's worth the time and effort you put into it."

As I gaze out the door, waiting for Delaney to return to me, I have to thank God again for her. *My special gift.*

62

DELANEY

My father has managed to act like a nice, normal man for the Christmas dinner, which we ate later than expected. All of us are stuffed and moving into the den where we have the tree set up.

We have a limited amount of time to open gifts, then Blaine and I need to get back to the hospital. We haven't told anyone about how we're going to be baptized in a few hours.

I printed out pictures of the Lake Tahoe cabin, as Blaine calls it. I tend to think of it more as a lodge, it's so huge. And I know my parents are going to be shocked by the gift.

Kent and Kate have quite a shock coming to them as well. Blaine has outdone himself this Christmas. With plenty of gifts under the tree, Blaine puts on a Santa hat and tosses me a green elf hat. "Care to play my elf once more? Last time this year, I promise," he says, ending with a ho, ho, ho.

I place the little pointy hat on my head and go to his side. "Okay, but next year I want to be a Christmas fairy. Not an elf."

"We'll see what we can do about that, Delaney," he says and hands me the first gift. "This one is for Tiffany and here's one for Kent too."

Taking the neatly-wrapped gifts, I hand them off to his brother, who hands his date hers. "Now, wait until everyone has one, please."

Nods of agreement assure me they will, and I go back to grab two more from Blaine, who says, "Kate and Randy."

I take those to them and watch my parents as they stare at the loads of presents under the tree. When I go back to Blaine, he hands me two more. "Your mother and father."

Handing them theirs, I find my father looking grim. "We weren't notified in time to buy you anything. I'm sorry."

"Dad, don't worry about that. Blaine and I need nothing in return." I step back, and Blaine stands up. "Okay, open them up."

Blaine and I hold hands in anticipation and see smiles everywhere we look as they all find the boxed sets of different perfumes and colognes we bought. It was the first time I had ever purchased such extravagant things. But I did enjoy it immensely!

The next round of presents gives them all manicure and pedicure sets in sterling silver. "You should never have to buy another set of nail clippers ever again," I say as they look their gifts over.

One more round of presents leaves them each with titanium bracelets for the men and diamond earrings for the ladies. Everyone seems really happy with their gifts.

Kate notices the grins Blaine nor I can manage to wipe off of our faces, as we know the best is yet to come. "You two look like a couple of cats who ate canaries."

Blaine reaches under the tree to retrieve the four small boxes and letter-sized envelopes that go with each box. He hands Kent his, Kate hers, then my parents theirs. "I hope you like this, Mr. and Mrs. Richards. It comes from the heart." He looks at his brother and sister. "You guys too. I really thought a lot about this, and with Delaney's help, we found what we think are perfect gifts for you all."

They all are looking at the small boxes and the long envelopes and all seem curiously confused. "Open them!" I say, and Blaine comes back to me.

He wraps his arm around my shoulders and pulls me in tight to his side, leaving a kiss on my cheek. I can feel his excitement, and I bet he can feel mine too as we watch them discover the gifts he's given them.

My mother is shaking her head as she looks at the set of keys on a keyring that says, 'There's no place like home.'

Dad's face is stoic, the expression he usually wears, as he opens his box to find a set of keys. His keyring is a souvenir from Lake Tahoe, with the city's name on it. "What does this mean?" he asks as he looks at me.

Kate rips open the envelope with an excited rush and shouts, "It means Blaine has bought us all new homes!" She pulls the pages with the pictures of her brand-new, upscale Houston home out and looks at them as I watch her eyes go shiny with emotion. "Blaine! How gorgeous!" Then she's up and hugging him with all she has.

Kent opens his envelope and looks at the picture of his country home with acreage and a brand-new tractor sitting outside the red barn. "Blaine, no way!" He's up and hugging him, too, after he pulls his sister off of him.

I make my way to my parents, who are looking over all the pictures of their new home and not quite understanding them. "How do you guys like that?"

"Is it a vacation?" Mom asks me.

"Can we pick when to take it?" Dad asks.

Kneeling down in front of them, I place one of my hands on each of their legs. "That's no vacation. That is your new home in Lake Tahoe. It comes with a full staff. It'll be like you're living a vacation. It's Blaine's gift to you. He knows it won't make up for all you've lost, but he's got more to make up for that."

"We can't take this." Dad looks at me with a frown. "We couldn't even afford to pay the taxes on this behemoth."

"You will after you get the settlement he's giving you for ruining your tire business. So feel free to thank him for this." I stand up and hold out my hands to help them up.

They look at one another as they have a silent conversation, using only their eyes. Then mom takes my hand. "We can accept it. Come on. This is our time, honey. The hard times are officially over."

I see a misty expression on my father's face. The first of its kind. "Are the tough times really behind us, Delaney?"

With a nod, I take his hand, too, help them up, and take them to Blaine. His brother and sister have left him alone to show one another and their dates their new homes.

"How do you like the place?" he asks my parents.

"It looks beyond my comprehension of what a house is," mom says, then reaches out for him and pulls him in for a hug. "Thank you. Thank you so much."

Dad clears his throat and mom steps back. "Well, Vanderbilt, you have surprised me. I have to say this is one heck of a home you've given us. We'll have to relocate. Change our lives up completely."

"Yes, you will," Blaine says, then wraps his arm around me and pulls me back to him. "And I hope we'll be welcomed visitors to your new home."

I had taken my engagement ring off so they wouldn't ask any questions and had given it to Blaine to hold. He pulls it out of his pocket and holds it up. "I gave this ring to your daughter last night. She's agreed to marry me. We're going to be married on New Year's Eve. We'd love it if you stayed with us until then so you can be at the wedding." He slips the ring back on my finger. The weight of it was missed.

I sigh as I look at it, then at my parents. Mom's hands are over her mouth and dad's eyes are very narrow. I hold my breath to see what he's going to say or how he'll act with this news.

When his face blooms into a smile, I can breathe again as he says, "Well, congratulations!"

Mom's crying as she says, "It looks like things are changing for us all."

Blaine and I are pulled into a group hug as mom cries, and I pat her on the back. "Things are changing. Don't worry. All the changes are going to be positive."

"I can't believe this," dad says as he ends the hug. "Yesterday, I hated this man. But now that I've actually met him and see how happy he's made you, that feeling has left me. It's so odd how something you've felt for a long time can vanish."

I'm overjoyed to hear him say that, and I fall back into Blaine's arms. I run my hand over his cheek and smile at my parents. "Things can change in a flash. I, for one, am glad that can happen. And, now, we need to get to the chapel at the hospital where Blaine and I are going to be baptized by the preacher who will officiate the wedding ceremony in a week."

"Oh, Lord!" Mom says. "Next week! There's so much to do. How will you ever get that all done in time?"

"Hopefully, with your help, Mom."

"Count me in," Kate jumps up and says as she raises her hand.

Tiffany joins her. "You can count on me too, Delaney."

Kent and Randy look at each other and shrug, then stand up as Kent says, "You have us too, guys."

Then it's me who starts crying with the show of solidarity to help Blaine and I become one. "You guys are all the best!"

Blaine laughs and pulls me into his chest to help hide my tears. His kiss on top of my head comforts me. "I think she's saying she really appreciates your help. With it, this little wedding of ours should go smoothly, and then we can all get on with our lives. There's so much to get done this week. But with everyone's help, we'll manage."

"We need to go change our clothes. Whoever wants to come with us is more than welcome. And whoever doesn't, we understand. You all have lives too. I know we've taken up a lot of your Christmas day," I tell them as I turn back to look at everyone and wipe my eyes.

Tiffany tugs at Kent's hand. "I should stop by my parents' place. Would you like to come with me?"

His smile says he would. "Yeah. Then we can go look at my new home."

Blaine further surprises him. "It's furnished and there's even food in the kitchen. My staff took care of everything. Take some clothes and stay there. Everything is on and ready for you. And the taxes are paid for the upcoming year too. There are no worries."

Tiffany's smile spreads even further across her pretty face. "Wow!"

"Wow is right," Kent says. "Thanks, Blaine. I'll do that. We're going to head out now."

With a wave, they leave, and Kate says, "I should let Randy go see his family too. Is everything on at my new house too, Blaine?"

"It is. Get you some clothes and go check it out," he tells her.

She looks at Randy, then back at Blaine. "Is it okay if Randy comes over?"

Blaine laughs as he looks at his sister. "Kate, the house is yours. And you're a grown woman. If you want him over, that's your call, not mine."

"Wow! Okay. I know that sounds stupid to ask that."

I hold up my hand, stopping her. "Not really. I know how they've kept you well-guarded all these years. Go have fun. Be careful driving around. I know the snow has stopped, but now it's getting dark and there may be ice."

Kate laughs and comes to hug me. "Yes, Mom. We'll be careful. Thank you too, soon-to-be sis. I love you guys. Call me for anything."

Then I watch them leave and wonder what mom and dad want to do. "You guys want to come with us?"

Mom shakes her head. "To be honest, it's been a long day and that bedroom with the attached bathroom is calling my name. There's so much to take in, and I think I'd like to spend the rest of the night alone with your dad, Delaney."

"I understand," I say and give them each a hug before we head off to our bedroom to change.

"You guys make yourself completely at home. There's wine in the chiller and all kinds of things to drink at the bar in the main living area. Feel free to roam around all you want to. My home is yours," Blaine says, making my heart jump, as I think he's the best man on the face of the Earth.

Leaning into him as we walk away from my parents, I find myself feeling as if I'm walking on air. "Is this all real, Blaine?"

His arm tightens around me. "If it's all a dream, please don't wake me up."

With a light laugh, I say, "Me neither. I want you to know I think you're the absolute best man in the world. You've given so much this holiday season. I know everything will happen for the best with your newfound faith."

"I think so too. And now to go make it official and start a new chapter in my life. One with hope, faith, love, and you, baby."

I giggle as he picks me up and carries me into our room. *He is gorgeous, sweet, and he is all mine. I could not be happier!*

63

BLAINE

December 30th:

As the light leaves the sky on the day before we're going to be married, I hold Delaney in my arms as we lie in our bed. "It has been one hell of a week, but it's behind us now. Tomorrow we start a new day, and by noon, we'll be man and wife."

"I cannot believe how exhausted I am," she says as she snuggles close to me. Her hand rests on my chest as she looks up at me. "I cannot believe this is all about to be over and we'll start living a normal life."

"Your parents will be off to Lake Tahoe tomorrow after the ceremony. And you and I will be off to honeymoon in Ireland. I have to tell you, I didn't think things would turn out quite like this."

"Neither did I." She turns and lays her head on my chest. "To think how I started out treating you makes me want to kick myself."

"I deserved it, Delaney. I thought of no one but myself. And that's over. This new year is all about change. I plan on making things right. And with what I saw happen at Christmas, I think doing business different will make us even more money. And spreading it out over more people is a thing that makes me happy."

"I know your parents are proud of you, Blaine," she says, and that means more to me than I think she realizes.

"Thank you, baby. I hope they are. I hope you are too."

"I am extremely proud of you. I can't think of a single thing you need to do to be a better man than you are right now." Her finger moves in a trail over my bare chest. "I'm going to rest up tonight for tomorrow. But tomorrow, on the jet to New York where we'll take off on the commercial flight to Ireland, I'm going to be all over you, Blaine. So you should get some sleep too."

Her words have visions going through my head that call for anything but sleep. But she's been so busy that it's almost inhuman what she's accomplished. She's managed to get her work done while still going shopping and making arrangements for our honeymoon.

With seeing how hard see's working to cover all of her bases, her boss had a change of heart and let her have the morning shifts, Monday through Friday, the way she asked for. Plus, she was able to get her a two-week vacation for the honeymoon.

It seems when you stop trying to accomplish things all on your own, things seem to fall into place. We've prayed every morning together before heading off to our prospective jobs. And each night before climbing into bed, we get on our knees beside the bed and thank the Lord for what he did for us and all the people we love and care about on that day.

It's a system that seems to be working. Terry and Colby were released from the hospital on Christmas day. Tammy went home two days ago. Her mom is going to work at our office next week. And little Adam went home today. The only one left in the hospital is Meagan and she's gained all but one pound, then she'll get to go home too.

The animosity between her father and me is over. He's all smiles when I go to visit her every day at lunchtime. I've made it a thing I do each weekday.

I go eat lunch with Delaney, then visit at least two kids there and give them small gifts of coloring books and a box of crayons. Not anything to spoil them, as some parents look at gifts that are too extravagant as bad things. But I give them something to help keep them entertained during such hard times in their lives.

It's always there, in the back of my mind, that our children might one day be in their shoes. It's something I hope never happens, but one never knows about these things.

There are no certainties in this life. And into each life a little rain must fall—that's something I recite to myself at least a few times each day when I see the bad things happening to innocent people. I always remind myself, it's not for me to understand these things. *They happen and that's that.*

I think often of the question I asked Meagan to ask my mother. Why is there suffering?

Her response makes me think all the time about that. Why are there bees? To make things grow, is that answer.

Why are there trees? To make air for the creatures here to breathe.

Why are there mountains? Lakes? Rivers? So many things to ask, but not all can be explained. And I think about what a boring world this would be if we knew all of the answers.

Somehow, I know my children will be inquisitive people, asking all kinds of things, the way I always have. All I can do is tell them the answers to things I know. But there will not be answers for everything.

My hope is that they, too, will learn to see some things are meant to be mysteries. Some things we will only learn the reasons for when we reach the other side, and maybe not even then. I recall Meagan telling me that my mother could answer some things, but she didn't know everything.

Perhaps there will never come a time when any of us know everything there is to know. In a way, that comforts me. It lets me know there's no need to worry about what I don't know or understand.

The main thing in life is to live it the best way you can think of. Not taking from others is a huge thing I had no conception of before my father passed on.

In the name of good business, I made my deals with people who could care less about the humans they employed. That's over, and if I could shut them down, I would. That's also a thing that's out of my hands.

So many things are out of our hands, and I know I'm not the only one who wishes more could be done. I do know this. I know my money will not help the people who practice such terrible things. Crimes against humanity are things I will watch for in any company I do business with. The slightest infraction will have them earning my business no longer.

And from what I've seen of my sales in all of my Bargain Bin stores, people are okay with paying a bit more for something made by reputable companies who value their employees and treat them well. Sales have gone up and the hate reviews have gone down.

Walking on the right path feels so much better than walking on the wrong path. This path is full of people who I love. The other one had me alone and secluded.

I've spoken with Delaney's father a few times about how he thought I'd made a deal with the devil to gain my money. And he wasn't that far off. Of course, I made no direct deal with the devil, but I did make deals with those oh whom I asked no questions.

In the back of my mind, if I wasn't absolutely sure that people were being treated terribly by the companies I did business with, then I was absolved of any guilt about that. I was wrong. I was hiding my head in the sand, and that's just as bad as knowingly participating in the business of making money off the mistreatment of people.

I won't be doing any of that again. And as Delaney makes small snoring sounds, I can see I had better get myself to sleep too.

Tomorrow is a big day for us!

64

DELANEY

December 31$^{st:}$
"Mom, did I give you the ring?" I call out, as I forgot who exactly I gave the wedding ring to that I'm supposed to put on Blaine's finger in a matter of minutes.

"Yes, dear. You gave it to me," she says as she smooths out the pale-blue dress I got for her to wear today.

This morning, at the crack of dawn, Mom, Kate, Tiffany, and myself all started the day with massages, pedicures, and manicures, and then hair and makeup were done at our place. We waited until getting to the hospital to change into our dresses.

I was relaxed, and now I'm turning into a disaster. Worry is consuming me, as I can't seem to find one of my shoes and I have to keep stopping what I'm doing to sit down as a sweat threatens me.

"Dear, Kate found your shoe." Mom produces my shoe, and I fan myself with relief.

"Good. I didn't want to go down the aisle in my bare feet, but I was preparing myself to do just that if the thing had been left at home somehow. This is nerve wracking, Mom. I wish I would've done what Blaine wanted and just gone to Vegas and gotten drunk so I wouldn't care what I looked like."

"I'd have been so disappointed if you'd done that." Mom helps me get my shoe on as the big white dress full of fluff hinders my progress. "And you're going to have such beautiful pictures to hang in your entry room now. You just need to settle down."

Kate enters the empty hospital room where I'm getting dressed, and she has a red cup in her hand. "Here you go, Nurse Richards. A much-needed calm-you-down drink."

"You snuck alcohol in here?" I whisper.

She nods. "I did. You need to chill, girl!"

Mom laughs as I take a sip and find it's a delicious margarita. "Oh my! I did need this. Thank you."

Mom takes a seat on the vacant hospital bed and plays with the string of pearls we bought her which hang around her neck. "Things have really turned around, pumpkin, haven't they?"

"They have," I agree and take another sip of the delicious drink.

"Your father and I got the settlement squared away, and later on, we'll be going by private jet to our new home. I'm just kind of going through the motions. It feels like a dream to me." She looks at me as I take another sip. "And when are we to expect grand-children?"

I nearly choke with her question. "Mom! Give us a minute or two. Okay?"

Kate laughs and Tiffany walks into the room, all ready and looking lovely, too, in her matching blue dress, just like Kate's and Mom's. "What's so funny?"

"Delaney nearly choked to death with her mother's question of when they were planning on having kids," Kate informs her.

"Kent told me they were already trying," she says, and Kate and I shush her.

Mom looks at me with narrowed eyes. "Delaney Richards, you're keeping secrets from me! You two are already on that?"

I nod and blush. "I'm afraid so. Blaine's in a real rush to get our family started. He wants a big one, so I assume time is of the essence in his eyes."

"A big family?" Mom asks as she shakes her head. "We'll see if you go that route. I was not about to go through that process again. One was plenty for me."

"I know," I tell her as I finish off the drink and do feel a whole lot calmer. "But Blaine wants a big family. Who am I to tell the man no? It's pretty obvious what that man wants, he gets."

In the hallway, I hear a commotion and the sound of heels echoing in the empty hall. "I heard he's going to be in the chapel for his wedding. Let's get him there," a woman's voice calls out.

Kate looks at me, then hurries to the door, peeking out of it then quickly closing it. "Damn!"

"What's going on?" I ask as I get out of the chair.

"There's a news crew out there. I bet they're looking for Blaine. I need to warn him," she says as she takes her phone out of her bra to call her brother.

"I'll handle this," I say as rage runs through me.

The press has been in contact with Blaine's office, asking for an interview since the news was leaked about the five miraculous recoveries of the kids he was visiting. I'm not sure who would've alerted the press to that, but someone did, and the reporters have been wanting to get him in their clutches. *A thing I think will end in disaster.*

Just as I get to the door, I feel a bunch of hands on me, holding me back. "No," Mom says. "Delaney, you don't want to end up on the news. Or even worse, in jail for assault. I can see the fury in your eyes. You'll knock that woman out if you get the chance."

"I will do that. She can't ruin my wedding day with this." I can't go anywhere, though, as they all hold me back.

"Blaine!" Kate shouts as he answers his phone.

"What? You sound pretty excited, Kate," he says. "Don't tell me Delaney is getting cold feet."

"No, it's not that. Where are you? You need to hide. A news crew is looking for you and they know you're going to be at the chapel."

"Shit!" he hisses. "I'm in a room two doors away from there. I can't believe they knew about this. This is totally private. Tell, Delaney I'm sorry about this. I should've given an interview before this so this wouldn't have happened."

"Don't apologize, Blaine," I call out. "This is no one's fault."

"She's slurring," he says. "Did you slip her a drink, Kate?"

"I'm slurring?" I ask, as I don't feel drunk. Well, maybe a little. Yeah, a little. I lean on the hospital bed and hiccup. "Damn, I'm drunk."

"Kate, you're in so much trouble. She hasn't eaten a thing since lunch yesterday. She was too busy packing and being nervous last night to eat a thing. Get her something like some crackers or something to help sober her up," he orders her, and she bolts out of the room.

"She's in trouble," I say, then lay on the bed. "And now I'm really tired."

Mom's eyes roll, and Tiffany looks worried as she says, "Delaney, you need to snap out of it. Try to sit up. Your eyes are looking very heavy. You should've told her you hadn't eaten."

"I know that now," I tell her as my eyes close. "But I need a little nap. Just a little one."

I hope this is still real when I wake up!

65

BLAINE

"He's not here yet," I hear the preacher tell the news crew in the hallway. "And you can't be here. This is a sacred place. I can call security to see you all out."

"We'll wait outside for him to leave then. I'm sure he has plans for after the wedding—to go on some extravagant honeymoon with his new bride. We'll get him then. He owes the world an explanation for how he gets everything he wants. First, he becomes a billionaire by selling crap, and then the kids he was visiting all have miraculous recoveries. Sources say he has an in with the devil, preacher. Is that the kind of person you want in your church?"

"The man has no in with the devil. You're being very dramatic. I baptized him only last week," he says.

"He was never religious before. What's happened to change him? Or is he faking a newfound religion for some reason? The people have a right to know about this. He may end up being a very dangerous man. So help me get the truth out of him. Help me find out if he actually made a deal with the devil like the man he ran out of business claims he did."

"I'm going out there to set the record straight," I say, but find Kent and Randy, as well as Mr. Richards, holding me back.

"You stay put," Delaney's father tells me. "I'll deal with her."

"No," I tell him as the other two continue to hold me back. "I can't let you do that, sir. This is my battle."

He turns to look at me and shakes his head. "Son, you are about to marry my daughter. You are about to be a part of my family. I protect what's mine. Today is about you and my daughter starting your own family. When you have kids, you'll understand what I'm doing. No one pushes any family of mine around. No one!"

And with that, he's out the door, and Kent says, "Damn! You got one tough father-in-law. Lord help that reporter. I think she's about to see the light."

We listen at the door as Mr. Richards calls out, "Hey you! Over here! What do you want with my son-in-law?"

The sound of several sets of feet moving quickly in our direction are heard, along with the female reporter's voice, "And who are you?"

"My name is none of your concern. My daughter is marrying the man you're planning on ambushing, and I'm here to tell you this ends now. You will never get an interview, mainly because this is no one's business. I overheard you talking to the preacher. I know you want to accuse Blaine of something evil, and I will not allow it. So, hit the road, or you'll be sorry."

Kent peeks out the door, then pulls his head right back in. "That cameraman has his camera on. Mr. Richards seems to have no idea they're videoing him."

Randy looks pissed and he goes out the door, leaving my brother and me alone. "Shit," I whisper. "What's he about to do?"

"Stop recording this instant," Randy shouts. "I'm Blaine Vanderbilt's attorney. I'll have you all charged if you don't stop videoing immediately!"

"Oh, shit," Kent says. "He's pulling some bullshit out of his hat now!"

"So, you think you can stop us from getting the truth about Blaine Vanderbilt, do you?" the reporter asks.

"Camera off, now!" he shouts again.

"Fine," a man says. I suppose it's the cameraman. "You have to know, we will get this story eventually."

"There is nothing to get. My client is cleaning up his business practices. He may have dealt with companies and people who weren't very good people, but those days are behind him. Leave the man alone to start his new life," Randy says.

I wait for the reporter to respond, but my phone rings, and all I hear after that is the sound of people running and the door being thrown open. They've found me, and the green light is on at the top of the camera.

"We're live with Blaine Vanderbilt," the dark-haired reporter says as she moves in, making me and Kent back up as they move into the room.

Pressing the button to send the call to voicemail, I stop moving and stand up straight. "Yes, you are. After harassing me for a week, you have me here, live, cornered in an empty hospital room on my wedding day. Please tell me what's so important you needed to interrupt our special day."

"The people want to know how it is you get everything you want. The wealth and the children's miraculous healing? All of it comes down to one night when you were seen leaving a warehouse that's known to be the meeting place of a group of satanic worshipers," she says, then pushes the microphone in my face.

"This is nothing more than a witch hunt." I look at my brother. "This is my brother. Ask him if I've ever exhibited any evil tendencies."

"Never," Kent says. "You're making yourself look ridiculous with these accusations. I'd expect this out of a cheesy tabloid. Never the local news."

A familiar voice comes from behind the camera crew. "I'm going to ask you only once to leave these premises. Then I'm calling law enforcement and pressing trespassing charges on your whole crew and your television station," the head of security, Mr. Davenport, says.

The reporter looks mad as a wet hen as she spins around. I hear a small voice come from the hallway, "What's happening?" It sounds like little Meagan.

"This is none of our concern," I hear her father say.

The reporter hurries out of the room, asking, "Are you one of the cured children?"

I hear her father say, "We're not doing any interviews."

"I just want to ask you about Blaine Vanderbilt. He's been accused of being a Satan worshiper," the reporter says.

"Satan?" Meagan asks, and I become furious as I come out of the room.

"Stop!" I shout. "Leave her alone. Leave that family alone! If you had a heart, you'd leave us all alone!"

Meagan's father is holding his tiny daughter in his arms as his wife stands next to him. She looks at the reporter. "Blaine Vanderbilt is not a bad man in any way. He has a host of people who will attest to the good in him. I, for one, don't believe a bad word anyone says about the man."

"Nor will I," Meagan's father says.

I smile as Meagan lifts her head off her father's shoulder and looks past the group of people and directly at me. "That man behind you is almost an angel. If you decide to report anything bad about him, I feel sorry for you. Then you will be the one doing a bad thing and that's never any good."

I watch the reporter lower her head. "Damn," she says under her breath. "Let's go." She turns to look at me, then gives me a weak smile. "Seems you have quite the fan club. You're willing to fight for them, and in my book, that makes you something other than evil. Sorry. I am not a reporter that reports lies. Sorry about this. It's just business. I was sent to get this interview."

"'It's just business' is something I used to say all of the time. That's the only evil I did, and I admit it was evil, and I will never live my life in that frame of mind again. You can report that if you'd like. But I'd really like it if you let this all go away. I'm trying to build a family with a very special woman, and I'd like a bit of privacy to do that."

With a nod, she and her crew leave us standing in the hallway that's grown a bit congested with onlookers. Meagan gives me a smile. "We came to see you get married."

"Well, let's get to that, shall we?" I say as we head to the chapel.

Her mother looks at me with a smile. "Meagan has something she wanted to tell you."

"You do?" I ask her as I run my hand over her head.

"I get to go home after your wedding," she says, filling me with complete joy.

The preacher looks happy, too, as he welcomes us into the chapel. "That's some great news," he tells Meagan.

Looking back, I find Delaney's father. "You should go get her now. I think it's time to get this show on the road."

With a nod, he's off to bring me my bride, and I go to wait for her. Then I recall the phone call I missed and look to find my sister was the one who called. I call her back and find her sounding like she's near tears. "Blaine, I've ruined your wedding."

"Do not tell me that, Kate. What's happened now?"

"She's out cold. The drink I gave her was too much for her to take. We can't get her to wake up and eat the crackers Tiffany got for her. You'll just have to wait for her to wake up. I'm so sorry," she wails.

"Damn it!" I whisper. "We'll wait then. And you are really in trouble, little sister!"

Making my way to the preacher, I can see he looks a little worried himself. "Are we having problems, Blaine?"

"We are," I say as I run my hand over my face. "My sister brought Delaney some kind of alcohol. Delaney hasn't eaten a thing since lunch yesterday and very little this entire week with her schedule and all the preparations. She's been exhausted every single night. I'm afraid she's passed out, and we'll just have to wait for her to wake up before we can do this."

"Oh my goodness. At least I have nothing else scheduled for today. We can wait."

I go to explain what's happened to the Sanders family when a bunch of people file into the little chapel. A woman is crying inconsolably. Two young men are holding her up and taking her to see the preacher.

A little girl translates for the Spanish-speaking family. "Help our mother, please, sir. We're here because my baby sister, who's just six months old, was hurt in a car wreck she and my mother were in. Mama is so upset with herself that we don't know what to do for her. Please help her."

So many people come into the chapel, filling the seats up. My party moves to the back row, then when I find more of the woman's family members standing, I gesture for my party to follow me and take our group to the cafeteria.

"What a tragedy," Mrs. Sanders says as we make our way out of the room.

Meagan looks at me as she walks in between her father and me. "Do you smell that honey and lemon smell?"

I take a deep breath and nod. "You think my mother's around?",

"I can't hear her like I did before. I guess because I'm all me again. But I could smell her when they walked into the room. I guess the poor baby is really bad off," she says with a sad face.

I'm shocked as her father stops, picks her up, and hugs her, then looks at me. "Can we all stop right here and pray for that child? Would everyone be okay with doing that?" he asks as he looks at every one of us.

Kent, Randy, and I all hold out our hands as we stop in the middle of the hallway, join hands, and bow our heads. Meagan says, "Blaine, I think you should say the prayer."

So I start a prayer for the baby none of us know a thing about, but we know one thing for sure. There's a baby girl in this hospital who is near death and we must send our prayers up for her.

In the midst of what was supposed to be a day about me and Delaney, I've found there may have been a reason for our delayed wedding. One never knows how things will turn out.

The best-laid plans, as they say.

66

DELANEY

"How long did I sleep?" I ask as I sit up and rub my eyes. My mother, father, soon to be sister-in-law, and my soon-to-be brother-in-law's new girlfriend stand around me.

"Finally!" my father says. "You've slept three hours." He looks at my mother. "She needs a bit of primping."

Kate and Tiffany spring into action, messing with my hair and makeup. "What happened?" I ask, then see Kate make a face.

"Oh no! You need to brush your teeth, Delaney!"

I look at Mom, nearly panicking. "Go to the nurses' station and ask for a toothbrush packet, please, Mom." Looking back at Kate, I ask, "I can't remember hardly anything. Did I pass out?"

"Yes, you did, and I am so sorry. I had no idea you were running on empty. I hope you can forgive me," she says with a very sorry expression.

Mom returns with the toothbrush packet, and I take it and go into the bathroom. Looking in the mirror, I see I don't look quite as pretty as I did before. A crease is running along one cheek where I was lying on the bed.

I can't believe I passed out. I feel fine now. Rinsing my mouth out, I dab the few drops of water away and decide I better use the bathroom while I'm here. Blaine will probably want to get going as soon as we get married.

I cannot believe I let myself get that way. That drink snuck up on me like a thief in the night. I can hear Kate on the phone with Blaine. "She's up. Are you guys ready?" Then she says, "You're kidding!"

Now, what?

As I walk out of the bathroom, I see Kate's face has fallen. "I really am sorry, Delaney!"

"What's the problem?" I ask as everyone looks very tired.

"There's a grieving family in the chapel. It would be terrible to ask them to leave," Kate says. "Blaine says he's sorry. Now we all have to wait."

"I'm going to grab you something to eat, pumpkin," Mom says and takes Dad with her to find me something.

I sit in the chair and wonder what happened to all the plans we made and why in the world so many things have gone wrong. Maybe this isn't the right thing to do. Maybe the powers that be are stopping this from happening.

Maybe I should end this whole thing!

I remember falling asleep and hoping I wouldn't wake up to find this had all been a dream, but maybe it's supposed to only be a memory. *A memory of what almost was.*

67

BLAINE

A chill runs through me as we sit at a table in the cafeteria. Then I see Meagan looking at me. "You shouldn't wait for the chapel, Blaine. You should get Nurse Richards and you should marry her anywhere."

When I look up, I see Delaney's mother and father coming into the nearly-empty cafeteria, and I get an idea. "I think you're right."

Getting up, I go to see the cashier, Shirley, who is still wearing a nametag that says, 'Mildred.' "Shirley, do you think it would be all right for us to have the wedding in here? We could make an aisle right through there and maybe dim all the lights like you do at night. What do you say?"

"I say, I'm on it. Help me out and I think we can have this place ready in five or ten minutes."

Getting my party to help, they begin to get things in order, and I go to talk to Mr. and Mrs. Richards. "We're going to have the wedding in here. If you'll go get her, we can start in ten minutes," I tell her father.

Her mother hurries after him. "I'll bring the preacher!"

With the plan in action, I hurry to assist with the moving of the tables and find a couple of people who were in there helping too. One of her nurse co-workers passes by, then comes back in. "What are you guys doing?" she asks.

Shirley tells her, as I'm just too busy to explain things. "Delaney and Blaine are getting married in here. You want to see if you can get the wedding march played on the speaker system for us?"

The other nurse runs off, and I find my heart pounding with excitement. *I think we're going to really pull this off!*

DELANEY

"No, Dad! I think this is all too many things going wrong. It's a sign!" I say as he tells me we're having our wedding in the cafeteria. "What about the beautiful pictures we're supposed to have at the quaint, little chapel? I don't want a case of pies in the background of our wedding photos!"

"You're acting spoiled," Dad tells me. "Now come on. He's waiting on you. I'm sure it will look great. Everyone is helping to make sure of that. It might not be what you planned, but the end result is that you two will be hitched, and that's all that really matters. Right?"

I look at Kate, who is nodding. Then Tiffany, who is also nodding. With one more look in the mirror, I find the crease in my cheek is gone, and I look a lot better than when I first woke up.

Looking up, I say a silent prayer. 'God, if this is the right thing to do, I'd love a sign right about now.'

Looking down, I find my heart slowing as I think about the lack of any sign. Then the speaker system crackles and the wedding march is playing overhead. I look up again with a smile. "Grab my bouquet, will you? I have a wedding to get to!"

BLAINE

One by one, I watch the people come down the makeshift aisle we created. Tiffany comes in on Kent's arm. Then Kate comes in on Randy's. The music goes on and on for what seems like forever, then I see my Delaney coming into the cafeteria. The lights are dimmed and someone found candles and placed them all over the place.

I can see her face, and she's amazed at the transformation of the cafeteria. Her eyes shimmer as she looks around and holds her father's arm as he brings her to me. Finally, she looks at me and a smile fills her face. "Hey," I say as I take her hand, which her father is giving to me.

"Hey," she says, then bites her lip. "You ready for this?"

With a nod, I take the woman who will be my wife and turn her to stand with me in front of the preacher who will lead us in saying the words that will hold us together forever and always.

And, now, I am sure we will all live happily ever after.

The End.

ABOUT THE AUTHOR

Mrs. Love writes about smart, sexy women and the hot alpha billionaires who love them. She has found her own happily ever after with her dream husband and adorable 6 and 2 year old kids. Currently, Michelle is hard at work on the next book in the series, and trying to stay off the Internet.
"Thank you for supporting an indie author. Anything you can do, whether it be writing a review, or even simply telling a fellow reader that you enjoyed this. Thanks

🌸 Created with Vellum

CPSIA information can be obtained
at www.ICGtesting.com
Printed in the USA
BVHW041506290121
599098BV00008B/572